The Changeling

Walter Besant

ESPRIOS DIGITAL PUBLISHING

The Changeling

NOVELS BY SIR WALTER BESANT & JAMES RICE.

Crown 8vo., cloth extra, 3s. 6d. each; post 8vo., boards, 2s. each; cloth, 2s. 6d. each.

READY MONEY MORTIBOY.

BY CELIA'S ARBOUR.

MY LITTLE GIRL.

THE CHAPLAIN OF THE FLEET.

WITH HARP AND CROWN.

THE SEAMY SIDE.

THIS SON OF VULCAN.

THE CASE OF MR. LUCRAFT.

THE GOLDEN BUTTERFLY.

'TWAS IN TRAFALGAR'S BAY.

THE MONKS OF THELEMA.

THE TEN YEARS' TENANT.

⁂ There is also a LIBRARY EDITION of the above Twelve Volumes, handsomely set in new type on a large crown 8vo. page, and bound in cloth extra, 6s. each; and POPULAR EDITIONS of THE GOLDEN BUTTERFLY, and of ALL SORTS AND CONDITIONS OF MEN, medium 8vo., 6d. each; cloth, 1s. each.

NOVELS BY SIR WALTER BESANT.

Crown 8vo., cloth extra, 3s. 6d. each; post 8vo., boards, 2s. each; cloth, 2s. 6d. each.

ALL SORTS AND CONDITIONS OF MEN. 12 Illusts. by BARNARD.

THE CAPTAINS' ROOM. With Frontispiece by E. J. WHEELER.

ALL IN A GARDEN FAIR. With 6 Illustrations by HARRY FURNISS.

DOROTHY FORSTER. With Frontispiece by CHARLES GREEN.

UNCLE JACK, and other Stories.

CHILDREN OF GIBEON.

THE WORLD WENT VERY WELL THEN. 12 Illusts. by FORESTIER.

HERR PAULUS: His Rise, his Greatness, and his Fall.

THE BELL OF ST. PAUL'S.

FOR FAITH AND FREEDOM. Illusts. by FORESTIER and WADDY.

TO CALL HER MINE. With 9 Illustrations by A. FORESTIER.

THE HOLY ROSE. With Frontispiece by F. BARNARD.

ARMOREL OF LYONESSE. With 12 Illustrations by F. BARNARD.

ST. KATHERINE'S BY THE TOWER. With 12 Illusts. by C. GREEN.

VERBENA CAMELLIA STEPHANOTIS. Frontis. by GORDON BROWN.

THE IVORY GATE.

THE REBEL QUEEN.

BEYOND THE DREAMS OF AVARICE. 12 Illustrations by HYDE.

IN DEACON'S ORDERS. With Frontispiece by A. FORESTIER.

THE REVOLT OF MAN.

THE MASTER CRAFTSMAN.

THE CITY OF REFUGE.

Crown 8vo., cloth, 3s. 6d. each.

A FOUNTAIN SEALED. With Frontispiece by H. G. BURGESS.

THE CHANGELING.

THE CHARM, and other Drawing-room Plays. By SIR WALTER BESANT and WALTER H. POLLOCK. With 50 Illustrations by CHRIS HAMMOND and JULE GOODMAN. Crown 8vo., cloth gilt, gilt edges, 6s.; blue cloth, plain edges, 3s. 6d.

FIFTY YEARS AGO. With 144 Illustrations. Crown 8vo., cloth, 5s.

THE EULOGY OF RICHARD JEFFERIES. Portrait. Cr. 8vo, cloth, 6s.

LONDON. With 125 Illustrations. Demy 8vo., cloth extra, 7s. 6d.

WESTMINSTER. With Etched Frontispiece by F. S. WALKER, R.E., and 130 Illustrations by WILLIAM PATTEN, etc. Demy 8vo., cloth, 7s. 6d.

SOUTH LONDON. With Etched Frontispiece by F. S. WALKER, R.E., and 118 Illustrations. Demy 8vo., cloth, gilt top, 18s.

SIR RICHARD WHITTINGTON. Frontispiece. Cr. 8vo., linen, 3s. 6d.

GASPARD DE COLIGNY. With a Portrait. Crown 8vo., art linen, 3s. 6d.

LONDON: CHATTO & WINDUS, 111 ST. MARTIN'S LANE, W.C.

THE CHANGELING

BY
WALTER BESANT
AUTHOR OF
"ALL SORTS AND CONDITIONS OF MEN," "A FOUNTAIN SEALED," ETC.

A NEW EDITION

LONDON
CHATTO & WINDUS
1899

THE CHANGELING

BY

WALTER BESANT

AUTHOR OF
"ALL SORTS AND CONDITIONS OF MEN," "A FOUNTAIN
SEALED," ETC.

A NEW EDITION

LONDON
CHATTO & WINDUS
1899

PRINTED BY
WILLIAM CLOWES AND SONS, LIMITED,
LONDON AND BECCLES.

CONTENTS.

CHAPTER

I.	Was it Substitution?
II.	The Only Witness Gone
III.	The Three Cousins
IV.	The Consulting-Room
V.	Guest Night
VI.	The Old Lover
VII.	The Master of the Situation
VIII.	The Cousins
IX.	One More
X.	Cousin Alfred's Secret
XI.	The Doctor's Dinner
XII.	The Other Child of Desertion
XIII.	A Midnight Walk

XIV.	THE FIRST MOVE
XV.	TWO JUMPS AND A CONCLUSION
XVI.	A WRETCH
XVII.	THE SECOND BLOW
XVIII.	A GRACIOUS LADY
XIX.	A CABINET COUNCIL
XX.	JOHN HAVERIL CLEARS UP THINGS
XXI.	"TO BE OFF WITH THE OLD LOVE"
XXII.	THE CLAN AGAIN
XXIII.	ONE MORE ATTEMPT
XXIV.	A HORRID NIGHT
XXV.	THE FIRST MOTHER
XXVI.	THE SECOND MOTHER
CHAPTER THE LAST.	FORGIVENESS

The Changeling

CHAPTER I.

WAS IT SUBSTITUTION?

"Pray be seated, madam." The doctor offered his visitor a chair. Then he closed the door, with perhaps a more marked manner than one generally displays in this simple operation. "I am happy to inform you," he began, "that the arrangements—the arrangements," he repeated with meaning, "are now completed."

The lady was quite young—not more than twenty-two or so—a handsome woman, a woman of distinction. Her face was full of sadness; her eyes were full of trouble; her lips trembled; her fingers nervously clutched the arms of the chair. When the doctor mentioned the arrangements, her cheek flushed and then paled. In a word, she betrayed every external sign of terror, sorrow, and anxiety.

"And when can I leave this place?"

"This day: as soon as you please."

"The woman made no objections?"

"None. You can have the child."

"I have told you my reasons for wishing to adopt this child"—he had never asked her reasons, yet at every interview she repeated them: "my own boy is dead. He is dead." There was a world of trouble in the repetition of the word.

The doctor bowed coldly. "Your reasons, madam," he said, "are sufficient for yourself. I have followed your instructions without asking for your reasons. That is to say, I have found the kind of child you want: light hair and blue eyes, apparently sound and healthy; at all events, the child of a sound and healthy mother. As for your reasons, I do not inquire."

"I thought you might like——"

"They are nothing to do with me. My business has been to find a child, and to arrange for your adoption of it. I have therefore, as I told you, arranged with a poor woman who is willing to part with her child."

The Changeling

"On my conditions?"

"Absolutely. That is—she will never see the child again; she will not ask who takes the child, or where it is taken, or in what position of life it will be brought up. She accepts your assurance that the child will be cared for, and treated kindly. She fully consents."

"Poor creature!"

"You will give her fifty pounds, and that single payment will terminate the whole business."

"Terminate the whole business? Oh, it will begin the whole business!"

"There are many reasons for adoption," the doctor continued, returning to the point with which he had no concern. "I have read in books of substituting a child—introducing a child—for the sake of keeping a title, or an estate, or a family."

The lady answered as if she had not heard this remark. "The mother consents to sell her child! Poor creature!"

"She accepts your conditions. I have told you so. Go your way—she goes hers."

The lady reflected for a moment. "Tell me," she said,—"you are a man of science,—in such an adoption——"

"Or, perhaps, such a substitution," interrupted the doctor.

"Is there not danger of inherited vice, or disease?"

"Certainly there is. It is a danger which you must watch in educating the child. He may inherit a tendency to drink: guard against it by keeping him from alcohol of any kind. He may show physical weakness; watch him carefully. But nine-tenths of so-called hereditary disease or vice are due to example and conditions of life."

"If we do not know the character of the parents—they may be criminals. What if the child should inherit these instincts?"

The doctor, who had been standing, took a chair, and prepared himself to argue the point. He was a young man, with a strong jaw and a square forehead. He had a face and features of rude but vigorous handling; such a face as a noble life would make beautiful in age, and an ignoble life would make hideous. Every man has as many faces as there are years of his life, and we heed them not; yet each follows each in a long procession, ending with the pale and waxen face in the coffin—that solemn face which tells so much.

"There is," he said, "a good deal of loose talk about heredity. Some things external are hereditary—face, eyes, figure, stature, hands, certainly descend from father to son; some diseases, especially those of the nervous kind; some forms of taste and aptitude, especially those which are artistic. Things which are not natural, but acquired, are never hereditary—never. If the boy's father is the greatest criminal in the country, it won't hurt him a bit, because he is taken away too early to have observed or imitated. The sons are said to take after the mothers; that is, perhaps, because they have always got the models before them. In your case, you will naturally become the child's most important model. Later on, will come in the male influence. If there is, for instance, a putative father——"

"There will be, of course, my husband."

The doctor bowed again. Then there was a husband living. "He will become the boy's second model," he said. "In other words, madam, the vices of the boy's parents—if they have vices—will not affect him in the least. Gout, rheumatism, asthma, consumption,—all these things, and many more, a child may inherit; but acquired criminality, never. Be quite easy on that point."

"My desire is that the child may become as perfect a gentleman at all points as his—as my husband."

"Why should he not? He has no past to drag him down. You will train him and mould him as you please—exactly as you please."

"You have not told me anything about the mother, except that she is in want."

"Why should you learn her name, or she yours?"

"I have no desire to learn her name. I was thinking whether she is the kind of woman to feel the loss of her child."

The doctor, as yet inexperienced in the feminine nature, marvelled at this sympathy with the mother whose child the lady was buying.

The Changeling

"Well," he said, "she is a young woman—of respectable character, I believe; good looking; in her speech something of a cockney, if I understand that dialect."

"The more respectable she is, the more she will feel the loss of her child."

"Yes; but there is another consideration. This poor creature has a husband who has deserted her."

"Then her child should console her."

"Her husband is a comedian—actor—singing fellow,—a chap who asks for nothing but enjoyment. As for wife and children, they may look out for themselves. When I saw him, I read desertion in his face; in his wife's face, it was easy to read neglect."

"Poor creature!"

"Now he's gone—deserted her. Nothing will do but she must go in search of him. Partly for money to help her along, partly because the workhouse is her only refuge, she sells her baby."

The lady was silent for a while, then she sighed. "Poor creature! There are, then, people in the world as unhappy as I myself?"

"If that is any consolation, there are. Well, madam, you now know the whole history; and, as it doesn't concern you, nor the child, best forget it at once."

"Poor mother!"

She kept harping on the bereavement, as though Providence, and not she herself, was the cause.

"I have told her that the boy will be brought up in ease—affluence even"—the lady inclined her head—"and she is resigned."

"Thank you. And when——?"

"You would like to go up to London this afternoon? Well, I will myself bring the child to the railway station. Once more, as regards heredity. If the child should inherit his mother's qualities, he will be truthful and tenacious, or obstinate and perhaps rather stupid; if his father's, he will be artistic and musical, selfish, cold-hearted, conceited."

The Changeling

"He might inherit the better qualities of both."

"Ah, then he will be persevering, high-principled, a man of artistic feeling—perhaps of power,—ambitious, and desirous of distinction. I wish, madam, that he may become so perfect and admirable a young man." He rose. "I have only, I think, to receive the money which will start this poor woman on her wild-goose chase. Thank you. Ten five-pound notes. I will take care that the woman has it at once."

"For your own trouble, Dr. Steele?"

"My fee is three guineas. Thank you."

"I shall be on the platform or in the train at a quarter before three. Please look about for an Indian ayah, who will receive the child. You are sure that there will never be any attempt made to follow and discover my name?"

"As to discovery," he said, "you may rest quite easy. For my own part, my work lies in this slum of Birmingham; it is not likely that I shall ever get out of it. I am a sixpenny doctor; you are a woman of society: I shall never meet you. This little business will be forgotten to-morrow. If, in the future, by any accident I were to meet you, I should not know you. If I were to know you, I should not speak to you. Until you yourself give me leave, even if I should recognize you, I should not speak about this business."

"Thank you," she said coldly. "It is not, however, likely that you will be tempted."

He took up an open envelope lying on the table—it was the envelope in which the lady had brought the notes,—replaced them, and put them in his pocket. Then he opened the door for the lady, who bowed coldly, and went out.

A few days before this, the same lady, with an Indian ayah, was bending over a dying child. They sent for the nearest medical man. He came. He tried the usual things; they proved useless. The child must die.

The child was dead.

The child was buried.

The Changeling

The mother sat stupefied. In her hand she held a letter—her husband's latest letter. "In a day or two," he said, "my life's work will be finished. In a fortnight after you get this, I shall be at Southampton. Come to meet me, dear one, and bring the boy. I am longing to see the boy and the boy's mother. Kiss the boy for me;" and so on, and so on—always thinking of the boy, the boy, the boy! And the boy was dead! And the bereaved father was on his way home! She laid down the letter, and took up a telegram. Already he must be crossing the Alps, looking forward to meeting the boy, the boy, the boy!

And the boy was dead.

The ayah crouched down on a stool beside her mistress, and began whispering in her own language. But the lady understood.

As she listened her face grew harder, her mouth showed resolution.

"Enough," she said; "you have told me enough. You can be silent?—for my sake, for the sake of the sahib? Yes—yes—I can trust you. Let me think."

Presently she went out; she walked at random into street after street. She stopped, letting chance direct her, at a surgery with a red lamp, in a mean quarter. She read the name. She entered, and asked to see Dr. Steele, not knowing anything at all about the man.

She was received by a young man of five and twenty or so. She stated her object in calling.

"The child I want," she said, "should be something like the child I have lost. He must have light hair and blue eyes."

"And the age?"

"He must not be more than eighteen months or less than a year. My own child was thirteen months old. He was born on December 2, 1872."

"I have a large acquaintance in a poor neighbourhood," said the doctor. "The women of my quarter have many babies. If you will give me a day or two, I may find what you want." He made a note—"Light hair, blue eyes; birth somewhere near December 2, 1872,—age, therefore, about thirteen months."

The Changeling

At a quarter before three in the afternoon a woman, carrying a baby, stood inside the railway station at Birmingham. She was young, thinly clad, though the day was cold; her face was delicate and refined, though pinched with want and trouble. She looked at her child every minute, and her tears fell fast.

The doctor arrived, looked round, and walked up to her. "Now, Mrs. Anthony," he said, "I've come for the baby."

"Oh! If it were not for the workhouse I would never part with him."

"Come, my good woman, you know you promised."

"Take him," she said suddenly. She almost flung him in the doctor's arms, and rushed away.

Above the noise of the trains and the station, the doctor heard her sobbing as she ran out of the station.

"She'll soon get over it," he said. But, as has already been observed, the doctor was as yet inexperienced in the feminine heart.

About six o'clock that evening the lady who had received the baby had arrived at her house in Bryanston Square.

"Now," she said, when she had reached the nursery, "we will have a look at the creature—oh! the little gutter-born creature!—that is to be my own all the rest of my life."

The ayah threw back the wraps, and disclosed a lusty boy, about a year or fifteen months old.

The lady sat down by the table, and dropped her hands in her lap.

"Oh," she cried, "I *could* not tell him! It broke my heart to watch the boy on his deathbed: it would kill him—it would kill him—the child of his old age, his only child! To save my husband I would do worse things than this—far worse things—far worse things."

Among the child's clothes, which were clean and well kept, there was a paper. The lady snatched it up. There was writing on it. "His name"—the writing was plain and clear, not that of a wholly uneducated woman—"is Humphrey. His surname does not matter. It begins with 'W.'"

The Changeling

"Why," cried the lady, "Humphrey! Humphrey! My boy's own name! And his surname begins with 'W'—my boy's initial! If it should be my own boy!—oh! ayah, my own boy come back again!"

The ayah shook her head sadly. But she changed the child's clothes for those of the dead child; and she folded up his own things, and laid them in a drawer.

"The doctor has not deceived me," said the lady. "Fair hair, blue eyes; eyes and hair the colour of my boy." The tears came into her eyes.

"He's a beautiful boy," said the nurse; "not a spot nor a blemish, and his limbs round and straight and strong. See how he kicks. And look—look! why, if he hasn't got the chin—the sahib's chin!"

It was not much: a dimple, a hollow between the lower lip and the end of the chin.

"Strange! So he has. Do you think, nurse, the sahib, his father, will think that the child looks his age? He is to be a year and a quarter, you know."

The ayah laughed. "Men know nothing," she said.

In a day or two the supposed parent returned home. He was a man advanced in years, between sixty and seventy. He was tall and spare of figure. His features were strongly marked, the features of a man who administers and commands. His face was full of authority; his eyes were as keen as a hawk's. He stepped up the stairs with the spring of five and twenty, and welcomed his wife with the sprightliness of a bridegroom of that elastic age. The man was, in fact, a retired Indian. He had spent forty years or so in administrating provinces: he was a king retired from business, a sovereign abdicated, on whose face a long reign had left the stamp of kingcraft. It was natural that in the evening of his life this man should marry a young and beautiful girl; it was also quite natural that this girl should entertain, for a husband old enough to be her grandfather, an affection and respect which dominated her.

He held out both arms; he embraced his wife with the ardour of a young lover; he turned her face to the light.

The Changeling

"Lilias!" he murmured, "let me look at you. Why, my dear, you look pale—and worried! Is anything the matter?"

"Nothing—nothing—now you are home again."

"And the boy? Where is the boy?"

"He shall be brought in." The ayah appeared carrying the child. "Here he is; quite well—and strong—and happy. Your son is quite happy—quite happy——" Her voice broke. She sank into a chair, and fell into hysterical sobbing and weeping. "He is quite—quite—quite happy."

They brought cold water, and presently she became calmer. Then the father turned again to consider the boy.

"He looks strong and hearty; but he doesn't seem much bigger than when you carried him off six months ago."

"A little backward with his growth." The mother had now recovered. "But that's nothing. He's made a new start already. Feel his fingers. There's a grip! Your own living picture, Humphrey!"

"Ay, ay. Perhaps I would rather, for good looks, that he took after his mother. Blue eyes, fair hair, and the family dimple in the chin."

When the doctor was left alone, he took the envelope containing the bank-notes from his pocket, and threw it on his desk. Then he sat down, and began to think over the situation.

"What does she do it for?" he asked. "Her own child is dead. There is no doubt about that; her face is so full of trouble. She wants to deceive her husband: at least, I suppose so. She will keep that secret to herself. The ayah is faithful—that's pretty certain. There will be no blackmailing in that quarter. A fine face she has"—meaning the lady, not the ayah. "Hard and determined, though. I should like to see it soften. I wish she had trusted me. But there, one couldn't expect it of a woman of that temperament—cold, reserved, haughty; a countess, perhaps. It's like the old story-books. Somebody will be disinherited. This boy is going to do it. Nobody will ever find it out. And that's the way they build up their fine pedigrees!"

The Changeling

The doctor was quite wrong. Nobody was to be disinherited; nor was there an estate. This you must understand, to begin with. The rest I am going to tell you.

"No clue," the doctor continued. "She is quite safe, unless she were to meet me. No other clue. Nobody else knows." He took up the envelope, and observed that it had part of an address upon it. All he could read, however, was one word—"Lady." "Oho!" he said; "there *is* a title, after all. It looks as if the latter half were a 'W.' There's a conspiracy, and I'm a conspirator! Humph! She's a beautiful creature!"

He fell into meditation on that subject which is always interesting to mere man—the face of a woman. Then his thoughts naturally wandered off to the conversation he had held with that memorable face.

"I *should* like, if I could, to learn how this job will turn out from the hereditary point of view! Will that interesting babe take after his father? Will he astonish his friends by becoming a low comedian? Or will he take after his mother, and become a simple, honourable Englishman? Or will he combine the inferior qualities of both, and become a beautiful and harmonious blend, which may make him either a villain of the deeper dye, or a common cold-blooded man of the world, with a touch of the artist?"

CHAPTER II.

THE ONLY WITNESS GONE.

One afternoon, about eighteen years later, certain mourning-coaches, returning home from a funeral, drew up before a house in Bryanston Square. There were three coaches. From the first descended a young man of twenty or thereabouts, still slight and boyish in figure. He had been sitting alone in the carriage.

From the second came a middle-aged man of the greatest respectability, to look at. He was so respectable, so eminently respectable, that he could not possibly be anything but a butler. With him was a completely respectable person of the other sex, who could be no other than a housekeeper.

In the third carriage there were two young maid-servants in black, and a boy in buttons. At the halting of the carriage they clapped their handkerchiefs to their eyes, because they knew what was expected on such an occasion; and they kept up this external show of grief until they had mounted the steps and the door was shut. The page, who was with them, had been weeping freely ever since they started; not so much from unavailing grief, as from the blackness of the ceremony, and the dreadful coffin, and the horror and terror and mystery of the thing. He went up the stairs snuffling, and so continued for the rest of the day.

The young gentleman mounted to the drawing-room, where his mother, sitting in a straight, high chair, more like an office-chair than one designed for a drawing-room, was dictating to a shorthand girl secretary. The table was covered with papers. In the back drawing-room two other girls were writing. For Lady Woodroffe was president of one society, chairman of committee of another, honorary secretary of a third; her letters and articles were on subjects and works of philanthropy, purity, rescue, white lilies, temperance, and education. Her platform advocacy of such works had placed her in the forefront of civilizing women; she was a great captain in Israel, a very Deborah, a Jael.

The Changeling

She was also, which certainly assisted her efforts, a very handsome woman still, perhaps austere: but then her eloquence was of the severe order. She appealed to the conscience, to duty, to responsibility, to honour. If sinners quailed at contemplating the gulf between themselves and the prophetess, who, like Jeremiah, had so little sympathy with those who slide backwards and enjoy the exercise, it was a perpetual joy to ladies of principle to consider an example so powerful.

She was dressed in black silk, but wore no widow's weeds; her husband, the first Sir Humphrey, had been dead four years.

The young gentleman threw himself into a chair. Lady Woodroffe nodded to her secretary, who gathered up her papers and retreated to the back drawing-room, closing the door.

"Well, mother," said the boy, carelessly, "we've buried the old woman."

"Yes. I hope you were not too much distressed, Humphrey. I am pleased that you went to the funeral, if only to gratify the servants."

"How could I refuse to attend her funeral?—an old servant like that. It's a beastly thing—a funeral,—and a beastly nuisance."

"We must not forget her services," the lady replied. "It was in return for those services that I kept her here, and nursed her through her old age. One does not encumber one's self with sick old women except in such cases as this."

"No, thank goodness." The young man was in no gracious mood. "Give me a servant who takes her wages and goes off, without asking for our gratitude."

"Still, she was your nurse—and a good nurse."

"Too ostentatious of her affection, especially towards the end."

"She was also"—Lady Woodroffe pursued her own thoughts, which was her way—"a silent woman; a woman who could be trusted, if necessary, with secrets—family secrets."

"Thank goodness, we've got none. From family secrets, family skeletons, family ghosts, good Lord, deliver us!"

The Changeling

"There are secrets, or skeletons, in every family, I suppose. Fortunately, we forget some, and we never hear of others. You are fortunate, Humphrey, that you are free from the vexation—or the shame—or the shock—of family secrets, which mean family scandals. Now, at all events, you are perfectly safe, because there is no one living who can create a family ghost for you, or provide you with a skeleton."

Humphrey laughed lightly. "Let the dead bury their dead," he replied. "So long as I know nothing about the skeleton, it can go on grinning in the cupboard, for aught I care.

"Did I tell you," the young man continued, after a pause, "of her last words?"

"What last words?"

"I thought I had told you. Curious words they were. I suppose her mind was wandering."

"Humphrey," said his mother, sharply, "what did she say? What words?"

"Well, they sent for me. It was just before the end. She was lying apparently asleep, her eyes shut. I thought she was going. The nurse was at the other end of the room, fussing with the tea-cups. Then she opened her eyes and saw me. She whispered, 'Low down, low down, Master Humphrey.' So I stooped down, and she said, 'Don't blame her, Master Humphrey. I persuaded her, and we kept it up, for your sake. Nobody suspects. All for your sake I kept it up,' Then she closed her eyes, and opened them no more."

"What do you understand by those words, Humphrey?"

"Nothing. I cannot understand them. She was accusing herself, I suppose, of something—I know not what. What did she keep up? Whom did she persuade? But why should we want to know?"

"Wandering words. Nurses will tell you that no importance can be attached to the last words when the brain wanders. Well, Humphrey, while you were at the funeral I unlocked her drawers and examined the contents. I found that she had quite a large sum of money invested. One is not in good service for all these years without saving

The Changeling

something. There is a little pile of photographs of yourself at various ages. I have put them aside for you, if you like to have them."

"I don't want them," he replied carelessly.

"I shall keep them, then. There is her wardrobe also. I believe she had nephews and nieces and cousins in her native village in India. All her possessions shall be sent out to them. Meanwhile, there is a little packet of things which she tied up a great many years ago, and has kept ever since. The sight of them caused me a strange shock. I thought they had been long destroyed. They revived my memories of a day—an event—certain days—when you were an infant."

"What things are these, then?"

"They were your own things—some of the things which you wore when you were a child in arms, not more than a few months old."

"Oh, they are not very interesting, are they?"

"Perhaps not." Lady Woodroffe had in her lap a small packet tied up in a towel or a serviette. She placed it on the table. "Humphrey, I always think, when I look at old things, of the stories they might tell, if they could, of the histories and the changes which might have happened."

"Well, I don't know, mother. I am very well contented with things as they are, though they might have given my father a peerage. As for thinking of what they might have been, why, I might, perhaps, have been born in a gutter."

"You might, Humphrey"—the widow laughed, which was an unwonted thing in her—"you certainly might. And you cannot imagine what you would be now, had you been born in a gutter."

"What's the good of asking, then?"

"Look at this bundle of your things."

"I don't want to look at them."

"No, I dare say not. But I do. They tell a story to me which they cannot tell to you. I am glad the old woman kept them."

Lady Woodroffe untied the parcel, and laid open the things.

The Changeling

"The story is so curious that I cannot help looking at the things. I have opened the bundle a dozen times to-day, since I found it. I believe I shall have to tell you that story some day, Humphrey, whether I like it or not."

"What story can there be connected with a parcel of socks and shoes?"

"To you, at present, none. To me, a most eventful story. The old nurse knew the story very well, but she never talked about it. See, Humphrey, the things are of quite coarse materials—one would think they were made for that gutter child we talked about."

Her son stooped and picked up a paper that had fallen on the floor.

"'His name is Humphrey,'" he read. "A servant's handwriting, one would think. What was the use of writing what everybody knew?"

"Perhaps some servant was practising the art of penmanship. Well"—she tied up the parcel again—"I shall keep these things myself."

She put the parcel on the table, and presently carried it to her room. Her son immediately forgot all about the old nurse's strange last words, and the parcel of clothes, and everything. This was not unnatural, because he presently went back to Cambridge, where there is very little sympathy with the sentiment of baby linen.

When the door closed upon her son, his mother sprang to her feet.

"Oh!" she clasped her hands. Can we put her thoughts into words—the thoughts that are so swift, into words that are so slow—the thoughts that can so feebly express the mind with words that are so imperfect? "I have never felt myself free until to-day. She is dead; she is buried. On her death-bed she kept the secret. She never wrote it down; she never told any one: had she written it I should have found it; had she told any one I should have heard of it before now. And all, as she said, for the sake of the boy. She meant her long silence. I feared that at the last, when she lay a-dying, she might have confessed. I sat in terror when I knew that the boy was at her death-bed. I thought that when Sir Humphrey died, and the boy succeeded, she might have confessed. But she did not. Good woman, and true! Never by a word, or by a look, or by a sigh, did she let me know that she remembered."

She breathed deeply, as if relieved from a great anxiety.

The Changeling

"I have thought it all over, day after day. There is nothing that can be found out now. The doctor would not recognize me. I suppose he is still slaving at Birmingham; he did not know my name. The mother never saw me. At last, I am free from danger! After all these years, I have no longer any fear."

Over the mantel hung a portrait of her late husband.

"Humphrey," she said, talking to it familiarly, "I did it for your sake. I could not bear that you should lose your boy. All for your sake—all for your sake I screened the child from you. At least you never knew that there is not—there has never been—the least touch of your nobility in the gutter child. He is mean; he is selfish. He has never done a kind action, or said a generous word. He has no friends, only companions. He has already all the vices, but is never carried away; he will become a sensualist, a cold and heartless sensualist. I am sorry, Humphrey, truly sorry, my most noble and honourable husband, that I have given you so unworthy a successor. Yet he is careful; he will cause no scandal. So far, my husband, your name is safe."

CHAPTER III.

THE THREE COUSINS.

"Is it possible?" they repeated, gazing each upon each in the triangular fashion.

Every incident in life is a coincident. That is to say, nothing happens as one expects. The reason is that no one considers the outside forces, which are unseen; very few, indeed, take into consideration the inside forces, which are obvious. The trade of prophet has fallen into decay, because we no longer believe in him; we know that he cannot really prophesy the coincidence: to him, as to us, the future is the unexpected. Wise folk, therefore, go about prepared for anything: they carry an umbrella in July; they build more ships when peace is most profound. The unexpected, the coincidence, gives to life its chief charm: it relieves the monotony; it breaks the week, so to speak. Formerly it might take the form of invasion, a descent upon the coast: dwellers by the seaside enjoyed, therefore, the most exciting lives possible. To-day it comes by telegraph, by post, by postal express. The philosopher of tears says that the unexpected is always disagreeable; he of smiles says that, on the whole, he has received more good gifts unexpectedly than thwacks. Mostly however, the opinion of the multitude, which is always right, is summed up in the words of the itinerant merchant—the man with the barrow and the oranges. "We expex a shilling," he says, "and we gits tuppence."

"Is it possible?"

These three people had arisen and gone forth that morning expecting nothing, and lo! a miracle! For they were enriched, suddenly, and without the least expectation, by the discovery that they were all three of common kin. Imagine the boundless possibilities of newly recovered cousinship! No one knows what may come out of it—an augmentation of family pride, an increase of family griefs, the addition of sympathy with the lowly, the shame and honour of ancient scandals, more money perhaps, more influence perhaps. It may be a most fortunate event. On the other hand—— But for the moment, these three had not begun to consider the other side.

The Changeling

"Is it possible?" Well, it is sometimes best to answer a question by repeating it. The place was a country churchyard; the time, a forenoon in July. In the churchyard was a group of four. They were all young, and two of them were of one sex, and two were of the other.

The girls were the first to arrive. They entered by a gate opening into the churchyard from a small coppice on the north side.

One of the girls, evidently the leader, had in her face, her form, her carriage, something of Pallas Athênê. She was grave—the goddess, I believe, seldom laughed; she was one of those girls who can smile readily and pleasantly, but are not anxious to hear good stories, like the frivolous man at his club, and really saw very little to laugh at even in the unexpectedness of men—nothing, of course, in the ways of women. Her seriousness was sweet in the eyes of those who loved her—that is to say, of all who had the privilege of knowing her. Her head was large and shapely—a shapely head is a very lovely thing in woman. Her figure matched her head in being large and full. Her features were regular, her cheek was ample, like that of a certain bronze Venus in the Museum. Her hair was light in colour, and abundant, not of the feathery kind, but heavy, and easily coiled in classical fashion. Her eyes were of that dark blue which is wickedly said to accompany a deceitful nature. If this is ever true, it certainly was not true of Hilarie Woodroffe. She was dressed in white, as becomes a girl on a summer morning, with a rose at her throat for a touch of colour. As a child of her generation, she was naturally tall; and being, as she was, a girl of the highest refinement and culture after such an education as girls can now command, and being, moreover, much occupied with the difficulties and problems of the age, she bore upon her brow an undoubted stamp of intellectual endeavour. Twenty years ago, such a girl would have been impossible. If you are still, happily, so young that you can doubt this assertion, read the novels—the best and the worst—of that time.

Her companion showed in her face and her appearance more of Aphrodite than the sister goddess. She looked as sprightly as L'Allegra herself; of slighter figure than the other, she was one of those fortunate girls who attract by their manner more than by their beauty. Indeed, no one could call her beautiful; but many called her charming. Her grey eyes danced and sparkled; her lips were always smiling; her

The Changeling

head was never still; her face was made for laughing and her eyes for joy; her hair was of the very commonest brown colour—every other kind of girl has that kind of hair, yet upon her it looked distinguished. The dress she wore—she had designed and made it herself—seemed craftily intended to set off her figure and her face and her eyes. In a word, she was one of those girls—a large class—who seem born especially for the delight and happiness of the male world. They are acting girls, singing girls, dancing girls, even stay-at-home girls; but always they delight their people or the public with their vivacity, and their cheerfulness, and their sympathy. By the side of the other girl she looked like an attendant nymph. I have always thought that it would be a pleasing thing to detach from Diana's train one of those attendant nymphs, whose undeveloped mind knew nothing but the narrow round of duty; to run breathlessly after the huntress, or to bathe with her in a cold mountain stream. I would take her away, and teach her other things, and make her separate and individual. But the fear of Dian has hitherto prevented me. Ladies-in-waiting, in other words, must have a dull time of it.

Both girls, of course, were strong, healthy, and vigorous: they thought nothing of twenty miles on a bicycle; they could row; they could ride; they could play lawn tennis; they would have climbed the Matterhorn if it had been within reach. They were such girls as we have, somehow, without knowing how, without expecting it, presented to modern youth, athletic and vigorous, of the last decade of the nineteenth century.

"This is my churchyard, Molly," said Hilarie. "You have seen the house—this place belongs to the house—and the whole of it belongs to the family history."

"It must be very nice to have a pedigree," said Molly—"ancestors who wore laced coats and swords, like the characters on the stage. My people, I suppose, wore smock-frocks. I gather the fact because my father never mentioned his father. Smocks go with silence."

"One would rather, I suppose, have a pedigree than not."

"Small shops, also, go with silence. I wonder why one would rather have a grandfather in a smock than in a small shop."

The Changeling

"I will tell you something of the family history. Let us sit down on this tombstone. I always sit here because you can see the church, and the alms-houses, and the school, if you like to take them together. So. Once there was a man named Woodroffe, who lived in this village, seised of a manor, as they say. He was a small country gentleman, an Armiger; I will show you his tomb presently, with his coat of arms. This man—it was five hundred years ago—had four sons. One of them stayed at home, and carried on the family descent; the second son was educated by the Bishop, and rose to the most splendid distinction. He actually became Archbishop of Canterbury and Lord Chancellor of England. Now, the father of these lads had friends or cousins—they came from the next village, where their descendants are living still—in the City of London. So the two younger sons were sent up to town and apprenticed, one to a mercer, and the other to a draper; and one of these became Lord Mayor—think of that!—and the other, Sheriff. There was a wonderful success for you! The effort seems to have exhausted the family, for no one else has ever distinguished himself. Stay; there was an Indian civilian of that name, who died some time ago, but I don't know if he belonged to the family. My own branch has always remained hopelessly undistinguished—squires, and plain gentlemen, and Justices of the Peace. They hunted, flogged vagabonds, and drank port. And, of course, after all these years, one does not know what has become of the citizens' descendants."

"Still, Archbishop, Lord Mayor, and Sheriff—that ought to last a long time."

"It has lasted a long time. Well, when they became old, these men resolved to show their grateful sense of the wonderful success which had been accorded to them. So they came back to their native village, and they replaced the little church by a beautiful and spacious church—there it is!"

Truly it was a great and noble church, of proportions quite beyond the needs of a small village; its tower and spire standing high above all the country round, its recessed porch a marvel of precious work. The windows and the clerestory and the roof may be seen figured in all the books on ecclesiastical architecture as the finest specimens of their style.

The Changeling

"Yes, this church was built by these brothers. They walled the churchyard—this is their old grey wall, with the wallflowers; they built the lych-gate—there it is—in the churchyard; they founded a school for the young—there it is"—she pointed to a small stone hall standing in the north-west corner of the churchyard. It was of the same period and of the same architecture as the church; the windows had the same tracery; the buttresses were covered with yellow lichen: a beautiful and venerable structure. From the building there came a confused murmur of voices. "And on the other side of the church they built an almshouse for the old—there it is"—she pointed to a long low building, also of the same architecture. "So, you see, they provided, in the same enclosure, a place of worship for the living, a place of burial for the dead, a school for the young, and a haven of rest for the old."

The sentiment of the history touched her companion, who looked about her, and murmured—

"It seems a peaceful place."

"Everything in the place seems to belong to those four brothers: the old house behind those trees, the broken cross at the gate, the ruined college in the village, the very cottages, all seem to me to be monuments of those four brothers."

"It is a beautiful thing owning such a house and such a place," said the other. "But I prefer your gardens to your churchyard, Hilarie, I confess."

Just then a young man, in a hired victoria, drove up to the gate and descended, and looked about him with an indolent kind of curiosity. He wore a brown velvet coat, had a crimson scarf with a white waistcoat, carried a pince-nez on his nose, had sharp and somewhat delicate features, carried his head high, and was tall enough to convey by that attitude, which was clearly habitual, the assumption of superiority, if not of disdain. And there was in him something of the artist. His face was pale and clean shaven; his lips were thin; his hair was light, with a touch of yellow in it; his eyes, when you could make them out, were of a light blue, and cold. His figure was thin, and not ungraceful. In a word, a young man of some distinction in appearance; of an individuality certainly marked, perhaps self-contained, perhaps selfish.

The Changeling

He walked slowly up the path. When he drew near the girls he raised his hat.

"Am I right," he asked, "in thinking this to be Woodroffe Church?"

"Yes. It is Woodroffe Church."

"The church built by the Archbishop and his brothers?"

"This is their church. That is their school. That is their almshouse. Would you like to go into the church? I have the key with me, and am going in at once."

At this moment they were joined by another young man, whose entrance to the churchyard was not noticed. He had been walking with light elastic step along the middle of the road. A small bag was slung from his shoulder by a strap; he carried a violin-case. His broad felt hat, his brown tweed suit, his brown shoes, were all white with the dust of the road. He passed the church without observing it; then he remembered something, stopped, came back, and turned into the churchyard.

He was quite a young man. His face was clean shaven—a mobile face, with thin lips and quick blue eyes. His hair, as he lifted his hat, was a light brown with a trace of yellow in it, growing in an arch over his forehead. His step was springy, his carriage free. His hair—longer than most men wear it,—the blue scarf at his throat, his long fingers, made one think of art in some shape or other. Probably a musician.

In the churchyard he looked about him curiously.

Then he turned to the group of three, and put exactly the same question as that proposed by the first young man.

"May I ask," he said, "if this is Woodroffe Church?"

The attendant nymph jumped up. "Oh!" she cried. "It's Dick!"

"You here, Molly?" he asked. "I never expected——"

"Hilarie," said the girl, "this is my old friend Dick. We were children together."

Hilarie bowed graciously. "I am pleased to know your friend," she said. "I was just telling this other gentleman that this is Woodroffe Church. We are going into the church: would you like to come too?"

The Changeling

Hilarie led the way, and opened the door of the south porch. Within, restorers had been at work. The seats which replaced the old oaken pews were machine-made, and new; they wanted the mellowing touch of two hundred years, and even then they would be machine-made still. The rood screen, as old as the Archbishop, was so polished and scraped, that it looked almost as much machine-made as the seats. Even the roof, after its scraping and painting, looked brand new. Yet they had not destroyed all the antiquity of the church: there were still the grey arches, the grey pillars, the grey walls and the monuments. There were many monuments in the church; two or three tablets in memory of former vicars; all the rest, shields, busts, and sculptured tombs, in memory of bygone Woodroffes. A low recessed arch in the north wall contained the figure of a Crusader. "He is one of the Woodroffes," said the guide. A recent tablet commemorated one who fell at the Alma. "He was another of them," said the guide. "You are walking over the graves of a whole family; they have been buried here from time immemorial. Every slab in the aisle, and every stone in the chancel, covers one of them."

In the north transept there stood a long low altar-tomb, with carvings on the sides, and a slab of grey granite on the top. Formerly it had been surrounded and covered by a white marble tabernacle richly carved; this was now broken away and destroyed, except a few fragments in the wall. The tomb itself was dilapidated; the granite slab was broken in two, yet the inscription remained perfectly legible. It was as follows:—

"Hic jacent
ROBERTUS WOODROFFE, Armiger,
et
HILARIS, Uxor Ejus,
Qui Robertus obiit Sep. 2, A.D. MCCCCXXXIX."

In the right-hand corner of the slab were the arms of the deceased.

"This tomb," said the guide, "was erected by the Archbishop, to the memory of his father."

On the opposite side of the south transept one of the common Elizabethan monuments was affixed to the wall. It represented figures in relief, and painted. The husband and wife, both in high ruffs, knelt

The Changeling

before a desk, face to face. Below them was a procession of boys and girls, six in number. Over their heads was a shield with a coat-of-arms—the same arms as on the other tomb. The monument was sacred to the memory of Robert Woodroffe, Knight, and Johanna his wife. Beneath the figures was a scroll on which the local poet had been allowed to do his worst.

> "After thy Dethe, thy Words and Works survive
> To shew thy Virtues: as if still alive.
> When thou didst fall, fair Mercy shrieked and swoon'd,
> And Charity bemoaned her deadly Wounde.
> The Orphan'd Babe, the hapless Widow cry'd,
> Ah! who will help us now that thou hast dyed?"

"They made him a knight," said the guide, "against his will. James the First insisted on his assuming the dignity. It was the only honour ever attained by any of this branch. They all stayed at home, contented to make no noise in the world at all. Well, I think I have shown you all the monuments."

"This is my ancestor," said the man with the violin-case, pointing to the first tomb. "Not this one at all."

"Why, the elder Robert is my ancestor also!" said the first young man, wondering.

"Good gracious! He is my ancestor as well!" cried Hilarie, in amazement. "All these Woodroffes belong to me, and I to them."

"Your ancestor? Is it possible?" she added, turning from one to the other.

"Is it possible?" the two men repeated.

"The Archbishop's elder brother is my direct ancestor," said Hilarie. "He is buried here beneath this stone."

"Mine was Lord Mayor Woodroffe," said the first young man. "He was buried in the Church of All Hallows the Less, where his tomb was destroyed in the Fire."

"And mine was the Sheriff," said the second young man. "He was buried in St. Helen's, where you may see his tomb to this day."

The Changeling

"Oh, it is wonderful!" Hilarie looked at her new cousins with some anxiety. The first young man seemed altogether "quite:" well-dressed, well-spoken, well-mannered, well-looking, of goodly stature, a proper youth. In fact, proper in the modern sense. His turn-out was faultless, and of the very day's—not yesterday's—mode. She turned to the other. Circumstances, perhaps, were against him: the dust with which he was covered; the shabby old bag hanging round his neck; his violin-case. A gentleman does not travel on foot, carrying a violin. Besides, his face was not the kind of face which comes out of Eton and Trinity. It was a humorous face; there was a twinkle, or the fag end of a smile, upon it. Such a girl as Hilarie would not at first take readily to such a face. However, he looked quiet, and he looked good-natured; his eyes, realizing the oddness of the situation, were luminous with suppressed laughter.

"Molly," he said, "please tell this lady—your friend—who I am."

"Hilarie, this is Dick Woodroffe. I suppose you have never heard of him. I never thought of his name being the same as yours. Dick is an actor. He sings and plays, and writes comediettas; he is *awfully* clever."

"Thank you, Molly. Add that I am now on tramp."

He looked with some contempt on the other young man.

"Since you are my cousin, Mr. Woodroffe, I hope we shall be friends."

Hilarie shook hands with him. "My name is Hilarie Woodroffe, and I am descended from the eldest brother. The old house, which I will show you presently, has remained with us. And you—are you really another cousin?"

She turned to the first comer.

"I hope so. My name is Humphrey Woodroffe."

"Oh, this is delightful! May I ask what your branch has been doing all these years?"

"I have a genealogy at home. We have had no more Lord Mayors or Archbishops. A buccaneer or two; a captain under Charles the First; a judge under William the Third; and an Anglo-Indian, my father, now dead, of some distinction."

"Your branch has done more creditably than mine. And yours, Cousin Dick?"

He laughed. "We went down in the world, and stayed there. Some of us assisted in colonizing Virginia, in the last century, by going out in the transports. There is a tradition of highwaymen; some of us had quarters permanently in the King's Bench. I am a musician, and a mime, and a small dramatist. Yet we have always kept up the memory of the Sheriff."

"Never mind, Dick," said Molly; "you shall raise your branch again."

He shook his head. "There is not so much staying power," he said, "in a Sheriff as in a Lord Mayor."

Hilarie observed him curiously. "Why," she said, "you two are strangely alike. Do you observe the resemblance, Molly?"

"Yes. Oh yes!"—after a little consideration. "Mr. Humphrey is taller and bigger. But they certainly *are* alike."

"Good Heavens! It is wonderful. The same coloured hair, growing in the same manner; the same eyes. It is the most extraordinary instance of the survival of a type."

The young men looked at each other with a kind of jealousy. They resented this charge of resemblance.

"Like that bounder?" said the look of the young man of clubs. "Like this Piccadilly masher?" was the expression on the speaking countenance of the man on tramp.

"After five hundred years." Hilarie pondered over this strange coincidence. "Let us go back to the churchyard."

At the porch she paused, and bade them look round. "Tell me," she said, "if you have ever seen a place more beautiful or more peaceful?"

The amplitude of the churchyard was in harmony with the stateliness of the church. An ancient yew stood in one corner; the place was surrounded by trees; the steps of the old Cross were hollowed by the feet of many generations; beyond the quiet mounds the dark trees with their heavy foliage made a fitting background; two or three of the bedesmen stood at their door, blinking in the sunshine.

The Changeling

"The almshouse is a reading-room now," said Hilarie. "The old people have quarters more commodious for sleeping, but they come here all day long to read and rest."

They stood in silence for a while.

The swifts flew about the tower and the spire; the lark was singing in the sky, the blackbird in the coppice. The air was full of soft calls, whispers-twitters of birds, the humming of insects, and the rustle of leaves. From the schoolroom came the continuous murmur of children's voices. Another old man passed slowly along the path among the graves towards the almshouse: it seemed as if he were choosing his own bed for a long sleep. Everything spoke of life, happy, serene, and peaceful.

"I am glad you came here," said Hilarie. "It is your own. When you know it you will love everything in it—the church and the churchyard, the trees and the birds, the old men and the children, the living and the dead."

Her eyes filled with tears. Those of the man with the violin-case softened, and he listened and looked round. Those of the other showed no response—they were resting with admiration upon the other girl.

"Come"—Hilarie returned to the duty of hostess,—"let me show you the house—the old, old house—where your ancestors lived."

She led the way to the gate by which she had entered. She conducted them along a path under the trees into a small park. In the middle of the park were buildings evidently of great age. They were surrounded by a moat, now dry, with a bridge over it, and beyond the bridge a little timbered cottage which had taken the place of gate tower and drawbridge. Within was a garden, with flowers, fruit, and vegetables, all together. And beyond the garden was the house. And surely there is no other house like unto it in the whole country. In the middle was a high-roofed hall; at either end were later buildings; beyond these buildings, at one end, was a low broad tower, embattled. The windows of the hall were the same as those of the church, the school, and the almshouse.

The Changeling

"You cannot wonder," said the girl, "that I love to call this house my own—my very own. There is nothing in the world that I would take in exchange for this house. Come in, Cousin Humphrey," she said hospitably. "And—and—my other cousin, Cousin Dick. Besides, you are a friend of Molly's. Come in. You are both welcome."

She opened the door. Within, the great hall had a stone bench running all round; the high-pitched roof was composed of thick beams, black with age; the floor was boarded; the daïs stood raised three or four inches for the high table; the circular space was still preserved beneath the lantern, where the fire was formerly made.

"Here lived Robert," said the chatelaine, "with his four sons. There was no floor to the hall then. The servants took their meals with the master, but below him. The men slept on the floor. This was the common living-room." She led the way to the north end. "Here was the kitchen, built out beyond the hall"—there were signs of women-servants—"and above it"—she led the way up a rude stair—"the solar of three or four rooms, where the lord and lady slept, and the daughters, and the women-servants. At the other end"—she led them to the south end of the hall—"was the lady's bower, where the lady with her maids sat at their work all day. And beyond is the tower, where the men-at-arms, our garrison, lay."

These rooms were furnished. "They are our sitting-rooms." Three or four girls now rose as Hilarie entered the room. She presented her cousins to them. "My friends," she said, simply. "Here we live; we take our meals in the hall. Our servants sleep in the gate-house; we in the solar. Confess, now, my newly-found cousins, is it not a noble house?"

She showed them the tower and the dungeon and the guard-room, all belonging to the Wars of the Roses. And then she led them back to the hall, where a dainty luncheon was spread on a sideboard. The high table was laid for about a dozen. The girls, to whom the cousins had been presented, trooped in after them. At the lower table stood the servants, the coachman and grooms, the gardener and his staff, the women-servants, the wives and children of the men. All sat down together at their table, which ran along the middle of the hall. Before Hilarie's chair, in the middle of the high table, stood an ancient ship in silver; ready for her use was a silver-gilt cup, also ancient; silver cups stood for each of her guests.

The Changeling

"We all dine together," she said—"my friends and I at our table, my servants below; we are one family. My ancestors"—her cousins sat on each side of her—"dined in this fashion. There is something in humanity which makes those friends who break bread together."

"It is like a picnic five hundred years back," said Humphrey. "I have heard talk, all my life, about this place. My father always intended to visit it, but at last grew too old."

Hilarie watched her two guests. The taller, Humphrey, had the manners of society; he seemed to be what the world, justly jealous, allows to be a gentleman. Yet he had a certain coldness of manner, and he accepted the beauty of this ancient place without surprise or enthusiasm.

"What are you by profession, Cousin Humphrey?" she asked.

"Nothing, as yet; I have been travelling since I left Cambridge." He laid his card before her—"Sir Humphrey Woodroffe."

"You have the title from your father. I hope you will create new distinctions for yourself."

"I suppose," he said coldly, "that I shall go into the House. My people seem to want it. There are too many cads in the House, but it seems that we cannot get through the world without encountering cads." He looked through his hostess, so to speak, and upon the third cousin, perhaps accidentally.

"You certainly cannot," observed the third. "For instance, I am sitting with you at luncheon."

"You will play something presently, Dick, won't you?"

Molly, sitting on the other side of the table, saw a quick flush upon her friend's cheek, and hastened to avert further danger. One may be a cad, but some cads are sensitive to an openly avowed contempt for cads.

Dick laughed. "All right, Molly. What shall I play? Something serious, befitting the place? Luncheon is over—I will play now, if you like." He looked down the hall. "That, I suppose, is the musicians' loft?"

"That is the musicians' gallery. It is a late addition—Elizabethan, I believe."

"The musicians' gallery? Well, Miss Woodroffe, I am the music. Let me play you something in return for the fine ancestors you have given me, and for your gracious hospitality."

He took up his violin-case, to which he had clung with fidelity, marched down the hall, climbed up into the gallery, and began to tune his fiddle.

"Hilarie," Molly said, "Dick plays in the most lovely way possible. He carries you quite out of yourself. That is why everybody loves him so."

However, the artist, standing up alone in the gallery, struck a chord, and began to play.

I suppose that the magic belonged to the fiddle itself. It is astonishing what magical powers a fiddle may possess. This was the most sympathetic instrument possible. It was a thought leader or inspirer. The moment it began, all the listeners, including the servants below the salt, sat upright, their eyes fixed upon the gallery, rapt out of themselves.

Hilarie, for her part, saw in a vision, but with a clearness and distinctness most marvellous, her ancestor Robert with Hilarie his wife. They were both well-stricken in years; they were standing in the porch with their eldest son, his wife and children, to receive their visitors. And first, across the drawbridge, rode the great Lord Archbishop and Lord Chancellor, followed by his retinue. When the Archbishop dismounted, the old man and his wife, and the son, and his wife, and his children went on their knees; but the Archbishop bade them rise, and kissed his parents lovingly. Meantime, the pages and the varlets were unloading pack-horses and pack-mules, because the Archbishop would not lay upon his father so great a charge as the entertainment of his following. And she saw next how the Lord Mayor and the Sheriff, his brother, rode up side by side, the Sheriff a little behind the Mayor, and how they dismounted and knelt for their father's blessing; and so all into the hall together, to take counsel for the great things they were minded to do for their native village.

The Changeling

Hilarie turned to her cousin on the right. "Cousin," she said, still in her dream, "we must think of our forefathers, and of what they did. We must ask what the Archbishop would have done in our place."

But her cousin made no reply. He was looking with a kind of wonder at Molly. Had the man never seen an attractive girl before? He had; but out of a thousand attractive girls a man may be attracted by one only.

And the music went on. What was it that the musician played? Indeed, I know not; things that awakened the imagination and touched the heart.

"No one knows," said Molly, "what he plays; only he makes one lost to everything."

As for herself, she had a delicious dream of going on the tramp with Dick, he and she alone—he to play, and she—— But when she was about to tell this dream, she would not confess her part in the tramp.

The music was over; the fiddle was replaced in its case; the musician was going away.

In the porch stood Hilarie. "Cousin," she said, "do you go on tramp for pleasure or for necessity?"

"For both. I must needs go on tramp from time to time. There is a restlessness in me. I suppose it is in the blood. Perhaps there was a gipsy once among my ancestors."

"But do you really—live—by playing to people?"

"He needn't," said Molly; "but he must. He leaves his money at home, and carries his fiddle. Oh, heavenly!"

"Why not? I fiddle on village greens and in rustic inns. I camp among the gipsies; I walk with the tramps and casuals. There is no more pleasant life, believe me!"

He began to sing in a light, musical tenor—

> "When daffodils began to peer,
> With heigh! the doxy over the dale,
> Why then comes in the sweet o' the year;
> For the red blood reigns in the winter's pale.

The Changeling

> The lark that tirra-lirra chants
> With heigh! with heigh! the thrush and the jay,
> Are summer songs for me and my aunts,
> While we lie tumbling in the hay."

"You are a strange man," said Hilarie. "Come and see me again."

"I am a vagabond," he replied, "and my name is Autolycus."

Dick took off his hat and bowed low, not in Piccadilly style at all; he waved his hand to Molly; he glared defiance at Humphrey, who loftily bent his head; and then, catching up his violin-case, he started off with a step light and elastic.

Humphrey, the other cousin, half an hour later, stood beside his carriage.

"I must congratulate myself," he said, "on the good fortune which has presented me to the head of my family."

"To two cousins, say."

"Oh! I fancy we shall not see much of Autolycus. Meanwhile, since you kindly grant me permission, I hope to call upon you again."

"I shall be very pleased."

As he drove away, his last look was not on Hilarie, but on the girl beside her—the girl called Molly—the nymph attendant. Some, the goddess charms; but more, the nymph attendant.

"What was she doing with all those girls?" he asked. "Making a home for them, or some such beastly nonsense, I suppose."

CHAPTER IV.

THE CONSULTING-ROOM.

The doctor's servant opened the door noiselessly, almost stealthily, and looked round the room.

There were half a dozen people waiting. One was an ex-colonial governor, who had been maintaining the empire with efficiency in many parts of the world for thirty years, and was now anxious to keep himself alive for a few years in the seclusion of a seaside town, if certain symptoms could be kept down. There was a middle-aged victim to gout; there was an elderly sufferer from rheumatism; there was an anæmic girl; there was a young fellow who looked the picture of health; and, sitting at one of the windows, there was a lady, richly dressed, her pale face, with delicate features of the kind which do not grow old, looking anxious and expectant.

They were all anxious and expectant: they feared the worst, and hoped the best. One looked out of window, seeing nothing; one gazed into the fireplace, not knowing whether there was a fire in it; one turned over the pages of a society journal, reading nothing; all were thinking of their symptoms. For those who wait for the physician, there is nothing in the whole world to consider except symptoms. They have got to set forth their symptoms to the physician. They have to tell the truth, that is quite clear. Still, the plain truth can be dressed up a little; it can be presented with palliatives. A long course of strong drinks may figure as a short course of weak whisky-and-soda. Perhaps the danger, after all, is not so grave. Patients waiting for the doctor are like persons waiting to be tried for life. Can a man take any interest in anything who awaits his trial for life—who hopes for an acquittal, but fears a capital sentence?

The doctor's manservant looked round the room, and then glided like a black ghost across the thick carpet. He stopped before the lady in the window.

"Sir Robert, madam, will see you."

The Changeling

There are some who maintain that the success of this eminent physician, Sir Robert Steele, M.D., F.R.S., is largely due to the virtues of his manservant. Certainly this usher of the chamber, this guardian of the portal, this receiver of those who bring tribute, has no equal in the profession. In his manner is the respect due to those who know where the only great physician is to be found. There is also an inflexible and incorruptible obedience to the laws of precedence, or order of succession. Thirdly, there is a soft, a velvety, note of sympathy in his voice, as one who would say, "Be of good cheer, sufferer; I bring thee to one who can relieve. Thou shalt not suffer long."

The rest of the patients looked at each other and sighed. He who would follow next sighed with increasing anxiety: his fate would soon be known. He who had yet to wait several turns sighed with impatience. It is hard to be tormented with anxiety as well as with pain. Those symptoms again! They may be the final call. Did Christiana, when the call came, repair first, in the greatest anxiety, to a physician! Or they may be only passing clouds, so to speak, calling attention to the advance of years.

The doctor, in his consulting-room, held a card in his hand—"Mrs. John Haveril." The name was somehow familiar to him. He could not remember, at the moment, the associations of the name. A physician, you see, may remember, if he pleases, so many names. To every man's memory belongs a long procession of figures and faces, with eyes and voices. But most men work alone. Think of the procession in the memory of a physician, who all day long sees new faces and hears new voices! "Haveril." He knew the name. Was she the wife of a certain American millionaire, lately spoken of in the papers?

"The doctor, madam, will see you."

The lady rose and followed him. All the patients watched her with the same kind of curiosity as is shown by those waiting to be tried towards the man who is called to the honours of the dock. They observed that she was strangely agitated; that she walked with some difficulty; that she tottered as she went; that her lips trembled, and her hands shook.

"Locomotor ataxis," whispered one. "I myself——"

"Or perhaps a break-up of the nervous system. It is my own——"

The Changeling

But the door was shut, and the patients in waiting relapsed into silence.

The lady followed the manservant, who placed a chair for her and withdrew.

Instead of sitting down, the patient stepped forward, and gazed into the doctor's face. Then she clasped her hands.

"Thank God," she cried; "he is the man!"

"I do not understand, madam. I see so many faces. The name—is it an American name?"

"You think of my husband. But I am English-born, and so is he."

"Well, Mrs. Haveril, even the richest of us get our little disorders. What is yours?"

"I have been very ill, doctor; but it was not for that that I came here."

"Then, madam, I do not understand why you do come here."

"You don't remember me? But I see that you don't." Her trembling ceased when she began to speak. "Yet I remember you very well. You have changed very little in four and twenty years."

"Indeed?"

"I heard some people at the hotel talking about you. They said you were the first man in the world for some complaints. And I remembered your name, and—and—I wondered if you were the man. And you are the man."

"This is a very busy morning, madam. If you would kindly come to the point at once. What do you want with me?"

"Doctor, I once had a child—a boy—the finest boy you ever saw."

"It is not unusual," the doctor began, but stopped, because the woman's face was filled with a great trouble. "But pray go on, madam."

"I had a boy," she repeated, and burst into a flood of tears.

The doctor inclined his head. There is no other answer possible when a complete stranger bursts into tears from some unknown cause.

The Changeling

"I lost the boy," she proceeded. "I—I—I lost the boy."

"He died?"

She shook her head. "No. But I lost my boy," she repeated. "My husband deserted me. I was alone in a strange town. My relations had cast me off because I married an actor. I was penniless, and I could find no work. I sold the boy to save him from the workhouse, and to get the money to follow my husband."

"Good Heavens! I remember! It was at Birmingham. Your husband's name was—was——?"

"His professional name was Anthony."

"True—true. I remember it all. Yes—yes. The child was taken by a lady. I remember it perfectly. And you are the deserted wife, and the rich American is your husband?"

"No. I followed my husband from place to place; but I had to cross the Atlantic. I came up with him in a town in a Western State. When I found him, he got a divorce for incompatibility of temper. I lost both my husband and my child, and neither of them died."

"Oh! And then—then you came back to look for the boy?"

"No; I married John Haveril. It was before he made his money."

"And now you come to me for information about the child, who must be a man by this time?"

"I've never forgotten him, doctor. I never can forget him. Every day since then I have thought of him. I said, 'Now he's six; now he's ten; now he's twenty.' And I've tried to think of him as he grew up. Always—always I have had the boy in my mind."

"Yes; but surely—— Perhaps you had no more children?"

"No; never any more. And last spring I fell ill—very ill. I was——"

"What was the matter?"

She told him the symptoms.

"Yes; nerves, of course. Fretting after the child."

The Changeling

"You know. The American doctor did not. Well, and while I was lying in my dark room, I had a dream. It came again. It kept on coming. A dream which told me that I should see my child again if I came to London. So my husband brought me over."

"And you think that you will find your child?"

"I am sure that I shall. It is the only thing that I have prayed for. Oh, you need not warn me about excitement; I know the danger. I don't care so very much about living; but I want that dream to come true. I must find the boy."

"You might as well look for him at the bottom of the sea. Why, my dear lady, your boy was intended to take the place of a dead child; I am sure he was. I know nothing at all about him. There is no clue—no chance of finding the child."

"Do you know nothing?"

"Upon my honour, madam, I cannot even guess. The lady did not give me her name, and I made no inquiries."

"Oh!" Her face fell. "I had such hopes. At the theatre, yesterday, I saw a young man who might have been my son—tall, fair, blue-eyed. Oh, do you know nothing?"

"Nothing at all," he replied decidedly. "And you came here," he went on, "remembering my name, and wondering whether it was the same man? Well, Mrs. Haveril, it *is* the same man, and I remember the whole business perfectly. Now go on."

"Where is that child, doctor?"

"I say that I don't know. I never did know. The lady gave me the money, received the child at the railway station. You brought it to the waiting-room. She had an Indian ayah with her, and the train carried her off, baby and all. That is all I can tell you."

Mrs. Haveril sighed. "Is that all?"

"Madam, since such precautions were taken, it is very certain that no one knew of the matter except the lady herself, and she will certainly not tell, because, as I have already told you, the case looked like substitution, and not adoption."

The Changeling

"What can I do, then?"

"You can do nothing. I would advise you to put the whole business out of your head and forget it. You can do nothing."

"I cannot forget it: I wish I could. The wickedness of it! Oh, to give away my own child only to run after that villain!"

"My dear lady, is it well to allow one single episode to ruin your life? Consider your duty to your second husband. You should bring him happiness, not anxiety. Consider your splendid fortune. If the papers are true, you are worth many millions."

"The papers are quite true."

"You yourself are still comparatively young — not more than five and forty, I should say. Time has dealt tenderly with you. When I knew you, in Birmingham, you were a girl still, with a delicate, beautiful face. How could your husband desert you? Your face is still delicate and still beautiful. You become the silks and satins as you then became your cottons. Resign yourself to twenty years more of happiness and luxury. As for that weakness of yours, it will vanish if you avoid excitement and agitation. If not — what did your American adviser warn you?"

She rose reluctantly. "I cannot forget," she said. "I must go on remembering. But the dream was true. It was *sent*, doctor; it was sent. And the first step, I am sure and certain, was to lead me here."

After a solitary dinner, Sir Robert sat by the fire in his dining-room. A novel lay on a chair beside him. Like many scientific men, he was a great reader of novels. For the moment, he was simply looking into the fire while his thoughts wandered this way and that. He had seen about twenty patients in the course of the day, and made, in consequence, forty guineas. He was perfectly satisfied with the condition of his practice; he was under no anxiety about his reputation: his mind was quite at ease concerning himself from every point of view. He was thinking of this and of that — things indifferent — when suddenly he saw before him, by the light of the four candles on the table, the ghost of a date. The figures, in fact, stood out, luminous, against the dark mahogany of his massive sideboard.

The Changeling

"December 2, 1872." He rubbed his eyes; the figures disappeared; he lay back; the figures came again.

"It's a trick of memory," he said. "What have I done to-day that could suggest this date?" The only important event of the day was the visit of his old patient, and the reminder about a certain adoption in which he had taken a part. Was the date connected with that event?

He got up and went into his consulting-room. There, on a shelf among many companions, he found his note-book of 1874. He remembered. The time was winter; it was early in the year. He turned over the pages; he came to his notes. He read these words: "Child must have light hair, blue eyes; age—must be born as nearly as possible to December 2, 1872, date of dead child's birth."

"That's the date, sure enough," he said. "And the brain's just been working round to it, without my knowledge—of its own accord—started by that poor woman. Humph!"

He put back the note-book, and returned to the dining-room.

He sat down by the fire again, crossed his feet, lay back, took up the novel, and prepared for a comfortable hour.

In vain. That business of the adoption came back to him. The letters on the page melted into dissolving views: he saw the poor woman crying over the child, and clutching at the money which would save the boy from the workhouse and carry her to her husband; he saw the Indian ayah taking the child from him, and the lady bowing coldly from the railway carriage. "A lady through and through," said the doctor.

The torn envelope was addressed to "Lady——" She was a woman of title, then. He got up; on the bookshelves of the dining-room was a Red Book.

"Now," he said, "if I go right through this book from beginning to end, and if I should find the heir to something or Lord Somebody, born on December 2, 1872, I shall probably come upon the victim of this conspiracy—if there has been a conspiracy."

Luckily he began at the end, at the letter Z. Before long, under the fourth letter from the end, he read as follows:—

The Changeling

"Woodroffe, Sir Humphrey Arundale, second baronet; born at Poonah, December 2, 1872; son of Sir Humphrey Armitage Woodroffe, first baronet, G.C.B., G.C.M.G., formerly Lieut-Governor of Bengal, by Lilias, daughter of the fifteenth Lord Dunedin. Succeeded his father in 1888. Educated at Eton and Trinity College, Cambridge. Is a captain in the Worcestershire Militia. Residence, Crowleigh, Worcestershire, and Bryanston Square, London. Clubs, 'Junior United,' 'Travellers,' and 'Oriental.'"

"That's my man!" cried the doctor, with some natural excitement. "I believe I've found him. Then there *has* been substitution, after all, and not adoption! But, good Lord! it's Lady Woodroffe! Lady Woodroffe! It's the writer and orator and leader! Oh, purity! Oh, temperance! Oh, charity! What would the world say, if the world only knew?"

He threw the book aside and sat down. "I told that woman," he reflected, "that I knew nothing about the lady who carried off her child. Well, I did not know then. But I do know now. Must I tell her? Why disturb things? She can never find out. Let her go back to her adopted land. And as for this—this substitution—I promised solemnly that I would not speak about the business, even if I were to chance upon that lady, without her leave. My dear Mrs. Haveril, go home to America and forget the boy who is now the second baronet. Go home; it will be best for your health. 'The first step,' she said. Strange! The first step. But not for you, dear lady, not for you."

CHAPTER V.

GUEST NIGHT.

"I am glad to see you again, Cousin Humphrey."

It was two months after the meeting in the churchyard. Hilarie's house was full; her guests overflowed into the village. It was, in fact, the first guest night of the season.

"This is the beginning of Term," she said. "You shall make acquaintance with the college."

"I have heard something about your college." He looked round the room, which was the lady's bower, as if in search of some one.

"You can take me in, and I will tell you more about it during dinner."

There were more than the house-party. The place is within an hour of Victoria, and a good many friends of the students had come out by train to see what the college was like; what it meant; and if it had come to stay.

A new social experiment always draws. First, it attracts the social wobblers who continually run after the last new gospel. Then it attracts those who watch social experiments from the outside. Thirdly, it attracts the New Woman herself; those who are curious about the New Woman; and those who hate the New Woman. Lastly, it attracts those who are always in search of material for "copy." For all these reasons, the guests present wore that expression of countenance called, by their friends, "thoughtful;" it should rather be called "uncertain." They looked about curiously, as if to find traces of the experiment in the furniture, on the walls, in the students' dresses; they listened in order to catch the note of the experiment in the air; they cast suspicious looks to right and to left, as expecting something to be sprung upon them. To be invited at all was to make them realize that they were in the very van and forefront of contemporary intellect; it also imposed upon them the difficult task of pronouncing a judgment without a "lead." Now, without a lead these philosophers are uncertain. Hence the aspect and appearance of the guests this evening. They did not know what to think or what to say of the college—no one had yet given them a lead; they were uncertain, and they would be expected to pronounce a judgment.

The oracle who waits for a "lead" is common among us; he takes himself seriously; he is said by his friends to have "made the most" of himself: not that he has distinguished himself in any way, but he has made the best out of poor materials, and he would have made himself a good deal bigger and better had the materials been richer. As it is, he reads all the thoughtful papers in all the magazines; he writes thoughtful papers of his own, which he finds a difficulty in placing; he sometimes gets letters into the papers giving reasons why he, being a very little man, cannot agree with some great man. This makes his chin to stick out. He even contrives to get people to read his letters, as if it matters a brass farthing whether he agrees or does not agree. Over a new social experiment, once he has got a "lead," this oracle is perfectly happy.

"We will talk presently," said Hilarie, turning to welcome new guests.

Humphrey stepped aside, and looked on while the room filled up. The students, he remarked, who were all dressed in white, with ribbons of their own individual choice, appeared to be a cheerful company of damsels. To be sure, cheerfulness belongs to their time of life, and to the profession of student, about which there should cling a certain lawless joyousness—a buoyancy not found in the domestic circle, a touch of the barrack, something of the camp, because they are recruits in the armies that fight against ignorance and prejudice. These white-robed students were full of cheerfulness, which bubbled over in laughter and happy faces. One is told that in some colleges there are students entirely given over to their studies, who wear dowdy dresses, who push back their hair anyhow behind their spectacles, who present faces of more than possible thoughtfulness. Here there were none such; none were oppressed with study.

Rightly considered, every college for young persons should be interesting. We have forgotten that there used formerly to be colleges for old persons; for priests, as Jesus Commons and the Papey on London Wall; for physicians; for surgeons; for serjeants-at-law; for debtors, as the Fleet; for the decayed, as an almshouse; for criminals, as Newgate; for paupers, as the workhouse. A college for girls is naturally more interesting than one for young men: first, because they are girls; next, because the male college contains so much that is disquieting,—ambition and impatience, with effort; strenuous endeavour to conciliate Fame, a goddess who presents to all comers at first a deaf ear, eyes that see nothing, and a trumpet silently dangling at her wrist; the resolution to compel Fortune, even against her will, to turn round that wheel which is to bear them up aloft. The strength of these ambitions stimulates the air—you may note this effect in any of the courts at Cambridge. One remembers, also, that in most cases Fame, however persistently wooed, continues to dangle the silent trumpet; while Fortune, however passionately invoked, refuses to turn the wheel; and that the resolution and determination of the petitioner go for nothing. One observes, also, that the courts of the colleges are paved with shattered resolutions, which make a much better pavement than the finest granite. One remembers, also, that there are found in the young man's college the Prig and the Smug, the Wallower, the Sloth, the Creeping Thing, and the Contented Creature. But pass across the road to the Woman's College. Heavens! what possibilities are there! What ambitions are hers! For her field is not man's field, though some pretend. Not hers to direct the throbbing engine, and make that thing of steel a thing of intelligence; not hers to command a fleet; not hers to make the laws. She does not construct lighthouses; she does not create new sciences; she does not advance the old; she never invents, nor creates, nor advances; she receives, she adapts, she distributes. How great are her possibilities! Though she neither creates nor invents, she may become a queen of song, a queen of the stage, a great painter, a great novelist, a great poet—great at artistic work of every kind. Or, again, while her brother is slowly and painfully working his way up, so that he will become a Q.C. at forty, a Judge at sixty, the girl steps at once by marriage into a position that dazzles her friends, and becomes a queen of society, a patron of Art, a power in politics. Far be it from me to suppose that the maidens of any college dream of possibilities such as these. Perhaps, however, the possibilities of maidenhood are never quite forgotten. There is another possibility also. Every great man has a mother. Do maidens ever dream of the supreme happiness of having a great man for a son? Which would a woman prefer, the greatest honour and glory and distinction ever won by woman for herself, or to be the mother of a Tennyson, a Gordon, a Huxley?

The Changeling

"Now, my cousin," said Hilarie. "The dinner is served."

So two by two they went into the old hall. It had been decorated since the summer. The lower part was covered with tapestry; the upper part was hung with armour and old weapons. There were also portraits, imaginary and otherwise, of women wise and women famous. Queen Elizabeth was there, Joan of Arc was there, George Sand, George Eliot, Elizabeth Barrett Browning, Jane Austen, Grace Darling, Rosa Bonheur, and many others. The male observer remarked, with a sense of omission, the absence of those queens of beauty whose lamentable lives make history so profoundly interesting. Where were Rosamond, Agnes Sorel, La Vallière, Nell Gwynne? Alas! they were not admitted.

"The house," said the president, taking her seat, "is much larger than it looks. With the solar and the lady's bower and the tower, we have arranged dormitories for forty and half a dozen sitting-rooms, besides this hall, which is used all day long."

The musicians' gallery had been rebuilt and painted. It contained an organ now and a piano, besides room for an orchestra. Six of the students were sitting there with violins and a harp, ready to discourse soft music during the banquet. There were three tables running down the hall, with the high table, and all were filled with an animated, joyous crowd of guests and residents.

"I want to interest you in my college," Hilarie began, when they were seated.

Humphrey examined the menu. He observed that it was an artistic attempt—an intelligent effort at a harmony. If only the execution should prove equal to the conception!

"At present, of course, we are only beginning. What are you yourself doing, however?"

"I follow—humbly—Art. There is nothing else. I paint, I write verse, I compose."

"Do you exhibit?"

"Exhibit? Court the empty praises or the empty sneers of an ignorant press? Never! I show my pictures to my friends. We confide our work to each other."

The Changeling

Hilarie smiled, and murmured something inaudible.

"And we keep the outer world outside. You, I fear"—he looked down the room—"admit the outer world. You lose a great deal. For instance, if this mob was out of your lovely house, I might bring my friends. It would be an ideal place for our pictures and our music, and for the acting of our plays."

"I fear the mob must remain." Hilarie began to doubt whether her college would appeal, after all, to this young man.

"What we should aim at in life," the artist continued, "is Art without Humanity."

"I should have said that Humanity is the basis of all Art."

Her cousin shook his head. "Not true Art—that is bodiless. I fear you do not yet belong to us."

"No; I belong to these girls, who are anything but bodiless."

"Your college, I take it, has something to do with helping people?"

"Certainly."

"My own view is that you cannot help people. You may give them things, but you only make them want more. People have got to help themselves."

"Did you help yourself?"

"Oh, I am born to what my forefathers acquired. As for these girls, to whom you are giving things, you will only make them discontented."

The president of the college looked round the hall. There were forty white frocks encasing as many girls, students at her college, and as many guests. There was a cheerful ripple of talk; one thought of a dancing sea in the sunlight. There were outbursts of laughter—light, musical; one thought of the white crests of the waves. In the music-gallery the girls played softly and continuously; one thought of the singing of birds in the coppice. The dinner was already half finished. There is a solid simplicity about these guest nights. A short dinner, with jellies, ices, and puddings, most commends itself to the feminine heart.

The Changeling

"Let me tell you my design, at least. I saw that in this revolution of society, going on so rapidly around us, all classes of women are rushing into work."

"A woman who works ceases to be a woman," Humphrey spoke and shuddered.

"I think of my great-grandmother Hilarie, wife of Robert, who lies buried in our church. She sat with her maids in the lady's bower and embroidered. She administered everything—the food and the drink and the raiment. She made them all behave with decency. She brought up the children, and taught them right and wrong. Above all, she civilized. To-day, as yesterday and to-morrow and always, it is the duty of woman to civilize. She is the everlasting priestess. This is therefore a theological college."

Her cheek flushed, her eye brightened. She turned her head, as if suspecting that she had said too much. Her cousin seemed not to have heard; he was, in fact, absorbed in partridge.

"Now that all women want to work, will they continue to civilize? I know not yet how things may go. They all want to work. They try to work, whether they are fit for it or not. They take men's work at a quarter the pay. I know not how it will end. They turn the men adrift; they drive them out of the country, and then congratulate themselves—poor fools! And for themselves, I chiefly dread their hardening. The woman who tries to turn herself into a man is a creature terrible—unnatural. I know the ideal woman of the past. I cannot find the ideal woman of the present."

"There isn't any."

"If we surrender the sacerdotal functions, what have we in exchange?"

"I don't know." The manner meant, "I don't care;" but Hilarie hardly observed the manner.

"I cannot alter the conditions, cousin. That is quite true. But there are some things which can be done."

Hilarie went on, at this point, to tell a story, for one who could read between the lines—which her cousin certainly could not—of a girl dominated partly by a sense of responsibility and duty; one who, being rich, must do something with her wealth, partly by that passion for power which is developed in some hearts—not all—by the possession of wealth; and partly by a deep sympathy with the sufferings and sorrows of her impecunious sisters.

There are always, as we know, at every moment of life, two courses open to us—the right and the wrong; or, if the choice is not so elementary, the better and the worse. But there comes to those of the better sort one supreme moment when we seem to choose the line which will lead to honour, or the line which will lead to obscurity. To the common sort the choice is only apparent, not real; men and women are pushed, pulled, dragged, shoved, either in the way of fortune or in the way of failure, by circumstances and conditions beyond our control. To them there is no free will. When the time of repentance arrives, we think that we choose freely. The majority cannot choose; their lives are ordered for them, with their sins and their follies. They might choose, but they are not able; they cannot see before them or around them. A fog lies about their steps; they stumble along with the multitude, getting now and then a pleasant bit, now and then a thorny bit. Some walk delicately along a narrow way, which is grassy and flowery, where the babbling brooks run with champagne, and the spicy breezes are laden with the fragrance of melons, peaches, and roast lamb. Some march and stagger along the broad way, thirsty and weary, where there is no refreshment of brooks or of breezes. It is an unequal world.

Such a supreme moment came to Hilarie after long consideration.

"I thought," she explained, "that if the Archbishop and his brethren were living to-day, they would do something for the women who work."

Her cousin slowly drank a glass of champagne. "Yes?" he asked, without much affectation of interest.

"I thought that if the Archbishop were living, he would like to found a college—not for priests, nor for old villagers, but for girls; not to teach anything, but to give them a place where they can go and stay. In this college we do not teach anything. There are no lectures. We need not do any work unless we please. Every girl does exactly what she pleases: some study, some paint—not after your school, I fear;

The Changeling

some practise music; in fact, they do just what they please. I believe that at least a dozen are writing novels, two or three are writing verse, one or two are working for examinations. In the evening we amuse ourselves."

"You give them all this?"

"Certainly. They come here whenever they please, and they can stay here for three months, or more if there is necessity. In three words, my cousin, I maintain an establishment of forty guests, and I fear I shall have to increase the number."

"And what's the good of it?"

"When the Archbishop built his school, he argued, first, that education is good even for the swineherd; next, that with education follow manners; and, thirdly, that it was good for himself to give. So, you see, it is good for the girls to get the rest and quiet; living thus all together in a college raises their standard of thought and manners; and, thirdly, it is good for me, as it was the Archbishop, to give."

"I do not feel myself any call to give anybody anything."

"Meantime, I keep before myself the great function of woman. She is, I say, the eternal priestess. She compels men into ways of gentleness and courtesy; she inspires great thoughts. By way of love she leads to the upper heights. But you do not feel these things."

"I do not, I confess."

"If the girls must work, I want them ever to keep before themselves the task laid upon them. They have hitherto civilized man from the home; they must now civilize him from the workshop. That, my cousin, is the meaning of this college."

"You've got some rather pretty girls in the place," said Humphrey.

"Oh, pretty! What has that to do with it?"

The music ceased. There was a general lull. The guests all leaned back in their chairs. The president knocked with her ivory hammer, and they all returned to the lady's bower.

In the drawing-room Humphrey left the president to the people who pressed in upon her, and wandered round the room, looking,

The Changeling

apparently, for some one. Presently he discovered, surrounded by a company of men, the girl who was called Molly. She, too, was dressed in white, and wore a cherry-coloured ribbon round her neck; a dainty damsel she looked, conspicuous for this lovely quality of daintiness among them all. At sight of her the young man coloured, and his eye brightened; then his face clouded. However, he made his way to her. She stepped out of the circle and gave him her hand.

"It is a week and more," he whispered, "since I have seen you. Why not say at once that you don't care about it any longer?"

"You are welcome to the college, Sir Humphrey," she replied aloud. "Confess that it is a pretty sight. The president was talking to you about it all dinner-time. I hope that you are interested."

"I think it is all tomfoolery," he replied ungraciously; "and a waste of good money too."

"Hilarie wants money to make happiness. You do not look in the best of tempers, Humphrey."

"I am not. I couldn't get enough to drink, and I have had to listen to a lot of stuff about women and priestesses."

"Good stuff should not be thrown away, should it? Like good pearls."

"I want to talk to you—away from this rabble. Where can we go?"

"I will take you over the college." She led the way into the library, a retired place, where she sat down. "Do you ask how I am getting on?"

"No, I don't." He remained standing. "You'll never go on the stage with my consent."

"We shall see." By her quick dancing eye, by her mobile lips, by the brightness of her quaint, attractive face, which looked as if it could be drawn into shapes like an india-rubber face, she belied his prophecy. "Besides, Hilarie wants me to become a tragic actress. Please remember, once more, Humphrey, that what Hilarie wishes I must do. I owe everything to Hilarie—everything."

"You drive me mad with your perverseness, Molly."

"I am going to please myself. Please understand that, even if I were engaged to you, I would keep my independence. If you don't like that,

The Changeling

take back your offer. Take it back at once." She held out both her hands, as if she was carrying it about.

"You know I can't. Molly, I love you too much, though you are a little devil."

"Then let me alone. If one is born in a theatre, one belongs to a theatre. I would rather be born in a theatre than in a West End square. Humphrey, you make me sorry that I ever listened to you."

"Well, go and listen to that fiddler fellow who calls you Molly. Curse his impudence!"

"Oh, if you had been only born differently! You belong to the people who are all alike. You sit in the stalls in a row, as if you were made after the same pattern; you expect the same jokes; you take the same too much champagne; you are like the pebbles of the seashore, all rounded alike."

"Well, what would you have?"

"The actors and show folk—my folk—are all different. As for kind hearts, how can you know, with your tables spread every day, and your champagne running like water? There's no charity where there's no poverty."

"I don't pretend to any charity."

"It is a dreadful thing to be born rich. You might have been so different if you had had nothing."

"Then you wouldn't have listened to me."

"Thank you. Listening doesn't mean consenting."

"You cannot withdraw. You are promised to me."

"Only on conditions. You want me to be engaged secretly. Well, I won't. You want me to marry you secretly. Well, I won't."

"You are engaged to me."

"I am not. And I don't think now that I ever shall be. It flattered me at first, having a man in your position following around. I should like to be 'my lady.' But I can't see any happiness in it. You belong to a different world, not to my world."

The Changeling

"I will lift you into my world."

"It looks more like tumbling down than getting lifted up. There is still time, however, to back out. If you dare to maintain that I ever said 'Yes,' I'll say 'No' on the spot. There!"

This sweet and loving conversation explains itself. Every one will understand it. The girl lived in a boarding-house, where she took lessons from an old actress in preparation for the stage. From time to time she went to stay with her friend—her benefactress—who had found her, after her father's death, penniless. At her country house she met, as we have seen, her old friend Dick, and the other cousin. The second meeting, outside the boarding-house, which the latter called, and she believed to be, accidental, led to other meetings. They were attended by the customary results; that is, by an ardent declaration of love. The girl was flattered by the attentions of a young man of position and apparent wealth. She listened to the tale. She found, presently, that her lover was not in every respect what a girl expects in a lover. His ideas of love were not hers. He turned out to be jealous, but that might prove the depth and sincerity of his love; suspicious, which argued a want of trust in her; ashamed to introduce her to his own people; anxious to be engaged first and married next, in secrecy; avowedly selfish, worshipping false gods in the matter of art and science; and, worst of all, ill-tempered, and boorish in his ill temper. Lastly, she was, at this stage, rapidly making the discovery that not even for a title and a carriage and a West End square ought she to marry a man she was unable to respect.

"We will now go back to the lady's bower," she said. "This talk, Humphrey, will have to last a long while."

CHAPTER VI.

THE OLD LOVER.

"My dear Dick!" Molly ran into the dining-room of her dingy boarding-house, which was also the reception-room for visitors. "At last! I thought you were never coming to see me again."

"It has been a long summer. I only came home last night."

"Sit down, and let me look at you." She put him in a chair, and turned his face to the light, familiarly holding it by the chin. "You look very well, Dick. You are browned by the summer's sun, that's all."

She released his chin, and lightly boxed his ears. They had always been on very friendly terms, these two.

"Well, Dick, tell me about your summer. Has it been prosperous? Have you had adventures?" She laughed, because she knew very well the kind of adventures that this young man desired.

"Adventures come to the adventurous, Molly."

"Oh, how I envied you that day when you turned up among the tombs, covered all over with dust, looking so fit and going so free! If I were only a man, to go off with you on the tramp!"

"I wish you were, Molly. We would go off together. I've often thought of it. You should carry a mandoline; I would stick to the fiddle. We would take a room at the inn, and have a little show. You should dance and sing and twang the mandoline. I should play the fiddle and do the patter. We should have a rare time, Molly."

"We should, oh, we should! Do you remember that time when daddy let me go with him, and you came too?"

"I do. I remember how charming you looked, even then! You were about fourteen; you wore a red flannel cap. You used to take off your shoes and stockings whenever we came to a brook, and wade in it with your pretty bare feet."

"And we rested on the trunks of trees in the woods, and had dinner in the open. And you talked to all the gipsies in their own language. And

The Changeling

one night we sat round their fire, and had some of their stew for supper. Oh! And we listened to the birds, and made nosegays of honeysuckle. And the people came to the inn at night while you played the fiddle, and daddy sang comic songs and did conjuring tricks. Oh, what a time it was!"

"And you danced. Don't forget your dance, Molly. I taught you that dance."

The girl laughed merrily. Then she threw herself into the attitude common to all dancing-girls in all ages and all countries—the arms held out and the foot pointed.

"I haven't forgotten it, Dicky. I only wish I could forget it." She sighed. "It would be better for me if I could."

"If we *could* go away together, Molly!" He took her hand and held it.

"Don't, Dick, don't! You make me feel a longing for the road and the country."

"There's nothing like it, Molly darlin', nothing! When the summer comes, I'm off. All the winter I live in a lonely flat, and am respectable."

"As respectable as you can be, Dick."

"Well, I put on dress clothes and get engagements. I don't mind, so that in summer I can be a tramp and a rogue and a vagabond."

"Not a rogue, Dick."

"I was born behind the scenes in a circus at St. Louis before my worthy parent ran away from his wife. It's in the blood, I suppose. I don't care, Molly, what they say." He sprang to his feet, and began to walk about. "There is no life like it. We don't want money; we don't try to be gentlefolk. We're not cooped up in cages. All we've got to do is to amuse the people. We're not stupid; we're not dull. We're not selfish; we are contented with a little. We're never tired of it. We're always trying some new business. My poor Molly, you're out of it. Pity, pity!" He sat down again, shaking his head. "And you born to it—actually born to it!"

The Changeling

"Well, I'm to have the next best thing to it. I'm to be an actress, at any rate."

"An actress! Well, that's something. Tell me about it, Molly."

"A serious actress—a tragic actress. It's all settled. I'm to show the world the real inwardness of Shakespeare. I'm to be the light and lamp of all other actresses. I'm to be another Siddons."

"You another Siddons? Oh, Molly!" He laughed, but not convincingly. The part of the scoffer was new to him. "You, with that face, with those lips, with those eyes? My child, you might be another Nelly Farren, but never another Siddons."

The girl laughed too; but only for a moment. Then she became serious.

"It's got to be, Dick. Don't tempt me. Don't make me unhappy. It would grieve Hilarie awfully if I failed or changed my mind—which is her mind."

"My cousin Hilarie hasn't the complete disposal of your life, has she?"

"She ought to have, because she saved my life. What should I have done, Dick, when daddy died and left me without a penny? There are relations about, I dare say; but I don't know where. My only chance was to get in somewhere. You were away. What could I do? Eighteenpence a night to go on——"

"No, no; not with that crew, Molly."

"There Hilarie found me. And she thinks she is doing the best thing in the world for me when she gets me taught to be a tragedy queen."

"You shall be a great actress, Molly. You shall rake in fifty pounds a week, and you shall wear long chains of diamonds, if you like."

"I've got ambition enough, if that counts for anything. I like that part of it where the great actress sweeps across the stage, with all the people shouting and clapping. Why, when daddy took me to the pit, and I used to watch the leading lady marching majestically—like this—with her long train, sweeping it back—so—I resolved to be an actress. And when she spoke the lines, I didn't care twopence about the sense, if they had any; I was thinking all the time how grand she

The Changeling

looked, and how splendid it must be to have all the world in love with you."

"You shall have it, Molly—if you like, that is. You were always ready to think about fellows being in love with you, were you not?"

"Why not? The stories and the plays and the songs are all about love. A girl can't help wanting all the world to be in love with her. At the theatre I used to see love and admiration on every man's face. The women's faces were not so full of love, I noticed."

"Oh, you noticed that, did you? At so early an age? Wonderful!"

"And now, Dick, now, you see, I've found out that it means work; and after all the work it may mean failure. Sometimes I think—Dick, I don't mind saying everything to you—girls who are beautiful—like me, in my way—were never intended to work; they were to be rewarded for their good looks by—you know—the prince, Dick."

"Sometimes it comes off," Dick replied thoughtfully. "There was Claribel Winthrop—Jane Perks her real name was—in one of my country companies; she married a young lord. But she worked desperately hard for it. All of us looked on and backed her up. It might come off that way; but I should be sorry, Molly. You're born for better things; you ought to have an empty purse."

"What should you say, Dick, if it was to come off that way?"

"Is there a young lord, then? Already?" He changed colour.

"He isn't a lord, but he is not far off, Dick; and I can have him if I like."

"What sort of a fellow, Molly? Oh, be very careful. It is the devil and all if he isn't the right sort. Do you like him?" His face twisted as if he could not find it in his heart to like him.

"He's a baronet. He's young. He wants to conceal things. His mother doesn't like show folk. He thinks most people are cads. He's rich."

"You don't mean to say it's that cousin of mine—not Sir Humphrey?"

She nodded her head. "You don't like him, I know. I'm afraid he's got a temper, and I don't know if I shall be able to put up with him."

"You haven't promised, have you?"

The Changeling

"He says I have. But I haven't, really. I am always reminding him that there is still time to draw back. But, Dick, think! To have plenty of money! To be independent!"

Dick groaned. "It's the greatest temptation in the world. Eve's apple was made of gold, and after she'd got it she couldn't eat it. You think of that, Molly. You can't eat a golden apple. Now, I could give you a real delicious Ribstone pippin." He sat down beside her, and took her hand again. "It's very serious, my dear." It is the manner of the stage to address the ladies so. It means nothing. Whether it is also the manner to take their hands, I know not. "You must be very careful, Molly. Will my other cousin, Hilarie, advise?"

"It's a secret, so far. But don't think about it, Dick. I've got to please Hilarie first. The young man will have to be considered next."

"Well, if there's nothing fixed — — Molly, I don't like the fellow, I own. I don't like any of the lot who talk about outsiders and cads, as if they were a different order. Still, if it makes you happy — Molly, I swear there's nothing I wouldn't consent to if it would make you happy." The tears stood in his eyes.

"My dear Dick," she said. "There's nobody cares for me so much as you." And the tears stood in her eyes as well.

The young man let go her hand, and stood up. "That's enough, Molly — so long as we understand. Now tell me about the studies. Are you really working?"

"Really working. But, oh, Dick, my trouble is that the harder I work the more I feel as if it isn't there. I do exactly what I am told to do, and it doesn't come off."

"But when you used to sing and dance — —"

"Oh, anybody could make people laugh."

The actor groaned. "She says — anybody! And she can do it! And they put her into tragedy!"

"Whenever I try to feel the emotion myself, it vanishes, and I can only feel myself in white satin, with a long train sweeping to the back of the stage, and all the house in love with me."

The Changeling

"This is bad; this is very bad, Molly."

"See, here, Dick, I'm telling you all my troubles. I am studying the part of Desdemona—you know, Desdemona who married a black man. How could she?—and of course he was jealous. I've got to show all kinds of emotion before that beast of a husband kills me."

"It's a fine part—none finer. Once I saw it played magnificently. She was in a travelling company, and she died of typhoid, poor thing! Yes, I can see her now." He acted as he spoke. "She was full of forebodings; her husband was cold; her distress of mind was shown in the way she took up trifles, and put them down again; she spoke she knew not what, and sang snatches of song; in her eyes stood tears; her voice trembled; she moved about uneasily; she clutched at her dress in agitation.

"'The poor soul sat sighing by a sycamore tree,
    Sing all a green willow.'"

"Why," cried the girl, "you make me feel it—you—only with talking about it! And I—alas! Have I any feeling in me at all, Dick?"

"Oh yes, it's there—it's there all right. There's tragedy in the most unpromising materials, if you know how to get at it. I think a woman's got to be in love first. It's a very fine thing for an actress to fall in love—the real thing, I mean. Then comes jealousy, of course. And after that, all the real tragedy emotions."

"Oh, love!" the girl repeated with scorn.

"Try again now; you know the words."

Molly began to repeat the lines—

"My mother had a maid called Barbara;
She was in love, and he she loved proved mad,
And forsook her; she had a song of 'Willow.'"

She declaimed these lines with certain gestures which had been taught her. She broke off, leaving the rest unfinished.

The effect was wooden. There was no pity, no sorrow, no foreboding in the lines at all. Dick shook his head.

"What am I to say to Hilarie?" she asked.

The Changeling

Dick passed his fingers through his hair. Then he sat down again, and began to laugh—laughed till the tears ran down his cheeks.

"You a tragedy queen!" he said. "Not even if you were over head and ears in love. Now, on the other hand, if I had my fiddle in my hand, and were to play—so—that air which you remember"—he put out his legs straight and sat upright, and pretended the conduct of a fiddle and bow—"could you dance, do you think, as you used to dance two years ago?"

She stood before him, seeming to listen. Then she gently moved her head as if touched by the music. Then she raised her arms and began to dance, with such ease and grace and lightness as can only belong to the dancer born.

"Thank you, Molly." He stood up as if the music was over. "We shall confer further upon this point—and other points. When may I come again to visit Miss Molly Pennefather?"

He caught her head in his hands and kissed her gaily on her forehead—after all, he had no more manners than can be expected of a tramp—and vanished.

"If Dick could only play 'Desdemona'!" she murmured, looking after him at the closed door. "Why, he actually *looked* the part. I suppose he has been in love. If I could only do it so!" She imitated his gestures, and broke out into singing—

"The poor soul sat sighing by a sycamore tree,
   Sing all a green willow."

"No," she said; "it won't do. I don't feel a bit like Desdemona. I am only myself, and I am filled with the most unholy longing for money—for riches, for filthy lucre, which we are told to despise."

Her eyes fell upon a newspaper, folded and lying on the floor. It had probably dropped out of Dick's pocket. She took it up mechanically, and opened it, expecting nothing. The sheet was one of the gossipy papers of the day, full of personal paragraphs. She glanced at it, thinking of the paragraphs about herself and her grand success, which would probably never appear, unless she could transform herself.

Presently her eye caught the word "millionaire," and she read—

The Changeling

"Among the *nouveaux riches*—the millionaires of the West—we must not, as Englishmen, forget to enumerate Mr. John Haveril, who has made his money partly by transactions in silver-mines, and partly by the sudden creation of a town on his own lands. He is said to be worth no more than two or three millions sterling, so that he is not in the very front rank of American rich men. Still, there is a good deal of spending, even in so moderate a fortune. Mr. Haveril is by birth an Englishman and a Yorkshireman. He was born about sixty years ago, and emigrated about the year '55. His wife is also of English origin, having been born at Hackney. Her maiden name was Alice Pennefather."

Molly looked up in bewilderment. "There can't be two people of that name!" she said. She went on with the paper—

"They have no children to inherit their wealth. They have arrived in London, and have taken rooms at the Hôtel Métropole."

That was all. She put the paper on the table. "Alice Pennefather! Why, she must be the Alice who disappeared—Dad's first cousin! But Alice married an actor named Anthony; Dad gave her away. He often wondered what had become of her. This Mr. Haveril is a second husband, I suppose. And now she's a millionairess! I think I might go and call upon her at the Hôtel Métropole. I will."

CHAPTER VII.

THE MASTER OF THE SITUATION.

The lady looked at the card. "Sir Richard Steele, M.D., F.R.S.," and in the corner, "245, Harley Street, W."

"Who is Sir Richard Steele?"

Her visitor came upstairs. He stood before her and bowed.

"I was right," he said. "I remember your face perfectly. But you do not appear to remember me, Lady Woodroffe."

"Indeed, Sir Richard. But if you will refresh my memory ——"

"I have to recall to you an incident in your life which happened four and twenty years ago."

"That is a long time ago." So far she suspected nothing.

"Yes; but you cannot have forgotten it. I have called, Lady Woodroffe, against my wish, to remind you of a certain adoption of a child a few days after the death of your own boy, at Birmingham, just about four and twenty years ago. It is impossible that you have forgotten the incident. I see that you have not." For the suddenness of the thing fell upon her like a paralytic stroke. She sat motionless, with parted lips and staring eyes. "You have not forgotten it," he repeated.

"Sir," she said, forcing herself to speak, "you talk of things of which I know nothing. What child? What adoption? Why do you come here with such a story?"

"Let me remind you again. You were passing through Birmingham with your child and an Indian ayah. The child was taken ill, and died. You called at my surgery—I was then a small general practitioner in a poor quarter of Birmingham—you asked me if I could procure a child for adoption. I understood that it was, perhaps, for consolation; I guessed that it was, perhaps, for substitution. You told me that the child was to have light hair and blue eyes; and for age it was to correspond tolerably nearly with that of your own lost child, whose

The Changeling

birth-date you gave me—December the 2nd, 1872. I have the date in my note-book. Now do you remember anything about it?"

"Nothing," she replied, with pale face and set lips; "nothing."

"I found you out, only yesterday, by means of this date. I was reminded of the date, and I suspected substitution. I therefore looked through the Red Book, and I came to the name of the present baronet. He was born, it is stated, on December 2, 1872—the exact date on which your own child was born. I looked out your address; I am here. I remember you perfectly. And I now find that my suspicions were correct."

"Do you accuse me of substituting a strange child for my own?" She spoke in words of indignation, but in a voice of terror.

"I merely state what happened—a transaction in which I took part. That is all, so far."

"Where is your proof? I deny everything. Prove what you say."

"It is very easy. I recognize in you the lady who conducted the business with me. I took the child myself to the railway station. I gave the child to the ayah, who took it to the carriage in which you were sitting."

"Proof! What kind of proof is that? You look in the Red Book, you find a date, and you make up a story."

"A man in my position does not make up stories. I am no longer a general practitioner; I am one of the leaders of my profession. I am no longer either obscure or poor. I have nothing whatever to gain by telling this story."

"Then, sir, why do you come to me with it at all?"

"Partly out of curiosity. I was curious to ascertain whether chance had directed me to the right quarter. I am satisfied on that score. Partly I came in order to warn you that the story may possibly be brought to light."

"How? how?"

"Since you are not concerned, it doesn't matter, does it? I may as well go." But he did not move from his chair.

The Changeling

"So far as I am concerned, there is no truth in it."

"In that case, I can do nothing except to tell the person who is inquiring what I know. I can send her to you. Consider again, if you please. There is no reason for me to hide my share in the transaction—not the least. And if you continue to declare that you are not the purchaser of the baby, I am freed from the promise I made at the time, to maintain silence until you yourself shall think fit to release me from my promise."

"Who is inquiring, then?"

"Is the story true?"

The lady hesitated; she quailed. The physician looked her in the face with eyes of authority. His voice was gentle, but his words were strong.

"You must confess," he said, "or I shall leave you. If you continue to deny the fact, I repeat that I shall feel myself absolved from my promise."

"It is true," she murmured, and buried her face in her hands.

"I only wanted the confirmation from your own lips. Now, Lady Woodroffe, be under no anxiety. I hope that this is the only occasion on which we shall discuss a subject naturally painful to you."

She sat without reply, abashed and humiliated.

"I remember," he said, "speaking to you then on the subject of heredity. Let me ask you if the boy has turned out well?"

"No. He turned out badly."

"About his qualities, now. His father was artistic in a way. He could sing, play, and act."

"This boy plays pretty well; he makes things which he calls songs, and smudges which he calls paintings. He is a prig of bad art, and consorts with other young prigs."

"His mother was, I remember, tenacious, honest, and careful."

"The boy is obstinate and ill-conditioned."

The Changeling

"Her qualities in excess. His father was handsome, selfish, and unprincipled."

"The boy is also handsome, selfish, and unprincipled."

"Humph! You speak bitterly, Lady Woodroffe."

"You know what I am, what I write, what I advocate."

"The whole world knows that."

"Imagine, then, what I suffer daily. Oh, how strong must be the force of hereditary vice when it breaks out after such an education!"

"It should make you a little more lenient, Lady Woodroffe. Your last papers on the exceeding wickedness of man would be less severe if you looked at home."

"This is my punishment. I must bear it till I die. But"—she turned sharply on her accomplice—"he must remain where he is. There must be no scandal. I cannot face a scandal. But for that he should have gone, long ago, back to his native kennel."

"Let him remain. No one but you can turn him out."

"Doctor—Sir Richard—can I really trust you?"

"Madam, hundreds of people trust me. I am a father confessor. I know all the little family secrets. This is only one secret the more. It is interesting to me, I confess, partly because I was concerned in the business, and partly because I was curious to know what kind of man would emerge from this boy's birth, and his education, and the general conditions of his life."

"I may rely upon that promise?"

The doctor spread out his hands. "Other people do rely upon my secrecy: why not you?"

"And you will not tell the boy? For that matter, if you tell him, I would just as soon that you told the whole world."

"I have long since promised that I would reveal the matter to no one unless you gave me leave."

She sighed. She leaned her head upon her hand. She sighed again.

The Changeling

"Let it be so," she said. "Consider me, then, as one of your patients. Let me come to you with this trouble of mine, which disturbs me night and day. It is not repentance, because I would do it again and again to shield that good and great man, my late husband, from pain. No; it is not repentance; it is fear of being found out. It is not the dread of seeing this young man turned out of the position he holds—I care nothing about him—it is fear of being found out myself."

"Madam, you can never be found out. There is only one person who knows the lady in question, and that is myself. I have only to continue the attitude which, till yesterday, was literally true—that I knew nothing about the lady, neither her name, nor her place of residence, nor anything at all—and you are perfectly safe. No one can find out the fact; no one even can suspect it."

"How has the question arisen, then? What do you mean by inquirers?"

"There is only one inquirer at present. She is certainly an important inquirer, but she is only one."

"She! Who is it?"

"The mother of the child."

"Quite a common creature, was she not?"

"I don't know what you call common; say undistinguished, born in the lower middle class—a nursery governess, married to a comedian first, and to an American adventurer next, who is now a millionaire. She called upon me, and began to inquire."

"Well, but what does she know?"

"Nothing, except that she parted with her boy when she was poor, and she would give all the world to get him back now that she is rich."

"He would not make her any happier. I can assure her of that."

"Perhaps not. She saw a young man somewhere, who reminded her of her husband. This made her remember things. She heard my name mentioned, and came to see if I was the man she knew in Birmingham."

"And then?"

"All I could say was—truthfully—that I knew nothing about the lady."

The Changeling

"What will she do?"

"I don't know. But she can discover nothing. Believe me, she can do nothing—nothing at all. It was well, however, to warn you—to tell you. The young man she saw may have been your son. It was at the theatre."

"He goes a good deal to the theatre—to see the girls on the stage."

"His true father was also, I believe, inclined that way. The best way, I take it, if I may advise——"

"Pray advise."

"One way, at least, would be to take the bull by the horns and bring them together. When she finds that the young man so like her husband is your son, she will at least make no further investigation in this direction."

"Do what you like," said the lady, sinking back in her chair. "I desire nothing except to avoid a scandal—such a scandal, Sir Richard; it would kill me."

"There shall be no scandal. The secret is mine." Sir Richard rose. "I promise, once more, to keep this secret till you give me permission to reveal it."

"Will you ever have to ask my permission?"

"On my honour, I believe not. I cannot conceive any turn of the wheel which would make such a permission desirable."

"My death, perhaps, might set you free; and it would rid society of a pretender."

"No. For then the scandal would be doubled. Your husband's name would be charged with the thing as well as your own. Rest easy, Lady Woodroffe. I will make her acquainted, however, with the young man."

The Changeling

CHAPTER VIII.

THE COUSINS.

The hall of a West End hotel on a fine afternoon, even in October, not to speak of June, is a spectacle of pious consolation in the eyes of those who like the contemplation of riches. Many there are on whose souls the sight of wealth in activity, producing its fruits in due season, pours sweet and balmy soothing. All those lovely costumes flitting across the hall, the coming and the going of the people in their carriages, the continual arrival of messengers with parcels, the driving up to the hotel or the driving off, the hotel porters, the liveries, the haughty children of pride and show who wear them—these things in a desert of longing illustrate what wealth can give, and how much wealth is to be envied; these things make wealth appear boundless and stable. Surely one may take such wealth as this to the halls of heaven! Inexhaustible it must be, else how could the hotel bills be paid? The magnificent person in uniform, with a gold band round his cap, makes wealth all-powerful as well as beautiful, else how could he receive a wage at all adequate to his appearance and his manners? The noble perspective of white tables through the doors on the right, and of velvet sofas through the doors on the left, proves the illimitable nature of the modern wealth of the millionaire, else how could those sumptuous dinners be paid for? The American accent which everywhere strikes the ear further indicates that the wealth mostly belongs to another country, which makes the true philanthropist and the altruist rejoice. "Non nobis, Domine," he chants, "but to our neighbours and our cousins." So long as there is accumulated wealth, which enables us to run these big hotels, and to maintain these costly costumes, and to keep these messengers on the trot, why should we grumble? All the world desires wealth. It is only at such places as the entrance-hall of a great hotel that the impecunious can really see with their own eyes, and properly understand, what great riches can actually do for their possessor. What can confer happiness more solid, more satisfying, more abiding, than to buy your wife a costume for two hundred guineas, and to live in such a hotel as this, with the

The Changeling

whole treasures of London lying at your feet, and waiting for your choice?

About half-past four, when the crush of arrivals was greatest, and the talk in the hall was loudest, another carriage and pair deposited at the hotel an elderly couple. The man was tall and thin; his features were plain, but strongly marked; his hair was grey, and his beard, which he grew behind his chin, was also grey. You may see men like him in face and figure, and in the disposition of his beard behind his chin, in every Yorkshire town—in fact, he was a Yorkshireman by birth, though he had spent the last forty years of his life in the Western States. His face was habitually grave; he spoke slowly. This man, in fact, was one of that most envied and enviable class—the rich American. In those lists which people like so much to read, the name of John Haveril was generally placed about halfway down, opposite the imposing figures 13,000,000 dollars. Reading these figures, the ordinary average Briton remarked, "Dollars, sir; dollars. Not pounds sterling. But still, two millions and a half sterling. And still rolling, still r-r-r-rolling!" The city magnate, reading them, sighs and says, "He cannot spend a quarter of the income. The rest fructifies, sir—fr-r-r-ructifies!"

John Haveril arrived at this pinnacle of greatness by methods which I believe are perfectly well understood by everybody who is interested in the great mystery of making money. It is a mystery which is intelligible, easy, and open to everybody. Yet only a very few—say, one in twenty millions—are able to practise the art successfully. A vast number try to cross that stormy sea which has no chart by which they can navigate their barques; rocks strike upon them and overwhelm them; hurricanes capsize and sink them. Disappointment, bankruptcy, concealment for life, flight, ruin, cruel misrepresentation, even open trial, conviction, sentence, and imprisonment are too often the consequences when persons who, perhaps, possess every quality except one—or all the qualities but one or two—in imperfection. Corners, rings, trusts, presidencies, the control of markets, monopolies, the crushing of competition, the trampling down of the weaker, disregard of scruple, tenderness, pity, sympathy, belong to the success which ought to have made John Haveril happy.

The fortunate possessor of thirteen millions—dollars—got out of the carriage when it stopped. He looked round him. On the steps of the

The Changeling

hotel the people drew back, hushed and awed. "John Haveril!" he heard, in whispers. He smiled. It is always a pleasure *monstrari digito*. He marched up the steps and into the hall, leaving his wife to follow alone.

This lady, whom we have already met in the doctor's consultation-room, was dressed in the splendour that belonged to her position. It is useless to have thirteen millions of dollars if you do not spend some of them in proclaiming the fact by silks and satins, lace and embroidery, chains of gold and glittering jewels. Mr. Haveril liked to see his wife in costly array. What wife would not willingly respond to such a pleasing taste in a husband? On this point, at least, the married couple's hearts beat as one — in unison. Mrs. Haveril, therefore, ought to have enjoyed nothing so much as the triumphal march across the hall, with all the people gazing upon her as the thrice happy, the four times happy, the pride of her country, the millionairess.

I do not think that she ever, under any circumstances, got the full flavour out of her wealth. You have seen her with the doctor; a constant anxiety weighed her down; she was weak in body and troubled in mind. She was no happier with the millions than if they had been hundreds. Moreover, she was always a simple woman, contented with simple ways — one to whom footmen, waiters, and grand dinners were a weariness. With her pale, delicate face, and sad soft eyes, she looked more like a nun in disguise than a woman rolling in gold.

Their rooms were, of course, on the first floor; such rooms, so furnished, as became such guests. Parcels, opened and unopened, were lying about on the tables and chairs, for they had only as yet been two or three days in London, and, therefore, had only begun to buy things. Tickets for theatres, cards of visitors, invitations to dinner, had already begun to flow in.

A waiter followed them upstairs, bearing a tray on which were cards, envelopes with names, and bits of paper with names. Mrs. Haveril turned them over.

"John," she said, "I do believe these are my cousins. They've found us out pretty soon."

It was, in fact, only the day after the arrivals were put in the papers.

The Changeling

John turned over the cards. "Humph!" he said. "Now, Alice, before these people come, let us make up our minds what we are going to do for them. What brings them? Is it money, or is it love?"

"I'm afraid it's money. Still, when one has been away for five and twenty years, it does seem hard not to see one's cousins again. 'Tisn't as if we came back beggars, John."

"That's just it. If we had, we shouldn't have been in this hotel. And they wouldn't be calling upon us."

"They're all waiting down below."

"Let 'em wait. What are we to do, Alice? They want money. Are you going to give 'em money?"

"It isn't my money, John. It's yours."

"'Tis thine, lass," the Yorkshireman replied. "If 'tis mine, 'tis thine. But leave it to me." He turned to the waiter who had been present, hearing what was said with the inscrutable face of one who hears nothing, "Send all these chaps and women up," he said. "Make 'em come up—every one. And, Alice, sit down and never move. I'll do the talking."

They came up, some twenty in number. One of the blessings which attend the possession of great wealth is its power in bringing together and uniting in bonds of affection the various members of a family. Branches long since obscure and forgotten come to the light again; members long since supposed—or hoped—to be gone away to the Ewigkeit appear alive, and with progeny. They rally round the money; the possessor of the money becomes the head of the family, the object of their most sincere respect, the source of dignity and pride to the whole family.

They trooped up the broad staircase, men and women, all together. They were old, and they were young; they presented, one must acknowledge, that kind of appearance which is called "common." It is not an agreeable thing to say of any one, especially of a woman, that he—or she—has a "common" appearance. Yet of Mrs. Haveril's cousins so much must be said, if one would preserve any reputation for truth. The elder women were accompanied by younger ones, their daughters, whose hats were monumental and their jackets deplorable: the ladies, both old and young, while waiting below, sniffed when

The Changeling

they looked around them. They sniffed, and they whispered half aloud, "Shameful, my dear! and she only just come home!"—deploring the motives which led the others, not themselves, to this universal consent. The men, for their part, seemed more ashamed of themselves than of their neighbours. Their appearance betokened the small clerk or the retail tradesman. Yet there was hostility in their faces, as if, in any possible slopping over, or in any droppings, from the money-bag, there were too many of them for the picking up.

They stood at the door, hesitating. The splendour of the room disconcerted them. They had never seen anything so magnificent.

Mrs. Haveril half rose to greet her cousins. Beside her stood her husband—of the earth's great ones. At the sight of this god-like person an awe and hush fell upon all these souls. They were so poor, all of them; they had all their lives so ardently desired riches—a modest, a very modest income—as an escape from poverty with its scourge, that, at the sight of one who had succeeded beyond their wildest dreams, their cheeks blanched, their knees trembled.

One of them boldly advanced. He was a man of fifty or so, who, though he was dressed in the black frock which means a certain social elevation, was more common in appearance, perhaps, than any of the rest. His close-set eyes, the cunning in his face, the hungry look, the evident determination which possessed him, the longing and yearning to get some of the money shown in that look, his arched back and bending knees, proclaimed the manner of the man, who was by nature a reptile.

He stepped across the room, and held out his hand. "Cousin Alice," he said softly, even sadly, as thinking of the long years of separation, "I am Charles—the Charlie of your happy childhood, when we played together in Hoxton Square." He continued to hold her hand. "This is, indeed, a joyful day. I have lost no time in hastening here, though at the sacrifice of most important business—but what are my interests compared with the reunion of the family? I say that I have lost no time, though in the sight of this crowd my action might possibly be misrepresented."

The Changeling

"You are doing well, Charles?" asked Mrs. Haveril, with some hesitation, because, though she remembered the cousinship, she could not remember the happy games in Hoxton Square.

"Pretty well, Alice, thank you. It is like your kind heart to ask. Pretty well. Mine is a well-known establishment. In Mare Street, Hackney. I am, at least, respectable—which is more than some can say. All I want," he stooped and whispered, "is the introduction of more capital—more capital."

"We cannot talk about that now, Cousin Charles." Mrs. Haveril pushed him gently aside; but he took up a position at her right hand, and whispered as each came up in turn.

The next was a man who most certainly, to judge by his appearance, was run down pretty low. He was dressed in seedy black, his boots down at heel, his tall hat limp.

He stepped forward, with an affectation of a laugh. "I am your cousin Alfred, Alice. Alf, you know." She did not remember; but she offered him her hand. "I had hoped to find you alone. I have much to tell you."

"A bankrupt, Alice," whispered Charles. "Actually a bankrupt! And in this company!"

"If I am," said Fortune's battered plaything, "you ought to be, too, if everybody had his rights."

Cousin Charles made no reply to this charge. Do any of us get our deserts? The bankrupt stepped aside.

Then a pair of ladies, old and young, stepped forward with a pleasing smile.

"Cousin Alice," said the elder, "I am Sophy. This is my daughter. She teaches in a Board school, and is a credit to the family, as much as if she had a place of business in Mare Street, I'm sure."

"Pew-opener of St. Alphege, Hoxton," whispered Cousin Charles.

And so on.

While the presentation was going on, a young lady appeared in the door. She saw the crowd, and held back, not presenting herself. She was none other, in fact, than Molly. Strange that a little difference in

The Changeling

dress and in associates should make so great a difference in a girl. Molly was but the daughter of a tenth-rate player, yet she was wholly different from the other girls in the room. She belonged to another species of humanity. It could not be altogether dress which caused this difference. She looked on puzzled at first, then she understood the situation, and she smiled, keeping in the background, waiting the event.

When they were all presented, Mrs. Haveril turned to her husband.

"John," she said, "these are my cousins. Will you speak to them, and tell them that we are pleased to see them here?"

John Haveril possessed three manners or aspects. The first was the latest. It was the air and carriage and voice of one who is in authority, and willing to exercise it, and ready to receive recognition. A recently created peer might possess this manner. The second was the air and carriage and voice of one who is exercising his trade. You may observe this manner on any afternoon near Capel Court. The third manner was quite different. It was his earliest and youngest manner. In this he seemed to lose interest in what went on, his eyes went out into space, he was for the time lost to the place and people about him.

On this occasion John Haveril began with the first manner — that of authority.

"Cousins," he said, "you are welcome. I take it you are all cousins, else you wouldn't have called. You don't look like interviewers. My wife is pleased to see you again, after all these years — five and twenty, I take it."

There was a general murmur.

"Very well, then. Waiter, bring champagne — right away — and for the whole party. You saw, ladies and gentlemen, a paragraph in the papers about Mr. and Mrs. John Haveril. Yes, and you have come in consequence of that notice. Very well."

"That's true," cried Cousin Charles, unable to resist the expression of his admiration. "To think that we should stand in the presence of millions!"

The Changeling

"And so you've come, all of you," said John of the thirteen millions, "to see your cousin again. Out of love and affection?"

"Some of us," said Cousin Charles. "I fear that others," he cast one eye on the bankrupt and one on the pew-opener, "have come to see what they can get. Humanity is mixed, Mr. Haveril. You must have learned that already. Mixed."

"Thank ye, sir. I have learned that lesson."

"To see our cousin Alice once more, to desire, Mr. Haveril, to see you—to gaze upon you—is with some of us, laudable, sir—laudable."

"Quite so, sir. Highly laudable."

"As for me," said the bankrupt, abashed, "I did hope to find Cousin Alice alone."

"And if Mr. Charles Pennefather," said the pew-opener, "means that he wants nothing for himself, let him go, now that he has seen his Cousin Alice! Let him go on down-trodding them poor girls in his place of business."

At this point, when it seemed likely that the family would take sides, the waiter appeared, bearing in his arms—I use the word with intention—a Jeroboam of champagne. He was followed by two boys, pages, bearing trays; and on the trays were glasses.

A Jeroboam! The sight of this inexhaustible vessel suggests hospitality of the more lavish: generosity of the less calculating: it contains two magnums and a magnum contains two bottles. Can one go farther than a Jeroboam? There are legends and traditions in one or two of the older hotels—those which flourished in the glorious days of the Regent—of a Rehoboam, containing two Jeroboams. But I have never met in this earthly pilgrimage with a living man who had gazed upon a Rehoboam. At the sight of the Jeroboam all faces softened, broadened, expanded, and began to slime with a smile not to be repressed. Cousin Charles thrust his right hand into his bosom, and directed his eyes, as if for penance, to the cornice.

"Now," said Mr. Haveril, "you came here to see your cousin again. You shall drink her health—all of you. Here she is. Not so hale and hearty as one could wish; but alive, after five and twenty years, or thereabouts. Now, boys, pass it round."

The glasses went round—the wine gurgled and sparkled. Cousin Charles gave the word.

"Cousin Alice!" he cried. "All together—after me!" He raised his glass. "Cousin Alice!" He emptied it at one draught.

"I think," said the pew-opener, in an audible whisper to her daughter, "that it would have been more becoming to offer port wine. I don't think much of this fizzy stuff."

"Hush! mother." The daughter had more reading, if less experience. "This is champagne. It's rich folks' drink, instead of beer."

The waiter and the boys went round again. The second glass vanished, without any toast. Eyes brightened, cheeks flushed, tongues were loosened.

"Cousin Alice," said the bankrupt, emboldened. "If I could see you alone——"

"Don't see him alone," whispered Cousin Charles. "Don't see anybody alone. They all want your money. They are leeches for sucking and limpets for sticking. Turn 'em over to me. I'll manage the whole lot for you. Very lucky for you, Cousin Alice, that I did call, just this day of all days, to stand between you and them."

But Cousin Alice made no answer. And they all began whispering together, and the whisper became a murmur, and the murmur a babble, and in the babble voices were raised and charges were made as of self-seeking, pretence, hypocrisy, unworthy motives, greed of gain, deception, past trickeries, known meannesses, sordidness, and so forth. And there was a general lurch forward, as if the cousins would one and all fall upon Alice and ravish from her, on the spot, her husband's millions.

But Cousin Charles, self-elected representative, stepped forward and held up his hand.

"We cannot part," he said. "It is impossible for you to leave me with my Cousin Alice——"

The Changeling

"Ho!" cried the pew-opener, "you alone with Cousin Alice!"

"See you alone, Alice," whispered the bankrupt, on whose weak nerves and ill-nourished brain the champagne was working.

"—without drinking—one more toast. We *must* drink," he said, "to our cousin's illustrious, noble, and distinguished husband. Long may he continue to enjoy the wealth which he so well deserves and which none of us envy him. No, my friends, humble and otherwise, none of us envy him. Mr. Haveril, sir, I could have wished that the family—your wife's family—which is, as you know, one of eminent respectability—an ancient family, in fact, of Haggerston——"

"Grandmother was a laundress," said the pew-opener. "Everybody knows that all the Haggerston people were washer-women in the old days."

"—had been better represented on this occasion by a limited deputation of respectability—say, by myself, without the appearance of branches, which should not have been presented to you, because we have no reason to be proud of them." He glanced at the decayed branch. "Sir, we drink your prolonged health and your perpetual happiness. We are proud of you, Mr. Haveril. The world is proud of you."

With a murmur, partly of remonstrance with the speaker's arrogance and his insinuations against their respectability; and partly meant for a cheer, the family drank the health of Mr. John Haveril.

"Thank ye," he said, with no visible emotion. "Now, take another glass—send it round, waiter—while I say something. It's just this." As he spoke his manner insensibly changed. He became the man of business, hard as nails. "I take it that some of you are here to see your cousin again, and some of you are here to get what you can, and some for both reasons. It's natural, and I don't blame anybody. When a body's poor, he always thinks that a rich man can make him rich, too. Well, he can't—not unless he makes over half his pile. And I'll tell you why. A chap is poor because he's foolish or lazy. Either he can't see the way or he won't stir himself. You can't help a blind man—nor you can't help a lazy man. If you give either of them what he wants, he spends it all, and then holds out his hand and asks for more." The bankrupt dropped his head, and sank into a chair. The champagne

The Changeling

helped him to apply this maxim to his own case. "The best thing that can be done for any one is to dump him down in a new country where he'll sink or swim. You, sir," he pointed a minatory finger to Cousin Charles, "you would like more capital, would you?"

"Not in the presence of this multitude, Mr. Haveril," Cousin Charles replied.

"Those who want capital, either here or anywhere else, have got to make it for themselves."

"So true—so true," said Cousin Charles. "Listen to this, all of you."

"Make it for themselves. Same as I did. How much capital had I to start with? Just nothing. Whatever you want, make it for yourself by your own smartness. There's nothing else in the world to get a man along but smartness. In whatever line you are, cast about for the prizes in that line and look out for opportunities. If you can't see them, who can help you? As for you, sir," he addressed the bankrupt, "you want money. Well, if I give you money you will eat it up, and then come for more. What's the use, I ask any of you?"

He looked round. Nobody answered. Cousin Charles, perspiring at the nose, murmured faintly, "So true—so true," but not with conviction. Some of the women wiped away a tear—they had taken four glasses of champagne, but fortunately a waiter does not quite fill up the glasses.

"Not one of you would be a bit the better off, in the long run, if I gave him a thousand pounds."

"Not to give, but to advance," said Cousin Charles.

"Not a bit the better off," John Haveril repeated. "Not a bit. We've got to work in this world—to work, and to think, and to lay low, and to watch. Those who can do nothing of all this had better sit down quiet in a retired spot. My friends, there's nothing shameful in taking a back seat. Most of the seats are in the back. Make up your mind that such is your lot, and you may be happy, though you've got no money. I've been poor, and now I'm rich. Seems to me I was just as happy when I was poor and looking out."

He paused for a moment.

The Changeling

"Alice doesn't want to throw you over. What then? Why—this. Any one of you who came to ask for something may do it in writing. Let him send me a letter—and tell me all about it. If it's a thing that will do you no harm, I'll do it for you. But I don't expect it is, only to feel that you've got somebody who'll give you what you ask for just because you ask for it. Why, there can't be in all the world anything worse for him. Remember that you've got to work for a living, to begin with; harder if you make your fortune, and harder still if you want to keep it. That's the dispositions of Providence, and I'm not going to stand in the way of the Lord. Go home, then. Take example by me, if you can. But if you came to coax dollars out of Alice, give it up."

The audience looked at each other ruefully. They did not know what to say in reply. Nor did they know how to get off. Nobody would move first. Cousin Charles stepped forward.

"Mr. Haveril," he said, "in the name of the family, worthy or unworthy, as the case may be; greedy or disinterested, as it may be; I thank you. Whatever words may drop from you, sir, will be treasured. What you have said are golden words. We shall, I hope, write them down and engrave them on the marble tombstones of our hearts. They will be buried with us. My friends," he addressed the family, "you can go."

"Not without you," said the pew-opener—"you and your respectability."

"Some of us will prepare that little note, I dare say—I fear so, Mr. Haveril," Cousin Charles went on. "In business, as you know, the introduction of capital is not a gift nor a charity; but I will explain later on, when these have gone."

"Not without you," said the lady pew-opener, planting her umbrella firmly on the carpet.

There was so much determination in her face that Cousin Charles quailed; he bent, he bowed, he submitted.

"On another, a more favourable occasion, then, when we can be private," he said. "Good-bye, Cousin Alice. You look younger than ever. Ah, if these friends present could remember you as I can, in the spring-time of youth and beauty, among the laurels and the

The Changeling

laburnums and the lilacs of Hoxton Square! Love's young dream, cousin; love's young dream." He grasped her hand, his voice vibrating with emotion. "Alice," he said, "on Sunday evenings we gather round us a little circle at South Hackney. Intellect and respectability. Supper at eight. I shall hope to see you there soon and often."

He then seized Mr. Haveril's hand. "If I may, sir—if I may."

"You may, sir—you may." He held out a hand immovable, like a sign-post.

"As men of business—men of business—we shall understand each other."

"Very like, very like," said Mr. Haveril, with distressing coldness.

He had fallen into his third manner, and his eyes were far off. He spoke mechanically.

Cousin Charles clapped his hat on his head and walked out. He was followed by the lady pew-opener, who called out after him over the broad balustrade—

"You and your respectability, indeed! Go and sweat your shop-girls! You and your respectability!"

CHAPTER IX.

ONE MORE.

"They are all gone, John," said Alice. "Oh, what a visit! I am ashamed! I never thought my people could have gone on so! As for Cousin Charles, he's just dreadful!"

One was left. The unfortunate bankrupt, overcome by the champagne, was asleep in his chair. John Haveril dragged him up by the collar.

"Now then, you, sir! What do you mean by going to sleep here?"

The unfortunate rubbed his eyes and pulled himself together. Presently he remembered where he was.

"Cousin Alice," he said, "are we alone?" He whispered confidentially. "They all want your money—particularly Charles. He's the most grasping, greedy, cheeseparing, avaricious, unscrupulous, bully of a cousin that ever had a place of business. Don't give him anything. Give it to me. I'm starving, Alice. I haven't eaten anything all day. It's true. I've got no work and no money."

"John, give him something."

"It's no good," said John. "He'll only eat it, and then ask for more."

"But give him something. Let him eat it."

John plunged his hand into his pocket. After the manner of the eighteenth century, it was full of gold.

"Well, take it." He transferred a handful to the clutch of the poor wretch. "Take it. Go and eat it up. And don't come back for more."

The man took it, bowed low, and shambled off. It made Alice ashamed only to see the attitude of the poor hungry creature, and the abasement of poverty.

"Well, Alice," said John, "we've seen the last of the family, until their letters begin to come in. Halloa! Who's this?"

For John became aware of the girl who had been standing beside the door, unnoticed. When all were gone, she stepped in lightly.

The Changeling

"Mrs. Haveril," she said—"I ought to call you Cousin Alice, but I am afraid you have had cousins enough. My name is Pennefather—Molly Pennefather."

"Why, I was a Pennefather—same as Charles, who's just gone out, and the ragged wretch who was Cousin Alfred."

"Yes; and others of the truly dreadful people who have just gone out. I don't know any of them. Fortunately, they wouldn't have anything to do with my poor old dad, because he disgraced the family and went on the stage. If they hadn't been so haughty, I might have had to know them now."

"Your father? Is he Willy Pennefather?"

"He was. But he died five years ago."

"He died? Poor Willy! Oh, John, if you'd known my cousin Will! How clever he was! And how bright! Dead, is he?"

"He was never a great success, you know, because he couldn't settle down. And at last he died. And I—— Well, I'm studying for the stage myself."

"Oh, you are Willy's daughter! My dear, you look straight. But there's been such a self-seeking——"

"I don't want your money, indeed!"

"Oh, but have you got money, my dear?"

"No; but some day I suppose I shall have—by my Art. That's the way to talk about the profession nowadays. Well, I mean that I don't want your money, Cousin Alice."

"If you haven't got any money and don't want any——" John began.

"You see, we are not all built like Mr. John Haveril," she interrupted, with a sweet smile. "Art, I am told, makes one despise money. When I am furnished with my Art, I dare say I shall despise money."

"Oh, coom now, lass!" From time to time, but rarely, John Haveril became Yorkshire again. "Despise the brass?"

"Not the people who have the brass. That is an accident."

"I don't know about accidents."

The Changeling

"Well, you've got money; once you hadn't. You're John Haveril all the same—see? Besides, it's quite right that some people should have money. They can take stalls at theatres. If you will let me be friends with you, Mr. Haveril, and won't look so dreadfully suspicious——"

"Well, I don't care," he said. "You look as if——"

"As if I was telling the truth. Shake hands, then."

Mrs. Haveril gave her a hand, and then, looking in her face, threw her arms round her neck.

"My dear child," she said, "you're the very picture of your father— Cousin Will. I thought there must be some one in the family fit to love." She hugged and kissed the girl with a sudden wave of affection. "Oh, Molly, my dear, I am sure I shall love you!"

"I'm so glad. Well, may I call you Alice? I will tell you what theatres to go to. Oh, I shall make myself very useful to you!" She clasped her hands, laughing—a picture of youth and truth and innocence. "Some time or other you shall see *me* on the stage."

"We get lots of actors out in the West—and actresses too. Some of them are real lovely," said John Haveril.

She laughed. "Oh! There are actresses and actresses. And some elevate their Art, and some degrade it. Now, let me see. Oh, father is dead, poor dear! I told you. And the rest of the family —— Well, you saw for yourself, cousin, they are not exactly the kind of people for a person of your consideration. You should lend them all some money—not much—and make them promise to pay it back on a certain day—next Monday week, at ten o'clock. It's a certain plan. Then you'll have no further trouble with them. Otherwise, they'll crowd round you like leeches."

"I can't let my own flesh and blood starve."

"Starve! Rubbish! They won't starve! What have they been doing while you've been away? Unless you encourage them not to work." And now she sank gracefully upon a footstool, and took her cousin's hands. "Oh," she said, "it is so nice to have a relative of whom one may be proud, after all those cousins. Oh, it must be a dreadful thing to have such lots of money! Why, I've got nothing!"

The Changeling

"You've had no champagne," said Cousin John, lifting his Jeroboam.

"Thank you, Cousin John, I don't drink champagne. Well, now, what can I do for you this afternoon?"

"I don't know, my dear. We neither of us know much about London, and we just wander about, for the most part, or drive about, and wonder where we are."

The girl jumped up. "Order a carriage and pair instantly. I shall drive you round and show you the best shops. You are sure to want something. As for me, remember that I want nothing. An actress appears in costume which the management finds. You, however, Alice, are different. You must dress as becomes your position."

"My dear child," said Alice, in the very first shop, "you *must* let me give you a dress—you really must."

"I don't want it, I assure you," she laughed. "But if it pains you not to give me one, why, I will take it."

She *did* take it. That evening there arrived at the boarding-house, addressed to Miss Pennefather, first a bonnet, for which five guineas would be cheap; a dress, the price of which the male observer could not even guess; a box of kid gloves, a mantle, and two or three pairs of boots.

"And, oh," said the girl, when she left the hotel that night, "what a *lovely* thing it is to feel that there will be no horrid mercenary considerations between us! You will admire my Art, but I shall not envy your money. Cousin John, admit that I am better off than you—one would rather be admired than envied."

She reached home. In her room lay the parcels and the packages. She opened them all. She put on the bonnet, she stroked the soft stuff with a caressing palm, she gazed upon the gloves, she held up the boots to the light.

"Am I a dreadful humbug?" she said. "I must be—I must be. What would Dick say? But one cannot—— No, one cannot refuse. I am not a stick or a stone. And Cousin Alice actually enjoyed the giving! But no money. Molly, you must not take their money."

CHAPTER X.

COUSIN ALFRED'S SECRET.

It was a few days later, in the forenoon. John Haveril was gone into the City on the business of keeping together what he had got—a business which seems to take up the whole of a rich man's time and more, so that he really has no chance of looking for the way to the kingdom of heaven. His wife sat at the window of her room in the hotel, contemplating the full tide of life below. She was not in the least a philosopher—the sight of the people, and the carriages, and the omnibuses, did not move her to meditate on the brevity of life as it moves some thinkers. It pleased her; she thought of places where she had lived in Western America, and the contrast pleased her. Nor was she moved, as a poet, to find something to say about this tide of life. The poet, you know, looks not only for the phrase appropriate, but for the phrase distinctive. Mrs. Haveril had never heard of such a thing. She only thought that there was nothing like it in the Western States, and that she remembered nothing like it in the village of Hackney. Molly was lying on the sofa, reading a novel.

One of the hotel pages disturbed her dreamery, which was close upon dropping off, by bringing up in a silver salver a dirty slip of paper, on which was written in pencil—

"Mr. Alfred Pennefather. For Mrs. Haveril. Bearer waits."

"Is it a man in rags? Is he a disgrace to the hotel?"

"Well, ma'am, he *is* in rags. As for his being a disgrace—he says he's your cousin." Here he laughed, holding the silver salver before his mouth.

"I wouldn't laugh at a poor man, if I were you. Why," said Mrs. Haveril, drawing a bow at a venture, "you've got cousins of your own in the workhouse. Send him up, right away," she added.

The man came in. The page shut the door quickly behind him, to conceal the figure of rags not often seen in that palatial place.

The Changeling

It was Alfred the Broken; strange to say, though it was less than a week since he had received that gift of golden sovereigns, the appearance of the man was as seedy as ever; his hat—a ridiculously tall silk hat with a limp brim—can anything look more forlorn?—his coat with ragged wrists; his boots parting from the soles; a ragged and decayed person, more ragged, more decayed, than before.

"Well?" the lady's voice was not encouraging. "You came here last week with the rest of them."

"I did, Alice—I did."

"You had champagne with the rest; you heard what my husband had to say: when the rest were gone, he gave you money. What have you done with that money? What do you want now?"

"I want to have a quiet talk with you."

The man had that sketchy irresolute face which foretells, in certain levels of life, social wreck. Not an evil face, exactly—the man with the evil face very often gets on in life—but with a weak face. You may see such a face any day in a police-court. First, it is a charge connected with the employer's accounts, then it is generally a charge of petty robbery. The last case I saw myself was one of boots snatched from an open counter. Between the first charge and the second there is a dreadful change in the matter of clothes; but there is never any change in face. As for Alfred Pennefather, one could understand that he had once been the gay and dashing Alf among his pals; that he had heard the midnight chimes ring; that he knew by experience the attractions of the public billiard-room, and the joys of pool; that he read the sporting papers; that he put a "bit" on his fancy; that whatever line of life he might attempt, therein he would fail; and that repeated failures would place him outside the forgiveness of his friends. For repeated misfortunes, as well as repeated follies, we can never forgive.

"You can talk," said his cousin. "This—young lady"—she was going to say "cousin of yours"—"does not count. Go on."

"I hoped, the other day, Alice, to find you alone. In that crowd of greedy impudent beggars and flatterers, I could not. I assure you I was ashamed of being in such company. As for Cousin Charles, if it had not been for you ——"

The Changeling

"Go on to something else, please. You all came for what you could get; now, what do you want?"

"I'll sit down." He took the most comfortable chair in the room, and stretched out his legs. "This is the lap of luxury. Alice, you're a happy woman."

"Oh! Go on."

"The world has been against me, Alice, from the beginning. Look at these boots. Ask yourself whether the world has not been against me. Don't believe what they say. Scandalous, impudent liars, all of them, especially Charles. No fault of mine. No, Alice. It's the world."

"What do you want, again?"

"I want an advance."

"Then do what my husband told you—write to him. What has become of the money he gave you? Is that spent already?"

"Don't call it spent, Alice. Debts paid, common necessaries bought."

"Debts! Who would trust you? Necessaries! Why, you are shabbier than ever."

"Well, I can prove to you, Alice, that the money was well laid out."

When, after many days, the man at the bottom of the ladder gets a few pounds in gold, the first temptation is to make a night of it. What? We are not money-grabbers. To-morrow for a new rig-out; to-morrow for the weary business of finding employment; to-night for joy and the wine-cup. When the morrow dawns the wine-cup still lingers in the brain—but the gold pieces—where are they? Gone as a dream—a splendid dream of the night. Thus, after a little sleep and a little slumber, poverty cometh again as a robber: and want as an armed man.

"Don't let's talk about money spent," he said cheerfully. "Let's talk about the future. I'm right down at the bottom of the ladder, Alice. Help me up."

If a man says that he is at the bottom of the ladder, he generally speaks the truth. It is one of those little things about which we are agreed not

The Changeling

to tell lies. And when he asks to be helped up, he always speaks with sincerity.

"I have no money of my own."

"You've things that make money." His eyes fell on a bracelet lying on the table.

Alice shook her finger at him. "Cousin Alfred," she said, "if you mean that I am going to give you my husband's presents for you to take to a pawnbroker, I will have you bundled out of the house. Now, tell me what you came for, before I ring the bell for the waiter."

He began to cry. He really was underfed and very miserable. "Oh! she's got a hard heart—and all I want is forty pounds—for the good will and stock-in-trade of a tobacconist—to become a credit to the family."

"I have no money of my own," Alice repeated. "If that is all you have to say, go away. My husband may come back at any moment."

"He won't. I watched. He's gone into the City on the top of a 'bus. With all his money, rides outside a 'bus. He's gone, and I mean, Alice——"

Molly rose and put down her novel. Then she advanced and seized the man, taking a combined handful of shirt-collar and coat-collar, which she twisted in her strong hand. He spread out his legs and hands; he struggled; the grip tightened; he rolled over; the coat-collar came off in her hand.

"Get up and go, you miserable creature!" she cried.

He rose slowly.

"Go!" said Molly.

"No coat-collar would stand such treatment," he said. "Pay me for the damage you have done to my wardrobe."

"Give him a shilling, Molly, and let him go."

"Wait a minute—wait a minute. Oh, don't be violent, Alice! I've got a secret. If you knew it, you'd give me money. I'll sell it for forty pounds."

"Sell it to my husband."

The Changeling

He got up feeling for his injured coat-collar. "This girl's so impetuous. May I sit down again?"

"No," said Molly. "Stand. If you don't tell your secret in two minutes, out you go."

"It's about your marriage, Alice. You were married about twenty-six years ago—it was in 1871, I remember. You married a play-acting fellow—Anthony by name——"

"That's no secret."

"Which wasn't his real name, but his theatrical name. His real name was Woodroffe."

"That is no secret, either."

"Your family wouldn't stand by you, being proud of their connections, although the only gentleman of the lot was myself—and I was in a bank."

"Oh, get on to your secret!"

"But, Cousin Will—Charles's brother—he stood by you, because he was in the play-acting line himself, and he got the boot, too, from the family. Will gave you away. You were married in South Hackney Church. After the wedding you went away. Will met me that same day; I remember I was a little haughty with him, because a bank clerk can't afford to know a common actor. He told me about it."

"What is your secret?"

"Two or three years later I met Will again, and borrowed something off him. Then he told me you had gone off to America."

"That is no secret."

"I'm coming to the secret. Don't you be impatient, Alice. It's my secret, not yours. Now, then. About fifteen years ago, I met a fellow at a billiard-table. He wouldn't play much, and he had some money, and so I thought—well—I got him to lodge with us. Mother kept lodgings in Myddleton Square in those days. He came; he said his name was Anthony, and he was a comedian from the States. We are coming to the secret now. Well, he stayed with us there a few weeks, and I took

The Changeling

some money off him at pool; but he never paid his rent, and went away."

"Go on."

"That was your husband, Alice—your husband, I say—your husband." His voice fell to a mysterious whisper.

"Well; and why not?"

"Well—if you will have it—I'll say it out loud. That was your husband. You married John Haveril because you thought your husband was dead. Perhaps you hoped he would never find you out. Very well. He's alive still. I've seen him. That's my secret."

"I care nothing whether he is alive or dead."

"That's bluff. He's alive, I say; and I know where he is at this very minute."

"Now you have told your secret, you may go," said Molly.

"I tell you," said Alice, "that I do not care to know anything at all about that man."

"Well—but—if he is living, how can you be anybody else's wife? Look here, Alice. I'm telling the truth. John Anthony, whose name is Woodroffe, is in London. Last week I met him by accident, but he doesn't remember me. We were engaged in the same occupation. Why should I conceal the poverty to which I am reduced by the hard hearts of wealthy friends? We were carrying boards in Oxford Street. At night we used the same doss-house."

"I tell you that I do not wish to hear anything about that man. If he is in poverty and wickedness, he deserves it."

"Wouldn't you help him now?"

"I tell you I have no money."

"But this man is your husband."

"I tell you again, I do not want to know anything about the man."

"Well, I can go and tell him that you're here, rolling in gold. Forty pounds I want, and then I'll become a credit to the family—as a tobacconist. Else you shall have your husband back again. I've only to set him on to you."

"I don't want your secret."

"Not to keep your husband from finding you out? Have you no heart, Alice?"

Molly pointed to the door. "Out!" she ordered. "Out, this instant!"

He turned away reluctantly. "I thought better of you, Alice. Well, it's a wicked world. Go straight, and you go downhill. Chuck your respectability, and you're like the sparks that fly upward. When I came here the other day, I thought I was coming to see a respectable woman."

"Out!" Molly advanced upon him.

He placed a chair in front of him. "I know where your husband is—in the Marylebone Workhouse Infirmary; that's where he is. I shall go to him. 'Anthony,' I shall say, 'your wife's over here—with another man.'"

Molly threw the chair down, and rushed at him.

He fled before the fire and fury of those eyes.

"Molly dear," Alice asked, "am I hard-hearted? I have not a spark of feeling left for that man; it moved me not in the least to hear of his wretched plight. He is to me just a stranger—a bad man—suffering just punishment."

"But his name is Woodroffe. That is strange, is it not?"

"Yes; his name is Woodroffe. He belonged, he always said, to a highly respectable family. That fact did not make him respectable."

"I wonder if he is any relation to Dick—my old friend, Dick Woodroffe. He's a musician now, and singer, too, and his father was a comedian before him."

"Well, dear, I don't know. As for that man in the infirmary, I dare say John will go and see if anything can be done for him. He deserted me

The Changeling

first, and divorced me afterwards, Molly, twenty-four years ago—for incompatibility of temper. That is the kind of man he is."

CHAPTER XI.

THE DOCTOR'S DINNER.

The secret of success is like the elixir of life, inasmuch as that precious balsam used to be eagerly sought after by countless thousands; and because, also like the elixir, it continually eludes the pursuer. One man succeeds. How? He does not know, and he does not inquire. A thousand others, who think they are as good, fail. Why? They cannot discover. But each of the thousand failures is ready to show you a thousand reasons why this one man has succeeded. First of all, he has really not succeeded; secondly, his success is grossly exaggerated; thirdly, it is a cheap success—the unsuccessful are especially contemptuous of a cheap success—they would not, themselves, condescend to a cheap success; fourthly, it is a success arrived at by tortuous, winding, crooked arts, which make the unsuccessful sick and sorry to contemplate—who would desire a success achieved by climbing up the back stairs? If a man writes, and succeeds in his writings, so that ordinary people flock to read him, he succeeds by his vulgarity. Or, he succeeds by his low tastes—who, that respects himself, would pander to the multitude? Or, he succeeds by vacuity, fatuity, futility, stupidity—what self-respecting writer would sink to the level of the fatuous and vacuous? He succeeds with an A, because he is Asinine; with a B, because he is Bestial; with a C, because he is Contemptible; and so on through the alphabet. Similar reasons are assigned when a man succeeds as a Painter, a Sculptor, a Preacher, a Lawyer. Now, Sir Robert Steele is one of the most successful physicians of the day. His success is easily understood and readily accounted for, on the principles just laid down, by those of his profession who have not by any means achieved the same popularity. He humours his patients—every one knows that; he has a soft voice and a warm hand—he makes ignoble profit out of both. Above all, he asks his patients—some of them—to the most delightful dinners possible.

The latter charge has a foundation in fact: he does ask a few of his more fortunate patients to dinner. More than this, he gives them a dinner much too artistic for most of them to understand. To bring Art

The Changeling

into a menu, to invent and build up a dinner which shall be completely artistic in every part, a harmonious whole; one course leading naturally to the next; a dinner of one colour in many tints; the wine gurgling like part of an orchestra, is a gift within the powers of very few. Sir Robert's reputation as a physician is justly, at least, assisted by his reputation as a great poetic creator of the harmonious dinner.

I think, having myself none of the *gourmet's* gifts, that the possession of them must cause continual and poignant unhappiness. It is like the endowment of the critical faculty at its highest. Nothing pleases wholly. When the critic of the menu dines out, alas, what false notes, what discords, what bad time, what feeble rendering, what platitude of conception, he must endure! Let us not envy his gifts, let us rather continue to enjoy, unheeding, dinners which would be only a prolonged torture to the sensitive soul of the perfect critic.

The doctor made his selections carefully from his patients and friends. He knew all the amusing people about town, especially those benefactors to their kind who consent to play and sing for after-dinner amusement; he knew all the actors, especially those who do not take themselves too seriously; he knew the men who can tell stories, sing songs, and are always in good temper. He loved them as King William loved the red deer; he esteemed them higher than princes; more excellent company than poets; more clubable than painters. Among his friends of the profession was Mr. Richard Woodroffe, whom the doctor esteemed even above his fellows for his unvarying cheerfulness and his great gifts and graces in music and in song. Him he invited to dinner on a certain evening, partly on account of these gifts and partly for another reason—the other guests were the Haverils, who would be useless in conversation; Miss Molly Pennefather, their cousin, who would not probably prove a leader in talk; Sir Humphrey Woodroffe, whom he invited for reasons which you know—and others, yet conscious beforehand that the young man would be out of his element and perhaps sulky; and two *umbræ*, persons of no account—mere patients—to make up the number of eight, the only number, unless it is four, which is permissible for a dinner-party. For the menu there was only one person to be considered; Dick, for instance, would eat tough steak with as much willingness as a Chateaubriand; Mr. Haveril knew not one dish from

The Changeling

another; Humphrey, whom he had met at his mother's table, would be the only guest capable of understanding a dinner. Moreover, Humphrey would have to be conciliated by the dinner itself, to make up for the company. The doctor therefore prepared a dinner of a few *plats* harmonized with the desire of pleasing a young man who was most easily approached, he had already discovered, by means of any one, or any group, of the senses. Dinner, as every artistic soul knows, appeals to a group of the senses, which is the reason why civilized man decorates his tables. Those unhappy persons to whom dinner is but feeding might as well serve up a single dish on one wine-case and sit down to it on another.

The reason, apart from his social qualities, why Sir Robert invited Richard Woodroffe to the dinner was not unconnected with a little conversation held at a smoking concert a few nights before. It was a very good smoking concert; a highly distinguished company was present; and the performers were all professionals.

Richard did his "turn," and then took a seat beside Sir Robert.

"I haven't seen you since last June, Dick, have I?"

"I've been on tramp."

"What do you go on tramp for?"

"Because I must when the summer comes. I can't stay in town—I take the fiddle and sling a hand-bag over my shoulders and go off."

"Where do you go?"

"Anywhere. First by train twenty miles or so out of London, and then plunge into the country at random."

"You tramp along the road. And then?"

"Well—you see—the real point is that I take no money with me—only enough for the first day or two—five shillings or so. The fiddle pays my way. I play for bed and supper in a roadside inn. The people of the village come to hear; sometimes I play and sing; sometimes I play for them to dance; then I collect the coppers; next day I go on."

"It sounds delightful for your audience. For me, listening to you is sufficient; as for the rest——"

The Changeling

"It's more delightful than you can believe. Why, I know all the gipsies and their language; sometimes I camp with them. And I know most of the tramps. Some excellent fellows among the tramps. And there's no dress-coat and no dinner-parties."

"What do you mean by saying that you must go?"

"Well, I don't know. It's something in the blood. It's heredity, I suppose. My father was a vagabond before me——"

"Did he also go on the tramp?"

"Well, he was always moving on. He was an actor—of sorts. Some of them still remember him over here, though he went to America five and twenty years ago."

"Do I remember him? Was his name Woodroffe?"

"His stage name was Anthony—John Anthony. His real name was Woodroffe."

"Anthony!" The doctor sat up. "Anthony? I have heard that name. Oh yes; I remember. Anthony! Strange! Only the other day——" he broke off.

"Did you hear that name coupled with any—creditable incident?"

"No—no, not very; it was in connection with a—a former wife.... How old are you, Dick?"

"I am two and twenty."

"Yes. I remember the case now—it was four and twenty years ago. One is always getting reminders. Dick, there's a young fellow of your name—a baronet—son of an Anglo-Indian; are you any relation to him?"

"I've met him. We are very distant cousins, I believe. The more distant the better."

"You don't like him? Well, he isn't quite your sort, is he? All the same, Dick, come and dine with me next Tuesday. You will meet him; but that won't matter. I expect some American people as well—rich people—*nouveaux riches*—the woman is interesting, the man is plain. They bring a girl with them—a girl, Miss Molly Pennefather. What's the matter?" For Dick jumped.

The Changeling

"Molly? I know Molly!—bless her! I'll come, doctor, even if there were twenty Sir Humphreys coming too. And after dinner I'll sing for you, if you like."

Now you understand why this selection was made. For the first time in his life, Sir Robert invited a company which could not possibly harmonize. There would be no talk worth having, his wine would be wasted, his *cuisine* would meet with no appreciation. But he would have them all before him—mother, son, stepson—if Richard could be called a stepson—half-brothers; and the master of the situation would study on the spot an illustration of heredity, unsuspected by the patients themselves.

Mrs. Haveril arrived, clothed chiefly in diamonds. Why not? Her husband liked her to wear those glittering things which help to make wealth attractive, otherwise we might all be contented with poverty. But the pale lady's delicate, nun-like face would have looked better without them. With her came Molly, now her daily companion. The girl was dressed, for the first time in her life, as in a dream—a dream of paradise; she wore such a frock, with such trimmings, as makes a maiden, if by happy chance she sees it in a window, gasp and yearn for the unattainable, yet go home thankful for having seen it; and humbled by the sense of personal unworthiness. Yet, what says the poet?

"Ah! but a man's reach should exceed his grasp,
Else what's a heaven for?"

The girl wore the dress with as little self-consciousness as one would expect. It was such a dress as she had seen upon the stage—elaborate, dainty, decorated; perhaps a little too old for her; but, then, an actress must be excused for a little exaggeration. Her *rôle* this evening was not a speaking part; she was only a lady of the court; meanwhile, she was on the stage, and it pleased her to find that her audience admired, though they could not applaud.

"I have invited to meet you," said the doctor, "two distant cousins; they bear the same name, and are of the same descent, but their families have gone off in different channels, I understand, for some hundreds of years. It is not often that people can claim cousinship after so long a separation. One of them is the only son of the late Sir Humphrey Woodroffe, a distinguished Anglo-Indian——"

"Woodroffe?" Alice asked. "It was my first husband's name."

"Very possibly he, too, was a cousin. The other is a young fellow called Richard Woodroffe."

"Again the name," said Alice.

"Yes; the distant cousin. He is a musician and a dramatist in a small and clever way."

"Dick is my oldest friend," said Molly.

"I am very glad, then, that he is coming to-night."

Sir Robert considered this young lady more attentively, because a girl who was Dick Woodroffe's oldest friend must be a young lady out of the common. There was, he observed, something certainly uncommon in her appearance, something which might suggest the footlights. Any old friend of Dick Woodroffe must suggest the footlights.

"It is strange," said the doctor, "to have three of our small party belonging to the same name."

The other guests arrived. The last was Humphrey. He looked round the room with that expression of cold and insolent curiosity which made him so much beloved by everybody. "Outsiders all," that look expressed. He greeted Dick with a brief nod of astonished recognition, as if he had not expected to meet him in a drawing-room. He stared at Mrs. Haveril's diamonds, and he smiled with some astonishment, but yet graciously, on Molly.

"You are properly dressed to-night," he whispered. "I have never seen you looking so well."

"Doctor," said Mrs. Haveril, as he led her down the stairs, "I wish I could go and sit in a corner."

"Why? You are trembling! What is the matter?"

"I feel as if I was in a dream. It is the sight of these two young men. One is the young man I saw at the theatre—the young man I told you of—so like my husband; the other is like him, too, but differently. I am haunted to-night with my husband's face."

"It is imagination. You have been thinking too much about certain things. Their name is the same as your husband's. Probably he, too, if you knew, was a distant cousin."

"It's not imagination; it is the fact."

"I am sorry you are so disturbed; but, above all, do not agitate yourself," he whispered, as they entered the dining-room.

"I will keep up, doctor; but it's dreadful to sit with two living images of your first husband."

From the ordinary point of view, the dinner was not so great a success as some of those given at this house. The conversation flagged. Yet, below the surface, everybody was interested. Humphrey took in Molly, but Dick sat on the other side of her, and told her stories about his last tramp; Humphrey, therefore, became sulky, and absorbed wine in quantities. Alice gazed at the two young men—her husband's eyes, her husband's mouth, her husband's voice, her husband's hair, in both of them—both like unto her first husband, yet both unlike; they were also like unto each other, yet unlike. She heard nothing that was said; she listened to the voice, she saw the eyes, and she was back again, after all those years, with that vagrant man, that vagabond in morals, as well as in ways, the man who so cruelly used her, the comedian and stroller.

The doctor also watched the two young men. They had, to begin with, many points of resemblance; they were alike, however, as brothers who often differ in disposition as much as strangers. The elder of the two—the doctor considered Mrs. Haveril—took after his mother, and was serious, at least. He thought of Lady Woodroffe's remarks about him: "Selfish." Yes; there was a way of eating his food and absorbing his wine that betokened a selfish pleasure in the food above the delights of society and conversation. He did not converse; he sat glum. "Ill-conditioned and bad-tempered," Lady Woodroffe said. The selfishness, and probably the bad temper, he inherited from the father. From his education he obtained, of course, the air of superiority, which, like the Order of the Garter, has nothing to do with intellect or achievement, or distinction. From his education also his features had probably acquired a certain manner which we call aristocratic.

The Changeling

He kept his guest in something like good temper by asking his opinion, pointedly, as if he valued his judgment, on the champagne. He had little talks with him on vintages and years and brands, in which the young man was as wide as most youths at the club where champagne flows. And he asked Sir Humphrey's opinion on the *plats*, and let the others feel that his opinion carried weight, so that his guest forgot something of Molly's perverseness in listening to her neighbour's stories, and of the intolerable nuisance of sitting down to dinner with such a company.

He turned to the other cousin—Dick. This fellow, like unto Humphrey, was yet so much unlike him that, to begin with, his face was as undistinguished as was his cousin's mind. Yet a clever face, capable of many emotions. He was full of life and talk, he was interested in everything, he could listen as well as talk—a young man of sympathy. The artistic side of him came from his father, as did also the nomad side of him; the sympathy and kindliness and honesty came to him from his unknown mother—one supposed.

As for John Haveril, he was chiefly engaged in considering the girl who had thus unexpectedly come into his life to cheer it with her brightness and her grace. I have never found any man so old or so self-made as to be insensible to the charms of sprightly maidenhood and youthful beauty. John Haveril was quite a homely person; he had not been brought up to think of beauty, and lovely dress, and charming airs and graces as belonging to himself in any way. It is this sense of being outside the circle which makes working men apparently deaf and blind to beauty adorned and cultivated. Why admire or think upon the unattainable? They might as well yearn after the possession of an ancient castle and noble name as after beauty decorated and set off. And now this girl belonged to them. He himself and his wife were only happy when this girl was with them; she came every day to see them; she drove out with them, took them to see things, taught them what to admire and what to buy, dined with them, consented graciously to accept their gifts, but refused their money.

At all events, she refused to take any. Yet she liked the things that money can buy—lovely frocks, gloves, hats, ribbons, laces, gold chains, and bracelets, and necklaces. To him contempt for money, combined with love of what only money can buy, seemed

The Changeling

incongruous. The contempt was only a phrase. Molly had been taught that Art ought to despise wealth; she had not been taught to despise the things artistic that money can buy. The rich man chuckled to think how much money can be spent upon a girl who despises it. He was pleased to make the girl happy by heaping unaccustomed treasures on her gratified shoulders. It was pleasant to be generous to a bright, happy, smiling girl, who kept him alive, and made him forget the burden of his riches. And as he thought of these things he fell into his third manner—that of the gardener—and his eyes went off into space.

After dinner Molly sat down to the piano and began to sing, in a full, flexible contralto, an old ditty about love and flowers, taught her by Dick himself, who possessed a treasure-house full of such songs, new and old, and of all countries, and in all languages. There is but one theme fit for a song—the theme of youth and love, and the sweet season of roses.

Humphrey stood listening. To this young man, perhaps to others, the effect of Molly's singing, as of her presence and of her voice and of her eyes, was to fill his mind with visions. They came to him in the shape of dancing-girls with tambourines and castanets. When a girl is endowed with the real faculty of singing, she may create in the minds of those who hear, those visions which best fit their inclinations and their natures. To this young man came the troop of dancing-girls, because his disposition inclined him that way: they sang as they danced, and they threw up white arms to a music of wild and reckless joy; they filled him with the longing, the yearning, for the delirium of youth and rapture which seizes every young man from time to time, and sometimes possesses him all the days of his youth, and casts him out long before his youth is over to the husks among the swine. Others, more fortunate, feel the yearning, too, but they make of it a stimulus and an incentive. There is no such rapture beneath the sky as young men dream of; yet the vision may make them poets, and may strengthen them for endeavour; and it may fill them with the worship of woman, which is the one thing needful for a man. Humphrey, wholly filled and possessed by this rapture, would not be cast forth to the husks, because—oh! sordid reason—his mother would pay his debts. Alas! poor Molly! and she so ignorant. She had no such vision—girls never do. When young men reel and tremble with the vision of

The Changeling

rapture inconceivable, girls have to be contented with a mild happiness. To them there comes no dream of gleaming arms—no imagined magic of voice and eyes and face. There is no such thing as a Prodigal daughter; the humble *rôle* of the Prodigal Girl is to minister, as with the white arms and the castanets, to the service of the Prodigal Son; for which she, too, has to go out presently to sit with the swine, and to maintain a precarious existence on the husks.

Molly had no such vision: yet by the mere power of her voice she could awaken this vision in the mind of a listener. It is a power which makes an actress; makes a queen; makes a lady of authority; whom all obey to whom that power appeals.

Molly, I say, had no respect at all for the flowery way; she could not understand, nor did she ask, why young men should want to dance hand-in-hand with the girls; nor why they like to crown their heads with roses; nor why they drink huge draughts of the wine that fizzeth in the cup, to make their heads as light as their feet.

She created, however, quite a different vision in the mind of the other young man. Dick knew all about the flowery way, and, in fact, despised it. You see, he belonged to the "service;" he played the fiddle for the dancers; like those who gather the roses, polish the floor, lay the cloth, open the champagne, cook the dishes, decorate the rooms, and write the songs; he belonged to the Show. The flowery way was nothing to him but a Show; the white arms amused him not; the soft cheeks he knew were painted; the smiles and the laughing looks were practised at rehearsals. As for Molly, she was his companion and a helpmeet; one to whom he would impart and give with all that he had, and who would in return love and cherish him. What is the Flowery way compared with the way of Love? This, and nothing else, is the real reason why the Show folk are so different from the other folk; there is no illusion to them; they are the paid dancers, makers of rosy wreaths, musicians and singers of the Flowery way.

Molly's song, therefore, opened another kind of vision to Master Richard. All he saw was a long road shaded with hills, and Molly in the middle of it marching along with him, singing as she went, and carrying the fiddle.

When the song was finished, Molly got up.

The Changeling

"May I sing you one of my own songs?" Humphrey asked her, paying no attention to the rest.

He sat down and struck a note and began a song. It had no melody; it was without a beginning and without an end; the words told nothing, neither a story nor a sentiment; like the music to which they were set, they began in the middle of a sentence and ended with a semicolon. His voice was good enough, but uncultivated. When he finished, he closed the piano, as if there was to be no more music after him.

"It is music," he said coldly, "of the advanced school. I am proud to belong to the music of the future—the true expression of Art in song."

"I will show you"—Richard opened the piano and took his place—"I will show you something of the music of the present."

With vigorous and practised fingers he ran up and down the notes; then he struck into an air—light, easy, catching, and began to sing the "Song of the Tramp"—one of his vagabond songs.

Mrs. Haveril sat watching the two young men. When Dick began, the other one turned away sullenly, and began to look into a portfolio of etchings, with the air of one who will not listen.

"Doctor," she whispered, "that young man sings and plays exactly like my husband. It might be the same. He would sit down and sing just that same way, as if nothing ever happened and nothing mattered. I wonder how men can go on like that, with age and sickness and the end before them. Women never can. Oh, how like my husband he is! The other is not like him in manner; not a bit; yet in face—oh, in face—and voice—and eyes—and hair! It is wonderful!"

"One can hardly expect the son of Sir Humphrey Woodroffe to be altogether like a comedian."

"Yet," she repeated, "so like him in face and everything; I cannot get over it."

Just then Humphrey looked up. There was just a moment—what was it?—a turn of the face; a look in the eyes, that made the doctor start.

"Heavens!" he thought. "He's exactly like his mother!"

Dick finished. John Haveril walked over to the piano before he got up.

The Changeling

"Mister," he said, "I like it. I find it cheerful. If you could see your way, now, to look in upon us of an evening, I think you might do good to my wife, who's apt to let her spirits go down. Come and sing to us."

"I will, with pleasure. When shall I come?"

"Come to-morrow evening. Come every evening, if you like, young gentleman. My wife doesn't care for the theatres much. If we could sit quiet at home, with a little lively talk and a little singing, she would like it ever so much better. You and Molly know each other, it appears. Come to dinner to-morrow, and see how you like us."

The party broke up. Sir Humphrey was left alone with the doctor.

"Stay for a cigarette." Sir Robert rang the bell. "I hope you liked the dinner and the wine."

"Both, Sir Robert, were beyond and above all praise. An artistic dinner is so rare!"

"It was thrown away upon some of my guests. However, if you will come another day, you shall meet a more distinguished company. I did not understand, Sir Humphrey, until this evening, the very strong resemblance you bear to your mother."

"Indeed! It is my father whom I am generally thought to resemble."

"Yes. You have, no doubt, a strong resemblance to him; but it is your mother of whom you remind me from time to time most strongly. It came out oddly this evening. The inheritance of face and figure and qualities interests me, and your own case, Sir Humphrey; the son of such a father and such a mother is extremely interesting." He took a cigarette. "Extremely interesting, I assure you."

CHAPTER XII.

THE OTHER CHILD OF DESERTION.

"Molly?" Richard arrived before the time, and found his old friend alone. "You here again? Last night I could not ask what it meant—the ineffable frock and the heavenly string of pearls. What does it mean?"

She had on another lovely frock with the same pearl necklace.

"It means, Dick," she replied, with much dignity, "that Alice—Mrs. Haveril—is my father's first cousin, and is therefore my own cousin. It also means, which you will hardly credit, that she is very fond of me."

"That is, indeed, difficult of belief. And you are a good deal with them? And this other frock, too, this thing—is it cloth of gold or samite?—was given to you by your cousin. Molly, Molly, have a care! The love of gold creeps upon one as a thief in the night."

"Dick!" She assumed an injured air. "When it affords them so much pleasure to give me things, why should I refuse? And confess, ridiculous creature, that you never saw me look so nice before!"

"You look very nice, Molly—very nice, indeed; but I never knew you look otherwise."

"You dear old boy!" She gave him her hand. "You always try to spoil a simple shepherdess."

"But, I say, Molly, is this kind of marble hall good for study? Does it bring you nearer to Mrs. Siddons? Does it suit the cothernus? Methinks the liquefaction of black velvet more befits the tragic muse than the frou-frou of the flowered silk."

"Very well put, Dick. I will remember."

"Tell me something about them, Molly. If I am to entertain them, you know——"

"Mr. John Haveril—whom I call John, for short—is slow of speech. Don't take that, however, for dulness. Everybody says he's as sharp as a razor. And he speaks slowly, and he's got a way while he talks of gazing far away."

"And madam? She looks like a saint in sadness because she's got to wear cloth of gold instead of sackcloth."

"She is in delicate health. Her husband is always anxious about her. Dick, he has many millions, and you always used to say that a man can't get rich honestly; but he does seem honest, and he's awfully fond of his wife."

"A man may be fond of his wife and yet not austerely honest. Go on, Molly, before they come in."

"Well, Dick," Molly lowered her voice, "she has something on her mind. I don't know what—she hasn't told me yet. But she will. It's some trouble. Sometimes the tears come into her eyes for nothing; sometimes she has fits of abstraction, when she hears nothing that you say; sometimes she becomes agitated, and her heart begins to flutter. I don't know what the trouble is, but it robs her life of happiness. She wants something. She goes to church and prays for it. If she were not such a good woman, I should think she had done something."

"What shall I play for her?"

"Play something that will rouse her. Play one of your descriptive things, Dick. I will play an accompaniment for you. Make the fiddle talk to her, as you know how. Nobody plays the fiddle quite so well as you, Dick."

They dined in the public room, where Molly observed, with profit, making mental notes, the dresses of the ladies. Dick, on his part, as an observer of manners, listened to the conversation and wasted his time. Most conversation in public places is naught; very few people can say anything worth hearing, either in public or in private; most people cannot forget that they are in a public place and may be overheard—but the modesty is passing away. The world follows the example of the young man who was admonished by Swift not to set up for a wit, "because," he said, "there are ten thousand chances to one against you." The young man took that advice, and is, therefore, unknown to history.

The Changeling

At this table the conversation was difficult, not so much because there was no wit among the small company, as because there were no opportunities for the display of wit. It is necessary for wit to have something to work upon; there can be no repartee where there is no talk. It is also difficult, if you think of it, to provide conversation for an elderly gentleman, who for the greater part of his life has been more accustomed to pork and beans than to *côtelettes à la Soubise*; who has habitually consumed bad coffee with his dinner, instead of claret and champagne; who is wholly ignorant of literature; has never looked upon a good picture; and has never heard of science except in connection with railways; who was originally apprenticed to a gardener; who in early life belonged to the Primitive Methodists. He might have discoursed upon shares and corners, but on such matters not even his own wife knew anything.

One is apt to imagine that the man who has rapidly made millions by playing upon the gambling spirit of the people, upon their greed, and their credulity, and their ignorance, must have moments, at least, of misgiving, perhaps of remorse. We talk of the ruined homes, the wrecks of families, the desolated hearths. Well, that is not the way in which the man who has succeeded where the rest all fail, looks at it. It is not the way in which John Haveril regards his own career. He puts it in his own way this evening at dinner. Unaccustomed to the society of the rich, Dick dropped some remark, slightly *mal à propos*, about money-making.

"In Yorkshire, sir," said John Haveril, "when a man buys a horse, he buys him as he stands. It's his business to find out that animal's faults. It's the business of the owner to crack up the animal. That's trading, all the world over. The man who wins, is the man who knows. The man who loses, is the man who gambles. I have never gambled."

"I thought it was all gambling."

"I buy stocks which I know are going up. I buy mines when there is going to be a run upon mines. I buy land where I know there will be built a town. Other people buy because they see others buying. The world gambles all the time. Men like me, sir, do not gamble. We buy for the rise in the market, which we understand."

"I know nothing, really," said Dick, abashed.

The Changeling

"No, sir; but you know as much as anybody. I have read in an English paper that I have ruined thousands. That is not true. They have ruined themselves. They buy in a rising venture, not knowing that it has risen too high, and they sell when it falls. My secret is, that I know."

"How do you know?"

"That, sir, I cannot explain. Why do you sing, and play that fiddle of yours better than anybody else? It is your gift, sir. So it's mine to know."

In spite, however, of these new lights on the mystery, or craft, of money-making, which were of little use to Mr. Haveril's guests, the conversation languished. The elder lady was pensive and sad; the marvels and miracles of the *chef* were thrown away upon her; she looked as if she longed to be upstairs again, lying on her sofa, looking out upon the full tide of human life surging round Charing Cross.

After dinner they took coffee in their private room. "Now," said Dick, taking out his violin, "I want to play something that will please you, Mrs. Haveril." He began to tune his instrument, talking the while. "Molly thinks that you would like a little foolish entertainment that I sometimes give—a descriptive piece. The fiddle describes, I only explain with a word or two, and Molly plays an accompaniment."

Molly took her place and waited.

"You must understand what we are going to talk about, first of all, otherwise you will understand nothing. Very good. I am just a strolling player, or a musician, as you please; I carry my fiddle with me, and I am on tramp. In my pocket there is no money. I earn my bed, and my supper, and my breakfast, with the fiddle and the bow. I take any odd jobs that I can get at country theatres, or at music-halls, or taverns, or anything. My girl is with me, of course. She can sing a little, and dance a little, so that on occasion we are prepared with a little show of our own. We carry no luggage except a bag with a few necessaries. It is my business to carry the bag. My girl carries the fiddle, which is lighter. Now you understand."

At the mention of the word "tramp," Mrs. Haveril, who had composed herself to quiet meditation at the window while the others talked, sat up and turned her head.

The Changeling

"So," Dick struck a chord—a bold, loud chord, which compelled the mind to listen. "We are on the road," he went on, talking in a monotone with murmurous voice, which became subordinated to the music, so that one heard the latter and forgot the former, insomuch that the music seemed by itself, and without any aid, to bring the scene before the eyes. It was the work of a magician. Molly played a running accompaniment which helped the illusion, if it added nothing more. Dick watched that one of his audience whom he desired to hold. After a little her eyes dropped; she sat with clasped hands, listening, carried away—enchanted by the sorcerer.

"We are on the road," he went on, "the broad, high-road, with banks of turf at the side. There is nobody else upon the road. We swing along; we sing as we go; it is morning; the village is behind us; another village is before us; we pick flowers from the hedge; we listen to the lark in the sky; and we catch the voice of the blackbird from the wood; we sit down in the shade when we are tired; we dine resting on a stile. The air is fresh and sweet; the flowers are all aflame in hedge and meadow."

As he played and as he talked, the listener heard the birds; the cool breeze of the country fanned her cheek; she saw the flowers; the sun warmed her; the hard road fatigued her; she listened to the birds in the woods, the rustle of the leaves, the whistling of the wind in the telegraph-wires; she sat in the grateful shade; she bathed her feet in the cool, running water.

Alice listened—carried away; her cheeks were flushed; she clutched the cushions of the sofa. Far away—out of sight—forgotten—were the grand rooms of the rich man's hotel; far away—forgotten—were the diamonds and the silks.

Dick watched, with grave and earnest face, the effect of his playing. With him it was always an experiment. He tried to mesmerize his people; to charm them into forgetfulness.

"Sometimes," he went on, "I get a place in a country theatre—in the orchestra, you know. This is the orchestra." He became, on the spot, a whole orchestra, blatant, tuneless, paid to make a noise; you heard all the discordant instruments played together. Alice sank back in her chair. She did not care much about the orchestra. Dick changed

The Changeling

quickly. "Sometimes I join a circus, and play in the procession through the town. The band goes first in a cart; you can hear how the bumping shakes the music." Indeed it did—the cart was without springs, and the road was uneven. "Behind us are the horses with the splendid riders." The music passed down the street, while the patter of the horses on the road was loud enough to be heard above the music. "Last of all the riders, before the clown and the rest of the people, is the Lady Equestrienne of the Haute École. At sight of her all the girls in the town yearn for the circus, and the hearts of all the young men sink with love and admiration." No. Mrs. Haveril cared very little for this part of the show, either. "Sometimes we come to a village, where there is a green. Then the people come out—it is a fine summer evening—and I play to them, and they dance. What shall it be? *Sellinger's Round*, or *Barley Break*? Take your partners—take your places; curtsey and bow, and hands across and down the middle, and up again and one place lower. Now then, keep it up—time—time—time." Again the lady sat up and listened with rapt face. Dick watched her closely. "Now we find a school-treat in a field—I play to them. Jump and dance; boys and girls, come out to play. Lasses and lads, take leave of your dads. Boys, don't be rough with the girls, but dance with each other. Now, hands all—and round we go, and round we go." Then the tears came into the pale lady's eyes. "Good-bye—we are on the road again. The sun is sinking; the swallows fly low; we shall have rain; luckily, we've got our supper in the bag. My girl, we must take shelter in this barn. Come—you are tired—I play my girl to sleep with a gentle lullaby. Sweet hay—sweet hay—it hath no fellow. Sleep, dear girl, sleep. Good night. Good night—Good night."

He stopped and laid down the fiddle, well pleased with himself. For that part of his audience to which he had played was in tears.

Molly jumped up. "Alice dear, what is the matter?"

"Oh, Molly, it is beautiful! Oh, it is beautiful! For I've done it. I know it all. I've been on tramp myself—just as he played it—with the fiddle, too—just as he made it. Oh, I know the country fair, and the village inn, and the circus, and all! I remember it all. When last I went on tramp I had my——!"

"Alice," her husband interposed. "Don't, my dear."

The Changeling

"It is four and twenty years ago. I remember it all so well. I had my — —"

"Alice"—her husband stopped her again.

She sighed. "Yes—yes. I try not to think of it. He deserted me after that last tramp. He couldn't bear the crying of the dear child. He deserted me, and when I found him again, in America, he put me away—by the law, as if he was ashamed of me."

"Desertion and divorce," said Dick, "were my mother's lot as well. She, too, was deserted and divorced. Is it a common lot?"

"His name," said Alice, "was the same as yours. It was Woodroffe—and you are strangely like him."

"My father's name was John Anthony Woodroffe."

Alice sprang to her feet and clasped her hands. "Oh, my dream—my dream! Is it coming true? You are—you are— — Oh, how old are you?"

She caught him by the arm, and gazed into his face as if seeking her own likeness there as well as her husband's.

"I am twenty-two."

"No; it is impossible." She sank back. "For a moment I thought you might be—my own boy. Yet you are his. Oh, it is strange! Who was your mother, then?"

"She was a rider in a circus."

"And he married her and deserted her?"

"Yes—and divorced her; and I know nothing more about him."

"He must have married your mother directly after he divorced me."

"No doubt he has treated a dozen women in the same manner since then," said Dick, with unfilial bitterness. "The fifth commandment always presented insuperable difficulties to me."

"Your mother was a player, too?" said Alice. "He always grumbled because I could not play."

"My mother was the Equestrienne of the Haute École that I talked about just now. She was represented on the bills as the Pride of the

The Changeling

States, the Envy of Europe, who had refused princes in the lands of tyrants, rather than forsake nature's nobility and the aristocracy of the republic."

"I remember, Dick," said Molly. "You used to tell my father all about it."

"I was born and brought up in the sawdust. And I played all the instruments in the orchestra one after the other. And I was afraid to go to church on account of that terrible announcement about the generations to follow the wicked man."

"He will suffer; he must suffer," said Alice. "But I have long since put him out of my mind."

"My mother never put him out of her mind. She died hoping that he would be made to suffer. For my own part, I hope that I may never meet him."

"My dream! My dream! First the doctor; then my husband's son. The past is returning."

Alice covered her face with her hands to hide the tears.

"Nay, nay," said her husband. "Keep quiet—keep quiet."

She sank back on the couch, and lay still, with closed eyes and pale face.

Molly felt her heart. "It is beating too fast," she said. "Let her be still awhile."

Thus the evening, which began with an attempt at mere amusement and entertainment, became serious.

Alice recovered and opened her eyes. "John," she said, "does he understand?"

"I think so," Dick replied. "You were my father's first wife. In order to be free, he divorced you. He then married my mother. Believe me, madam, my mother was wholly ignorant, to the last, of this history."

"Indeed, I believe it. I do not think there was a woman in America who would have married a man with such a record."

"At all events, my mother would not."

The Changeling

"And you are—my stepson."

"No." Dick considered. "If I were your stepson, my mother would have come first. I'm not your stepson. In fact, there isn't a word in the language to express the relationship. But—if I may venture——"

"Alice," Molly interposed, "make a friend of Dick, as you have of me. He will be the handiest, usefullest friend you can have. And he really is the best fellow in the world—aren't you, Dick?"

"Of course I am," he replied stoutly.

"As for trying to get money from you, he is incapable of it. Dick is one of the few people in the world who don't want money. You must call him Dick, though."

The pale lady smiled faintly. "Dick," she said, "if I may ... we have a common sorrow and a common misfortune—mine, to have married a bad man; you, to be his son. Can these things make a foundation for friendship?"

"Let us try," said Dick, with something like a moistening of the eye. He was a tender-hearted, sentimental creature, who could not bear to see a woman suffer.

Alice held out her thin, white hand. Dick took it and kissed it.

"If friendship," he said, "can exist between mistress and servant, then am I your friend. But if not, then your servant at your command."

"This place," John Haveril laid his hand upon Dick's shoulder, "is your home, and what we have is at your service."

"Dick," said Molly, "we are now a kind of cousins, and you are a sort of stepson of the house."

"So long, Molly, as you don't call me brother."

"John"—after the young people had gone—"did you tell him about his father?"

"No, I didn't." John sat down, and gave his reasons very slowly. "Why? This way, I thought. He's the young man's father; that's true. But he ran away from his wife and his child—twice, he did. That won't make the son respect the father much, will it? Next, Alice, I've been to see the sick man."

The Changeling

"You've been to see him, John? You are a good man, John. You deserve a less troublesome wife. When that creature in rags wanted to sell his secret, I pretended I didn't care. But I did. It made me sick and sorry to think of that poor, bad man, without a friend or a helper in his time of need. You are not jealous, are you, John? I did love the man once. He is a worthless, wicked man. You are not jealous, are you, John? I have no such feeling left for him. It is all pity—pity for a man who is punished for his sins."

"Not I, lass—not I. Pity him as much as you please."

"Tell me what he looks like."

"Well, he's like this young fellow Dick. Also, he's like that other chap—Sir Humphrey—more like him than the other. He's grey now, and thin, cheeks sunk in, and fingers like bits of glass. I told him who I was, but he only half understood. He won't desert any more women, I reckon. They've got stories about him at the Hospital—the boys there pick up everything. No, Alice. I don't think it would make this fellow they call Dick any happier to see his father. I'll go again. Don't think of him any more, my dear. Remember what the doctor said. Keep quiet."

CHAPTER XIII.

A MIDNIGHT WALK.

"Let me walk home with you," said Dick. "It is a fine night, and we can walk."

They left the hotel, and turned northwards across Trafalgar Square.

"The pale, worn face of that poor woman haunts me, Molly. It is a strange adventure."

"You will love her, Dick, as much as I do. But there is that trouble behind, whatever it is, that she has not yet told me."

Dick looked up and straightened himself. They were in the crowd — the crowd infect and horrible at the top of the Haymarket.

"It is really peaceful night," he said. "The air just here is corrupt with voices, and there are shapes about that mock the peace of darkness; but it is really peaceful night."

"And overhead are the stars, just as in the country."

"You are like the lady in *Comus*, Molly. These are only shapes and shadows that you see. They do not exist, except in imagination. They are the ghosts and devils that belong to night in streets."

Molly pressed a little closer to him, but made no reply.

What do men understand of the wonder, the bewilderment, with which a girl looks on the rabble rout, if ever she is permitted to see it? What does it reveal to her, this mockery of the peaceful night?

Presently they came to the upper end of Regent Street, which was quieter; and to Portland Place, which was quite deserted and peaceful; and then to the outer circle of Regent's Park, where they were beyond the houses, and where the cool wind of October fell upon their faces from the broad level of the park.

"It is almost country here. Let us walk in the middle of the road, Molly." He held out his left hand. Molly linked her little finger with his. "That is the way we used to walk what time we went on tramp, Molly."

The Changeling

"Yes, Dick; it was this way."

She was strangely quiet, contrary to her usual manner.

"You must never become a town girl, Molly, or a West End woman, or a society woman."

"I don't know, Dick. Perhaps I must."

They went on a little farther.

"Molly, I wanted to talk to you about something else, but I must talk about this evening. It's been a very remarkable evening. I am enriched by a kind of stepmother—a stepmother before the event, so to speak, not after—a relationship not in any dictionary. I am the child of a younger Sultana. Who would expect to meet in a London hotel, in the person of a middle-aged millionairess, the elder Sultana?"

"Ought one to be sorry for you, Dick? You couldn't have a better stepmother."

"Not sorry, exactly. But she recalls the sins of the forefathers. I have always understood that he was that kind of person. My mother, who took it wrathfully, was careful that I should know the kind of person he was. Her history halved the fifth commandment. This good lady takes it tearfully."

"She was thinking of her own dead child. For a moment she thought you were her son."

"Does one weep for a child four and twenty years after its death? There was more than a dead child in those tears."

"It was your playing, then. You never played so well. The violin talked all the time. It made me glow only to think of your birds and breezes and flowers."

"I shall call on her to-morrow. She wants to talk about it again. Molly, it's a wonderful thing."

"What is a wonderful thing?"

For he stopped.

"Woman is a wonderful thing. Acting, as you know, my poor Molly, makes real emotion difficult for us, because we are always connecting

The Changeling

emotion with its theatrical gesture. When we ought to weep, we begin to think of how we weep."

"You talk like a book sometimes, Dick. Where do you get all your wisdom?"

"Not from books. Come on tramp with me, and you shall learn where I get it, Molly. All the thoughts worth having come to a man as he walks along the road, especially by night. Books can't tell him anything. I say that we can't help connecting emotion with the stage way of expressing it. This makes us quick to understand emotion when we do see it without the stage directions. Which is odd, but it's true. An actor born is a kind of thought-reader."

"What are you driving at, Dick?"

"I mean that an actor knows real emotion, just because it isn't like the stage business."

"Well, what then?"

"I was thinking of that poor pale lady, Molly. It's four and twenty years since her husband deserted her, and she thinks about him still. There isn't room in a woman's heart for more than one lover in a life, that's all."

"What then?"

"It's the lingering passion that she thinks was extinguished long ago. Poor old Haveril is all very well, but he hasn't the engaging qualities of the light comedian. Good, no doubt, at making money, and without the greater vices; but, Molly, my dear, without the lighter virtues. And these she remembers."

"Well, but that isn't what lies on her mind. You will be a thought-reader, indeed, Dick, if you can read what is written there."

They walked on together, side by side, in silence. Then the figure of the pale, fragile, sad woman went out of their thoughts. They returned, as is the way with youth, to themselves.

"You are happy, Molly?" he asked.

"I am happy enough," she sighed.

The Changeling

"Most of us are. We make ourselves as happy as we can. Of course, nobody is entirely happy till he gets all he wants. For my own part, I want very little; and I am very nearly quite happy, because I've got it all except one thing, Molly."

"Hadn't we better talk about the wisdom acquired on tramp?"

"That is just what I am doing, my dear child. To-night the stars are out, the skies are clear, the air is fresh. I smell the fragrant earth across the park. I can almost believe that we are miles and miles from a town. And I want to have a real talk with you, Molly."

"Will you let me talk first?"

"Certainly, if you won't abuse the privilege. But leave time for me to answer. We mustn't throw away such a chance as this."

"I know what you want to say very well. I don't ask you to put it out of your head, because—— Oh, Dick, you know very well that I like you ever so much! You are the only kind of brother I ever had."

"By your leave, Molly, you never had any brother. You might have had the kindness to call me pal, or cousin, or comrade, or companion, or confidential clerk, even—but not any kind of brother. That relationship doesn't exist for you. I might as well call myself the child of that good lady, being only a kind of posthumous stepson. Now, Molly, you may go on."

"I only mean so that I can tell everything to you."

"That is permitted. Now I shall not interrupt."

"Very well. First of all, Hilarie is anxious about my appearance. So am I. She remains firm in the belief that I am the tragedian of the future."

Dick shook his head. "Vain hopes! Fond dreams!"

"You know, don't you, Dick, that it is impossible?"

"Comedy, light and sparkling, if you please, Molly. As soon as your name is made, I shall write a part for you on purpose. You shall take the town by storm—you yourself, as you are, witch and enchantress."

"Which makes it the more unfortunate that I'm compelled to go in for the other business."

The Changeling

"What about advertising 'Lady Macbeth,' and getting ready a burlesque?"

Molly took no notice of this suggestion. "Hilarie thinks the time is now approaching when I ought to make my *début*. Dick, I declare that I don't care one farthing about disappointed ambition. I told you so before. But I do care about disappointing Hilarie. And that weighs on my soul more than anything almost—more than the two other things."

"What are the two other things?"

"I am coming to them. Either of them, you see, would bring consolation—of sorts—for disappointed ambition. First, your cousin, Sir Humphrey——"

"Oh! He goes on making love, does he?"

"He goes on pressing for an answer. What answer shall I give him?"

"I will try to answer as if I was a disinterested bystander. You must consider not what he wants, but what you want."

"He offers me position and—I suppose—wealth. He wants me to marry him secretly, and to live out of the world, while he smooths matters with his mother."

Dick stopped in the middle of the road. "What?" he cried. "He wants you to marry him secretly? The—the—no, I won't use names and language. Marry him secretly and go into hiding? Why? Because you love the man? But you don't. Because he will make you Lady Woodroffe? But he won't—he will hide you away. Because he is rich? My dear, I know all about him. He has no money at all. The money is his mother's; she could cut him off with a shilling, if she liked. Because he is clever? He isn't. He's the laughing-stock of everybody, except the miserable little clique that he belongs to; they talk of Art—who have no feeling for Art; they hand about things they call Art, which are——"

"That will do, Dick."

"Add to this that he is a moody, ill-conditioned beast. If he loves you, it's because any man would love you. He'd be tired of you in a week. I know the man, my dear; I've made it my business to find out all about him. He is unworthy of you—quite unworthy, Molly. If you loved him

The Changeling

it might be different; I say, might, because then there might be some lessening of the misery you would draw on your head—I don't know, it might only mean greater misery—because you would feel his treatment more."

"You are incoherent, Dick."

"Could you marry a man without loving him, Molly? I ask you that."

"Here is a seat," said Molly, evading the question, which is always a delicate one for girls. Should they—ought they—ever to marry without love? One would rather not answer that question. There are conventions, there are things understood rather than expressed, there are imaginations, men are believed to be what they are not, the secret history of men is not suspected, there are reasons which might possibly make love quite a secondary consideration. It is not, indeed, a question which ought to be put to any girl.

"Here is a seat," Molly repeated. "It is chilly; but I am tired. Let us sit down for a minute, Dick."

He pressed his question. "Could you possibly marry this fellow, Molly, when you cannot respect him or love him?"

"About loving a man, Dick. I suppose it's quite possible to marry anybody, whether you love him or not. Whether a girl can screw up her courage to endure a man all day long when she doesn't like him, I don't know. Women have to do a great many things they don't like. Very few women can afford to choose——"

"You can, Molly."

"And if a man is a gentleman, he may be trusted, I suppose, not to do horrid things. He wouldn't get drunk; he would be tolerably kind; he would not spend all the money on himself; he would not desert one; he wouldn't throw the furniture about."

"That's a contented and a lowly state of mind, Molly."

"Well, and you must consider what a man may have to offer. Money; position; independence. You should listen to girls talking about these things with each other."

"Go on, Molly. It's a revelation."

The Changeling

"Not really, Dick? Why, as for love, I don't know what it means. I don't, indeed."

"Don't tell lies, Molly," he said, pressing her fingers.

"I mean that I don't love Sir Humphrey a bit."

"In that case, why not present him with the Boot?"

"He won't leave me alone. He hangs about the street, waiting for me when I go to my lesson. He comes to the college when I am staying with Hilarie, and, oh, Dick, can't you understand the temptation of it?"

"No, I can't."

"Well, then, try to understand it. Here I am, a girl with no money, dependent on Hilarie, who is all sweetness and goodness, yet dependent; and this man, who may be—very likely—all that you say, offers me this promotion."

"You ought not to be tempted. He is insulting you. If he means what he says, why doesn't he take you by the hand and lead you to his mother? He won't. He wants to hide you away. But he shall not, Molly—he shall not, so long as I breathe the upper air."

Molly made no reply. What was there to say?

"Fine love! Very fine love!" Dick snorted.

"I don't think I care much about his being all that you say, Dick, because, if I have no particular regard for him, I should not inquire, and I should not mind. I suppose he would be tolerably well-behaved with me."

"Then you are credulous, Molly, because he can't behave well to anybody."

"And while I am pulled this way and that way with doubts, Hilarie is wanting me to make my first appearance and to conquer the world; and my teacher thinks I shall do pretty well, and learn by experience, and I know the contrary, because you say so, Dick."

"Certainly. Quite the contrary."

"And you are always telling me what you want."

"I want you, Molly. Nothing short of that will satisfy me."

The Changeling

"Then comes another temptation—worse than anything."

"What is that?"

"It's Alice. She wants me——"

"Does she hiss 'diamonds' in your ear?"

"No. She says that she's so fond of me she cannot live without me, and she wants me to live with them altogether. And John chimes in. Says he will adopt me, and make me his heiress. Think of that, Dick! Millions! All for me—for me, the daughter of a failure."

"Molly." Dick spoke with solemnity suitable to the occasion. "This goes to the very root of things. You can't go on tramp with me if you begin to hanker after millions. No one ever heard of a great heiress talking to a gipsy or dancing in a barn. It can't be done. The weight of the dollars would nail your very heels to the boards."

"But, Dick, they're my own people, you know."

"My child"—Dick rose, for it was getting cold—"this is the most alarming temptation of all. It must be stopped right away. Look here, Molly," they were standing face to face under the lamp-post beside the railings of the park, "you know very well that you are only shamming. You love me; and I—well, shall I say it?"

"Stage people have no emotions, Dick. You said so yourself just now."

"This is not an emotion. It is part of me. I live in it; I breathe it; I only exist, my Molly, because of you. There isn't any stage gesture to signify my state of mind. The stalls would be disturbed in their little minds if one put this passion into visible representation. Even the gallery wouldn't understand. Put your arms on my shoulders, Molly."

She obeyed; she was quite as tall as her lover, and she had no difficulty in throwing her arms quite round his neck, which she did. If she blushed, the stars, which blink because they are short-sighted, could not see it. The lamp on the lamp-post is, of course, used to such things.

"You are the best girl in the world," he said, "the best and the dearest; and I promise you, Molly—the best and the dearest—that Humphrey shall never marry you, and that Mrs. Siddons shall never have a rival in you, and that you shall never become Miss Molly Pennefather

Haveril, heiress of millions, with decayed dukes and barefooted barons languishing after you."

He kissed her on the forehead and the lips. The girl made no reply, except to draw a long breath, which might have meant remonstrance, and might equally well mean satisfaction.

She took up the violin-case. "If I must carry the fiddle," she said, "let me see how it feels."

He made no objection. The action was a symbol. He accepted it as a visible expression of acquiescence, and so, side by side, in silence, they walked home under the stars and the lamp-posts.

CHAPTER XIV.

THE FIRST MOVE.

"No, my children," Alice replied. It was two days later. They were sympathetic children; they would feel for one. "I am not afraid to tell you what troubles me day and night. I am not afraid, but I am ashamed."

"You need not be ashamed," said Molly, stoutly. "Whatever you did must have been well done."

Alice sighed. "I wish I could think so. Sit down, one on each side of me, and I will tell you. Take my hand, Molly dear."

She was lying on a couch. In these days she was troubled with her heart, and lay down a good deal. So lying, with closed eyes, she had the courage to tell her story—the whole of it—suppressing nothing: the terrible sale of her child. She told them all.

"My child was taken away," she concluded. "It was the choice of that for him, or the workhouse. My people would do nothing for me. Partly they were poor—you know them, Molly—and some of them were Methodists, and serious. So I thought of the child's welfare; and I thought I should find my husband with the money, and so—and so——"

"You let him go." Molly finished the sentence.

"I have never known a day's peace since—never a day nor a night without self-reproach. We've prospered—oh, how we've prospered! everything we touch turns to gold! And not a single day of happiness has ever dawned for me, because I meet the reproachful eyes of my boy everywhere!"

"But you gave him to a lady who would treat him well."

"The doctor promised for her. But how am I to know that she has treated him well? If I could only find out where he is! And then came that dream!"

"What dream?"

The Changeling

"It came three times, by which I know that it is a true dream. Three times! Each time as vivid and plain as I see you two. I was sick; I thought I was dying, but I wasn't. And I know, now, that I shall not die without seeing my boy. That I know because, in the dream, some one, I don't know who, pointed to England, and said, 'Go over now—this very year—this fall, and you shall find your boy. If you wait longer, you will never find him.' That was a strange dream to come three times running, wasn't it?"

"Strange. Yes; a very strange dream."

"So we came. John will do anything I ask him. We shall lose—I don't know how much—by coming away. But he came with me. We've been here three weeks. Now listen. First, I found out, by accident, the doctor who took my child away. To be sure, he says he knows nothing more about him, but it is a first step; and now I've found my husband's second son,—that is a second step. And both by accident, that is, both providential. What shall I find next?"

"I think," said Molly, with profound sagacity, "that you should give Dick a free hand, and tell him to search about. You don't know how wise Dick is. He gets his wisdom by tramping at night. Let him think for you, dear. You want some one to think for you."

Mrs. Haveril turned to Dick. "Can you help me, Dick?"

He rose slowly, and began to walk about the room. "Can I? Well, I could try. But I confess the thing seems difficult. It's a new line for me, the detective line. Four and twenty years ago. We don't know who took the child—where she took the child; whether it is still living; whether the lady who took it is living. We want to find the clue."

"Dick," said Molly, "if we had a clue, we shouldn't want your assistance. Find one for us."

He sat down at the piano. "Ideas come this way often." He played a few chords and got up. "Not this morning. Well, let us see. The doctor says he doesn't know. If he doesn't, who can? Who else was there? An Indian ayah. Where is that woman? No mark on the child? No. Nothing put up with the clothes? A rattle. Ah! People don't keep rattles. And a paper with his Christian name. People don't keep such papers. And so the child disappears. How shall we find him after all

The Changeling

these years? Have you anything to suggest? Do you suspect anybody in the whole wide world?"

"No. There's only the young man I met at the doctor's. He's so wonderfully like your father, and like you, too. But they say he's the son of some great man. He's bigger than you, Dick. Your mother was a little woman, I should say."

"She was slight, like most American women."

"This young man is tall. Your father was a personable man; and he's big—much like my family. Dick, when I first saw him, my heart went out to him. I thought, 'Oh, my boy must be like you, tall and handsome!'"

"Would it not be better, dear lady, to make up your mind to forget the whole thing? Consider, it is so long ago."

"I would if I could. But I can't. No, Dick, I can never forget it."

"Force yourself to think about something else. It seems so desperately hopeless."

She shook her head. "When you play, my thoughts go out after him, whether I will or not. I am sitting with my son somewhere, or walking with him, or talking with him. I dream of him at night. Perhaps he is dead—because I dream of him so much. But I cannot think of him as dead. Oh, Dick, if you could find my son for me!"

"My dear lady, I will do what I can."

"You must think," said Molly, "morning, noon, and night, about nothing else. Consult your violin; you may whisper it into the piano-case."

"Yes, yes—meantime. It's no use going to see the doctor. He says he doesn't know. But if he called upon the woman at her hotel, he must have inquired for her by name."

"He did not. She came to him."

"Her own child was dead. Did she come to the place before the child died, or after?"

"I cannot tell you."

The Changeling

"Who else was concerned? Let us consider. An Indian ayah. Now, one doesn't bury a child and adopt another child without other people knowing it. You can't do it—servants must know. Perhaps the child was substituted. That has been done, I believe. But servants must know the secret. Then there are the undertakers who buried the child; the place where it is buried. If we knew the name of the child, I believe it would be easy, after all, to trace it. Then there is the place where the child died; it isn't often that a child dies in a hotel. There are the doctors who attended the child—they might remember the case. If we only knew the name of the child! Without that, we are powerless."

"I told you, Dick," said Molly, "that we want you to find the clue. If we knew the name of the child, we could go on quite easily without you."

"Very likely," he continued.

"There was no concealment; it was an open adoption known to everybody concerned, who were only three people."

"Then, why did the lady conceal her name?"

"She was probably anxious that the child should not know his relations at all. Perhaps, Dick, if you were to go away and think for a bit," Molly insisted.

"Oh yes; presently! Meantime there is one very simple way. Will you spend some money?"

"John will let you spend as much as you please."

"Very well, then." He sat down and took pen and paper. "The most simple way is to advertise. Let the world know what you want. Offer a reward. Same as for a lost dog. What do you think of this?—

"'Whereas, in the month of February, 1874, a child was adopted by a lady unknown in the city of Birmingham, the mother of the child will be most grateful to the lady who adopted it, if she will send her name and address to—' What shall we say? 'R. W., care of the hall porter, Dumfries Flats.'

I will receive the letters."

"But the reward?"

"I am coming to that, Molly.

The Changeling

"'In case of the lady's death, a reward of £100 will be paid for such information as will enable the child, now a young man of twenty-six, if he is living, to be identified. Nothing will be given for any information except such as is capable of proof. No persons will be received, and no verbal communications will be heard.'

There, Molly, what do you think of that?"

It might have been observed that neither then, nor afterwards, did Richard consult Mrs. Haveril. He took the conduct of the case into his own hands and Molly's.

"Dick! I knew you were awfully clever. I think it a splendid way!"

As if such a thing as an advertisement was entirely novel and previously unknown.

"Yes," said Dick, contemplating the document with pride, "I flatter myself that it is a good idea. Looks well on paper, doesn't it?" He held it at arm's length to catch the noontide sun. "'Whereas'—there's a legal 'note,' as they say, about it. Well, now, Molly, let us see how this will work. If the adoption was real, somebody must know of it—whether the lady is living or dead. Then we shall get a reply in a day or two——"

"In a day or two! Alice! Think of that!"

"If it was a substitution, we shall get no reply from the lady; but then, we may expect that other people know about it—servants and such. Then the reward comes in."

"Oh, isn't he clever, Alice? In a week—at least—you shall have your boy."

"Now I go," Dick concluded, with one more admiring glance at the paper before he folded it up, "and put the advertisement in the leading papers all over the country, and keep it going for a week, unless we hear something. Let us live in hope meantime."

Sir Robert read the advertisement over his breakfast. "Ah!" he said. "She has found an adviser; she means business; she will spend money. What is the good? She can just prove nothing. I am the master of the situation."

The Changeling

Yet there remained an uneasiness. For, although he was the master of the situation, it might be at the cost of declaring—or swearing in a court—that he still knew nothing as to the name and position and residence of the lady.

Lady Woodroffe read the advertisement as well. One of her secretaries pointed it out to her as an interesting item in the day's news. She read it; she held the paper before her face to hide a guilty pallor; her heart sank low: the dreadful thing was already in the papers. Soon, perhaps, it would appear again, with her name attached to it.

Next morning a letter was received by the advertiser. It enclosed the advertisement, cut out of a paper, with these words, "You need not advertise any more. The child has been dead for twenty years."

"Now"—Richard read the letter twice before he began to think about it—"what does this mean? If it was adoption, why not come forward? If it was substitution, then the child may be dead or he may not. I don't think he is, for my part. I believe it is a try-on to make us give over. We shall not give over, dear madam."

He continued the advertisement, therefore, for another week. Yet there came no more letters and no discovery.

"Oh, Dick, and I have been waiting day after day!"

"We must change the advertisement. The anonymous letter proves pretty clearly that there is reason for concealment. Else, why did not the writer sign her name? It was in a lady's handwriting—not a servant's. The adoption, therefore, to put it kindly, was not generally known. Let us alter the advertisement. We will now put in a few more details. We will leave the mother out; and we will no longer address the lady."

In consequence of this resolution, the following advertisement appeared next day:—

> "Whereas, in the month of February, 1874, in the city of Birmingham, a child, adopted by a lady to take the place of her own, recently dead, was taken to the railway station; was there delivered to the lady and carried to London;—a reward of TWO THOUSAND GUINEAS will be given to any person who will give such information as may lead to the discovery and identity of the

child. Nothing will be given for proffered information which does not lead to such discovery and identity. No advance will be made for expenses of travelling, or any other expenses. And no person will be received who offers verbal information. Address, by writing only, to R. W., care of the Hall porter, Dumfries Flats."

I dare say that many of my readers will remember the interest—nay, the racket—created by the appearance of this strange series of advertisements, which were never explained. The mystery is still referred to as an illustration of romance in upper circles. Some of the American papers quoted it as another proof of the profligacy of an aristocracy, concluding that it was the substitution of a gutter child for the Scion of a Baronial Stock.

This time there were shoals of answers. They came by hundreds; they came from all parts of the country. One would think that adoption by purchase was a recognized form of creating heirs to an estate. One railway porter wrote from Birmingham, stating that he remembered the affair perfectly well, because the lady gave him sixpence; that he saw the lady into the carriage, carrying the baby, which was dressed in white clothes with a woollen thing over its face; that on receipt of travelling money, and a trifle of £5 on account, he would run up to London and identify the baby. Another person conveyed the startling intelligence that she herself was the mother of the child; that she could tell by whom it was adopted. "My child," she said, "is now a belted earl. But my conscience upbraids me. Better a crust with the reward, than the pricks of a guilty conscience."

A third wrote with the warmth of a man of the world. Did the advertiser believe that he was such a juggins as to give away the story without making sure of the reward? If so—— But the writer preferred to think that he was dealing with a man of honour as well as a man of business—therefore he would propose a sure and certain plan. There must be in delicate affairs a certain amount of confidence on both sides. The writer knew the whole history, which was curious and valuable, and concerned certain noble houses; he had the proofs in his hands: he was prepared to send up the story, with the proofs, which nobody could question after once reading them, by return of post. But there must be some show of confidence on both sides. For himself, he was ready to confide in their promise to pay the reward. Let them confide to some extent in him. A mere trifle would do—the twentieth part of the reward—say a hundred pounds. Let the advertiser send this sum to him in registered letter, care of the Dog and Duck, Aston Terrace, Birmingham, in ten-pound notes, and by return post would follow the proofs.

Or if, as might happen—the writer thought it best in such matters to be extremely prudent—the advertiser did not trust this plan, he had a brother in a respectable way in a coffee-house and lodgings for single men, Kingsland Road. Let the money be deposited in his hands, to be held until the proofs and vouchers had been received. Nothing could be fairer than the proposal.

And so on. And so on. Richard greatly enjoyed these letters. Human faces, he said, may differ; legs are long or short; eyes are straight or skew; but the human mind, when two thousand pounds are involved, is apparently always the same. Meantime, which was disappointing, he was not a bit advanced in his inquiry.

Sir Robert read this advertisement as well. "She is well advised," he said. "She's going the right way to work. They calculate that servants know, and they offer a big reward. If that doesn't fetch them, there'll be a bigger. But it's no good—it's no good. Nobody knows what I know."

He thought it best, however, to reassure Lady Woodroffe.

"I hoped," he said, "that we should have no further occasion to speak about a certain transaction. I suppose, however, that you have heard of certain advertisements?"

"I have. Do you think——?"

"I do not think. Nay, I am certain. Lady Woodroffe, remember that there is only one person who knows the two women engaged in that transaction. I stood between them. I am not going to bring them together unless you desire me to do so. I came to say this, in case you should be in the least degree uneasy."

"Thank you, Sir Robert," she answered humbly. She trusted in that square-jawed, beetle-browed man; yet she was humiliated. "I certainly confide in you."

The Changeling

He got up. "Then I will waste your time no longer. You are always at work—I see and read and hear—always at work—good works—good works."

Her lips parted, but she was silent. Did he mean a reflection on the one work that had not been quite so good? But he was gone.

The advertisement was repeated in all the papers. England, Scotland, Ireland, the Colonies, knew about this adoption, and the anxiety of the mother to recover her son.

At this stage of the investigation, the subject began to be generally talked about. The newspapers had leading articles on the general subject of adoption. It was an opportunity for the display of classical scholarship; of mediæval scholarship; of historical scholarship; cases of pretence, of substitution, are not uncommon. There are noble houses about which things are whispered—things which must not be bruited abroad. The subject of adoption, open or concealed, proved fertile and fruitful to the leader-writer. One man, for instance, projected himself in imagination into the situation, and speculated on the effect which would be produced on a young man of culture and fine feeling, of finding out, at five and twenty, that he belonged to quite another family, with quite another set of traditions, prejudices, and ideas. Thus a young man born in the purple, or near it; brought up in great respect for birth, connections, and family history, with a strong prejudice in favour of an aristocratic caste; suddenly discovers that his people belong to the lowest grade of those who can call themselves of the middle class, and that he has no kind of connection with the folk to whom he has always believed himself attached. What would be the effect upon an educated and a sensitive mind? What would be the effect upon his affections? How would he regard his new mother—probably a vulgar old woman—or his new brothers and sisters—probably preposterous in their vulgarity? What effect would the discovery have upon his views of life? What upon his politics? What upon his opinions as to small trade, and the mean and undignified and sordid employments by which the bulk of mankind have to live?

At dinner-tables people talked about this mysterious adoption. What could it mean? Why did not the lady come forward? Was it, as some of the papers argued, clearly a case of fraudulent substitution? If not,

The Changeling

why did she not come forward? She was dead, perhaps. If so, why did not some one else come forward? If, however, it really was a case of substitution, then the position was intelligible. For instance, the case quoted the day before yesterday by the *Daily News*; that was, surely, a similar case. And so on; all the speakers wise with the knowledge derived from yesterday's paper. Are we sufficiently grateful to our daily papers and our leader-writers, for providing us with subjects of conversation?

The subject was handled with great vigour one night at Lady Woodroffe's own table. Sir Robert was present; he argued, with ability, that there was no reason to suppose any deception at all; that in his view, the lady had adopted the child, and had resolved to bring up the child in complete ignorance of its relatives, who were presumably of the lowlier sort; that she had seen no reason to take her servants into her confidence, or her friends; and that she now saw no reason to let the young man learn who his real relations were. And he drew a really admirable sketch of the disgust with which the young man would receive his new cousins. Lady Woodroffe, while this agreeable discussion was continued, sat at the head of her table, calm, pale, and collected.

Then there appeared a third advertisement. It was just like the second, except that it now raised the reward to ten thousand guineas. It also included the fact that the child had been received at the Birmingham station by an Indian ayah.

This advertisement caused searchings of heart in all houses where there had been at any time an Indian ayah. The suggestion in every one of these houses was that a child had died, and another had been substituted. The matter was discussed in the servants' hall at Lady Woodroffe's. The butler had been in service with Sir Humphrey and his household for thirty years.

"I came home," he said, "from India with Sir Humphrey. We came to this house. My lady and the *ayah*—she that died six or seven years ago—were already here with the child—now Sir Humphrey."

"Did you know the child again?"

The Changeling

"Know the child? I'd know Sir Humphrey's child anywhere. Why, I saw him every day till he was six months old. A lovely child he was, with his light hair and his blue eyes."

"Did my lady come from Birmingham?"

"What would my lady be doing at Birmingham? She came straight through from Scotland from her noble pa, Lord Dunedin. The ayah told us so."

The page, who was listening, resigned, with a sigh, the prospect of getting that reward of ten thousand guineas.

Lady Woodroffe, upstairs, read the third advertisement, and grew faint and sick with fear.

Sir Robert read the advertisement. "Very good," he said. "Very good indeed. But if there had been any one who knew anything at all, there would have been an answer to the offer of two thousand pounds. Let them offer a million, if they like."

"Dick," said Molly, "it seemed very clever at first. But, you see, nothing has come of it."

"On the contrary, something has come of it. Mind you, the whole world is talking about the case. If it was a genuine adoption, the unknown woman would certainly have come forward."

"Why?"

"Because there could be no reason for concealment. As it is, she remains silent. Why? Because there has been substitution instead of adoption. She has put forward another baby in the place and in the name of the dead child."

"How can you prove that?"

"I don't know, Molly. I believe I have missed my vocation. I am a sleuth-hound. Give me a clue; put me on the scent, and let me rip."

His face hardened; his features grew sharper; his eyes keener; he bent his neck forward; he was no longer the musician; he was the bloodhound looking for the scent. The acting instinct in him made him while he spoke adapt his face and his expression to the new part he played. To look the part is, if you consider, essential.

CHAPTER XV.

TWO JUMPS AND A CONCLUSION.

The advertisements produced no answer except from persons hoping to make money by the case—such as the railway porter, who could swear to the baby, the lady who was really the mother, or the detective who wanted a good long-staying job. There seemed no hope or help from the advertisement. Well, then, what next?

By this time Richard Woodroffe, though never before engaged upon this kind of business, found himself so much interested in the subject that he could think of nothing else. He occupied himself with putting the case into a statement, which he kept altering. He carried himself back in imagination to the transference of the baby; he saw the doctor taking it from the mother and giving it to an ayah in the railway station. And there he stopped.

His friend Sir Robert was the doctor—his friend Sir Robert, who knew all the theatrical and show folk, as well as the royal princes and the dukes and illustrious folk. Well, he knew this physician well enough to be certain that a secret was as safe behind those steady, deep-set eyes as with any father confessor. That square chin did not belong to a garrulous temper, that big brain was a treasury of family secrets; he knew where all the skeletons were kept; this was only one of a thousand secrets; his patients told him everything—that was, of course, because he was a specialist in nervous disorders, which have a good deal to do with family and personal secrets. Fortunately, personal secrets are not family secrets.

There is a deep-seated prejudice against the upper ten thousand in the matter of family secrets. They are supposed to possess a large number of these awkward chronicles, and they are all supposed to be scandals. Aristocratic circles are supposed to be very much exposed to the danger of catching a family secret, a disease which is contagious, and is passed on from one family to another with surprising readiness. They are supposed also to be continually engaged in hushing up, hiding away, sending accomplices and servants cognizant of certain transactions to America and the Antipodes, even dropping them into dungeons. They are believed to be always trying to forget the last scandal but one, while they are destroying the proofs of the last scandal. For my own part, while admitting the contagion of the disorder, I would submit that an earl is no more liable to it than an alderman, a baron no more than a butcher. Middle-class families are always either going up or going down. With those which are going up there is an immense quantity of things to be forgotten. We wipe out with a sponge a deplorable great-aunt, we look the other way when we pass her grave; we agree to forget a whole family of cousins; we do not wish ourselves to be remembered more than, say, thirty years back; we desire that no inquiry, other than general, shall be made into our origins. In a word—if we may compress so great a discovery in a single sentence—the middle class—the great middle class—backbone, legs, brain, and tongue, as we all know, of the country—the class to which we all, or nearly all, belong—is really the home and haunt of the family secret.

This secret, however, was not in the ordinary run—not those which excitable actresses pour into the ears of physicians. Moreover, if the theory was true, it was a secret, Richard reflected, as much of the doctor's as of the lady's. And, again, since adoption became substitution, although the young doctor may have assisted in the former, the old doctor might not be anxious for the story to get about now that it meant the latter.

Here, however, were the facts as related by Alice herself.

An unknown lady, according to the doctor's statement, called upon him and stated that she was anxious to adopt a child in place of her own, which she had just lost by death.

This was early in February, 1874.

The lady stated further that she wanted a child about fifteen months of age, light-haired, blue-eyed.

(The child she adopted was thirteen months of age.)

(Did the child die in Birmingham? As the lady was apparently passing through, did the child die at a hotel?)

Dr. Steele called upon Alice, then in great poverty and distress, and asked her if she would let the child be adopted, or whether she would suffer it to go into the workhouse. She chose the former alternative, and accepted the sum of fifty pounds for her child.

The money was paid in five-pound notes. She did not know the numbers.

There were no marks on the child by which he might be identified.

On the child's clothes, before giving him up, the mother pinned a paper, giving his Christian name—Humphrey.

He was the son of Anthony Woodroffe. In the Woodroffe family there was always a Humphrey.

Nothing else, nothing else—no clue, no suggestion, or hint, or opening anywhere, except resemblance. The strange likeness of this young man Humphrey to himself haunted Dick; he looked at himself in the glass. Any one could see that his features, his hair, his eyes, were those of Humphrey. Differences there were—in stature, in expression, in carriage. Dick was as elastic and springy as the other was measured and slow of gait. As for that other resemblance, said by Alice to be even more marked—that between Humphrey and Anthony Woodroffe, the actor, John Anthony—it was even more remarkable. These resemblances one may look for in sons and in brothers, but not in cousins separated by five hundred years. Another point which he kept to himself was the resemblance which he found in Humphrey to Alice, his mother by theory. It was not the same kind of resemblance as the other—features, face, head, all were different; it was that resemblance which reminds—a resemblance not defined in words, but unmistakable. And all day long and all night Dick saw this resemblance.

He put down the points—

- 1. The strongest possible resemblance—so stated by the mother of the adopted child—of son to father.

- 2. A strong resemblance as between brothers or sons of the same father.

- 3. A resemblance—was it fancy of his own?—as between mother and son.

The Changeling

- 4. The lady who adopted the boy must have belonged to an Indian family, because there was an ayah with her.

- 5. The age of the child adopted corresponded very nearly with the age of Sir Humphrey.

He went to the British Museum and consulted "Debrett." He took the trouble to go there because he did not possess the volume, and none of his friends had ever heard of it. There he read, as the doctor had read a few weeks before, that the present holder of the Woodroffe baronetcy was Humphrey Arundale, second baronet, son of the late Sir Humphrey, etc., born on December the 2nd, 1872.

There was nothing much to be got out of that little paragraph. But, as Dick read it again and again, the letters began to shift themselves. It is astonishing how letters can, by a little shifting, convey a very different meaning. This is what he read now—

"Woodroffe, Humphrey, falsely calling himself second baronet, and son of the late Sir Humphrey, really son of one John Anthony Woodroffe, distant cousin of Sir Humphrey, vocalist, comedian, and vagabond, by Alice, daughter of Tom, Dick, or Harry Pennefather, engaged in small trade, of Hackney; born in 1873, sold by his mother in February, 1874, through the agency of Sir Robert Steele, M.D., F.R.S., Ex-President of the Royal College of Physicians, now of Harley Street, to Lilias, Lady Woodroffe, daughter of the Earl of Dunedin, who passed him off as her own child.

"Collateral branches—Richard, son of the late John Anthony Woodroffe, by Bethia, his second wife, after he had divorced and deserted the above mentioned Alice, October 14, 1875; unmarried, has no club, musician, singer, comedian, vagabond."

He put back the volume. "It's a very remarkable Red Book," he said; "nobody knows how they get at these facts. Now, I, for my part, don't seem able to get at the truth, however much I try; and there 'Debrett' has it in print, for all the world to read."

He then looked up the same work twelve years before. He found under the name of Woodroffe the fact that Sir Humphrey the elder retired from active service, and returned to England early in February, 1874.

The Changeling

"The old man came home, then," he said, "at the very time when the adoption was negotiated. At that very time. How does that bear on the case? Well, if his own child died, there was perhaps time to get another to take its place before he got home."

Now, Dick in a small way was a story-teller; he was in request by those who knew him because he told stories very well, and also because he told very few, and would only work when he could capture an idea, and when a story came of its own accord; he was the author of one or two comediettas; further, he had been on the stage, and had played many parts. From this variegated experience he understood the value of drawing your conclusion first, and putting together your proofs afterwards: perhaps the proofs might fail to arrive; but the conclusion would remain. Geometry wants to build up proofs and arrive at a conclusion which one would not otherwise guess. Who could possibly imagine that the square on the side opposite the right angle is equal to the sum of the squares on the sides containing the right angle? Not even the sharpest woman ever created would arrive at such a conclusion without proofs. In law also, chiefly because men are mostly liars, exact proof is demanded—proof arrived at by painfully picking the truth out of the lies. This young man, for his part, partly because he was a story-teller and a dramatist, partly because he was a musician, found it the best and readiest method to jump at the truth first, and to prove it afterwards. He arrived at this conclusion, which perfectly satisfied him, without any reason, like a kangaroo, by a jump. In fact, he took two jumps.

It is always a great help in cases requiring thought and argument and construction—because every good case is like a story in requiring construction—to consult the feminine mind; if you are interested in the owner, or tenant, of a certain mind, it makes the consultation all the better. Richard Woodroffe consulted Molly every day. By talking over the case again and again, and by looking at it in company, one becomes more critical and at the same time clearer in one's views. There were, as you know, many reasons why Richard should consult this young lady, apart from her undoubted intelligence.

"Why, Molly," he asked—"why—I put it to your feminine perceptions—why was this good lady so profoundly moved by the mere sight of the fellow? She wasn't moved by the sight of me. Yet I

The Changeling

am exactly like him, I believe. It was at the theatre. She was in a private box; he was one of a line of Johnnies in the stalls. She was so much affected that she had to leave the house. She met him again at Steele's dinner. She was affected in the same way. Why? She is presumed never to have seen the fellow before; she certainly has not seen him for twenty-four years. Why, I ask, was she so much affected? She tells me that the sight of him always affects her in exactly the same way—with the same mysterious yearning and longing and with a sadness indescribable.

"Wait a minute. Hear me out. Is it his resemblance to a certain man—her first husband? But again, I am like him, and she does not yearn after me a bit. What can it be except an unknown sense—the maternal instinct—which is awakened in her? What is it but his own identity, which she alone can understand—with her child?"

"Dick," said Molly, "it's a tremendous jump. Yet, of course——"

"Of course. I knew you would agree with me. The intuitions—the conclusions—the insight of women are beyond everything. Molly, it is a blessed thing that you are retained in this case. The sight of you is to me a daily refresher; the look of you is a heavy fee; and the voice of you is an encouragement. Stand by me, Molly—and I will pull this half-brother of mine down from that bad eminence and ask him, when he stands beside me, with an entirely new and most distinguished company of cousins, how he feels, and what has become of his superiority. You shall introduce him to the pew-opener, and I will present him to the draper."

Again, there was the second jump. "I ask you that, Molly. Do you imagine that the doctor is really and truly as ignorant as he would have us believe, of the lady's name? He knows Lady Woodroffe; he asks her son to dinner. To be sure, he knows half the world. If he attended the dead child, of course he would have known her name. But I suppose he did not. If so, since the lady came to him immediately after the death, he might have consulted the registers, to find what children of that age had died during a certain week in Birmingham—if the child did die there, of which we are not certain. Even in a great city like Birmingham there are not many children of that age dying every day; very few dying in hotels; and very few children indeed

The Changeling

belonging to visitors and strangers. Molly mine—if the doctor did not know, the doctor might have known. Is that so? Deny it if you can."

"I suppose so, Dick, though really I don't see what you are driving at."

"Very well, then. We go on. Why did the doctor go out of his way to invite Humphrey to meet his true mother? Now, I know Dr. Steele. He's an awfully good fellow—charitable and good-natured; he'll do anything for a man; but he's a man of science, and he's always watching and thinking and putting things together. I've heard him talk about heredity, and what a man gets from his ancestors. Now, I'm quite certain, Molly—without any proof—I don't want any proof. Hang your hard-and-fast matter-of-fact evidence! I am quite certain, I say, that Steele invited Humphrey and his mother and myself in order to look at us all and watch differences and likenesses. You see, the case may be a beautiful illustration of hereditary qualities. Here is a young man separated from his own people from infancy. There can be no imitation; and now, after twenty years and more, the man of science can contemplate the son, brought up in a most aristocratic and superior atmosphere; the mother, who has always remained in much the same condition except for money; and another son, who has been brought up like his father, a vagabond and a wanderer—with a fiddle. It was a lovely chance for him. I saw him looking at us all dinner-time; in the evening, when I was playing, I saw him, under his bushy eyebrows, looking from Humphrey to his mother. I wondered why. Now I know. The doctor, Molly, is an accomplice."

"An accomplice! Oh! And a man in that position!"

"An accomplice after the act, not before it. My theory is this: Dr. Steele met the lady after he came to town. How he managed to raise himself from the cheap general practitioner to a leading London physician, one doesn't know. It's like stepping from thirty shillings a week to being a star at fifty pounds; no one knows how it's done. Do you think Lady Woodroffe was useful in talking about him? If I wrote a story, I should make the doctor dog the lady's footsteps and coerce her into advancing him. But this isn't a story. However, I take it that he met her, recognized her, and that they agreed that nothing was to be said about this little transaction of the past. Then, of course, when Alice turned up unexpectedly, and asked where the child was to be seen,

The Changeling

there was nothing to do except to hold up his hands and protest that he knew nothing about the child."

"But all this is guess-work, Dick."

"Yes. I am afraid we have nothing before us but guess-work. Unless we get some facts to go upon. Look here. A woman is standing on one side of a high wall; another woman is on the other side of the wall. There is a door in the wall; Sir Robert keeps the key of that door in his pocket. There is only one key, and he has it. Unless he consents to unlock the door, those two women can never meet. And so my half-brother will remain upon his eminence."

They fell into a gloomy silence.

Dick broke it. "Molly, what about our good friend, the mother of this interesting changeling?"

"She is strangely comforted by the reflection that the matter is in your hands. Dick, you have found favour in her sight and in her husband's."

"Good, so far."

"And she is firmly persuaded that you will bring the truth to light. She still clings to her dream, you know."

"Does she talk about Humphrey? Was she taken with him?"

"She says little. She lies down and shuts her eyes. Then she is thinking of him. She likes me to play, so that she may think about him. When we drive out, I am sure she is looking for him in the crowd. If he were to call, she would tell him everything. And I am certain that she dreams of heaping upon him all that a young man can possibly desire as soon as she gets him back."

"I hope the poor soul will not meet with disappointment. But I fear, Molly—I fear." He relapsed into his gloomy silence. "I hold the two ends of the chain in my hands, but I cannot connect the ends. I might go to Steele and show him what I suspect. He would only laugh at me. He laughs like the Sphynx, sometimes. If I went to Lady Woodroffe, I should be handed over to her solicitors, and by them conducted to the High Court of Justice; I should hear plain speaking from the Judge on the subject of defamation of character. Everybody would believe that I was a black-mailer. I should be called upon to pay large sums of

The Changeling

money as damages; and I should have to go through the Court of Bankruptcy."

The mind of this inquirer had never before been exercised upon any matter more knotty than the presentation of a simple plot, or the difficulty of getting people off the stage. Sometimes, in moments of depression, he even doubted his own conclusions—a condition of mind fatal to all discovery, because it is quite certain that the eye of faith first perceives what the slow piecing together of facts afterwards proves. You must perceive the truth, somehow, first before you can prove it. Perhaps it is not the truth which is at first discerned. In that case, the seeker after truth has at least an imaginary object by which to direct his steps. It may lead him wrong; on the other hand, it may help him to recover the clue which will lead him straight to the heart of things. In a word, one wants a theory to assist all research in things of science or in things of practice.

"Dick," said Molly, "about those registers."

"What about them?"

"Why, that the doctor might have found the name of the child by simply looking into the registers."

"If the child, that is to say, died in Birmingham."

"Yes—if it died in Birmingham. Well, then, Dick—if the doctor could search those registers——" She stopped for a moment. They always do it on the stage, to heighten the effect.

"Well, Molly?"

"Why can't you?"

Dick sat down suddenly, knocked over by the shock of this suggestion.

"Good Heavens, Molly! Oh the depth and the height and the spring and the leap of woman's wit! Why can't I? why can't I? Molly, I am a log, and a lump, and a lout. I deserve that you should take my half-brother. No—not that! Good-bye, good-bye, incomparable shepherdess!" He raised her hand and kissed it. "I fly—I hasten—on the wings of the wind—to Birmingham—the city of Hidden Truth—to read the Revelations of the Register."

CHAPTER XVI.

A WRETCH.

Hilarie sat alone in the deep recesses of the western porch of the old church. Although it was November, this sheltered porch was still warm; the swallows that make the summer, and their friends the swifts, were gone; the leaves which still clung to the trees were red and brown and yellow; the grass which clothed the graves no longer waved under the breeze with light and shade and sunshine; none of the old bedesmen were walking the churchyard; even the children in the school were silent over their work, as if singing only belonged to summer; and the wind whistled mournfully in the branches of the yew. Her face, always so calm and restful to others, was troubled and disturbed as she sat by herself.

She held two letters in her hand. One of them was open. She had already read it twice; now she read it a third time. It was from Molly, and it ran as follows:—

> "Dearest President of the only college where they teach sweet thoughts and gracious manners and nothing else—where they have only one professor, who is the president and the chaplain and all the lecturers—I have not seen you for so long a time that I am ashamed. Now I am going to tell you why. I must make confession, and then I must ask your advice. I can do this much better by writing than by talking, so that I will write first and we will talk afterwards. I have to tell you most unexpected things, and most wonderful events. They are full of temptations and quandaries.
>
> "First, for my confession. Your ambition for me has been that I should be ambitious for myself. I have done my best to meet your wish; I have tried to be ambitious in the best way—your way. You thought that I might make a serious attempt at serious acting— that I might become a queen of tragedy. Alas! I have felt for some time that I must abandon the attempt. I cannot portray the emotions, I cannot feel the emotions, of tragedy; my nature is too shallow; I cannot realize a great passion. I only know that it must

produce in voice, and face, and speech, and gesture, changes and indications that cannot be taught. As for me, when I try, I become either stilted or wooden. The passion does not seize me and possess me. Ambition, of a kind, is not wanting. I like to imagine myself a great actress, sweeping across the stage with a velvet train; I like to think of the people rising and applauding; but, as for the part, I am not moved at all. I think about nothing but myself. If I look in the glass, I am told that I have not the face for tragedy. If I begin to declaim, I cannot feel the words. I am just like the young man who kept on dreaming that he was a great poet, until he made the disagreeable discovery that in order to be a great poet it is absolutely necessary to write great poems. My dear Hilarie, I must put a stop to this attempt at once. I have been a burden to you for five long years. Let me not load you with more than is necessary. I don't say anything about thanks, because you know—you know.

"Dick—you remember Dick, my father's old young friend—the Dick that turned up on tramp that day you three cousins met—tells me that in comedy I should do well. You shall hear, directly, that it is quite possible that I may change the buskin for the sock—which he says is the classical way of putting it. He tells me that an expressive face—mine can screw up or be pulled out like an indiarubber face—a tall figure, and a fairly good voice, are wanted first of all; and that I have all three. But you will see directly that poor Dick is not quite a disinterested person. Still, he may be right, and I must say that if I am to go on the stage, I would rather make them laugh than cry. It must be much more pleasant to broaden their faces with smiles than to stiffen them with terror at the sight of the blood-stained dagger.

"The stage seems the only profession open to a girl like me, if I am to have a profession at all—which you will understand directly is no longer absolutely necessary. I was born behind the footlights, Dick was born in the sawdust; so there seems a natural fitness. However, until I knew you all, my acquaintances were these folk; I have never learned to think of myself as belonging to the world at all. To my young imagination the world consisted of a great many people, whose only occupation was to scrape money

The Changeling

together in order to buy seats at a theatre. Some made things, some painted things, some built things, some contrived things, some wrote things; they were extremely industrious, because their industry brought them tickets. The shops, I imagined, were only established and furnished for the purpose of providing things wanted by the show folk. I have never, in fact, got rid of that feeling. The show was everything; all the world existed only to be dramatized. Even the Church, you see, could be put upon the stage. So, as I said, the stage is the only profession for me, if I am to choose a profession.

"There is another thing. I suppose I got this idea, too, from my upbringing. It is that to be an actress is the one honourable career for a woman. Not to be a great actress—but just an actress, that's all. I believe that the people who really belong to this profession from one generation to another, don't really care very much about being great actors; they are just content to belong to the profession, just as most doctors have no ambition to become great doctors, but are just content with being in the profession. In acting it is the new-comer who wants to be great. There is something comfortable and satisfying in a position of humble utility. I may possibly become the housemaid of farce, with a black daub upon my face.

"The next thing is about my newly discovered cousin, Alice Haveril. She is the kindest of women—next to one. She heaps kindnesses upon me. She loads me with dresses, gold chains, bonnets, gloves, and would load me with money if I could take it. But I will not have that form of gift.

"I am very much with her, because she has no friends here, and her husband is much engaged with his affairs. She is in most delicate health, with a weak heart. She has a terrible trouble, the nature of which I have recently learned; and she wants some one with her constantly. I spend most of the day with her; I drive with her, go shopping with her, read to her, and talk to her.

"Now, dear Hilarie, here is my temptation. My cousin Alice wants me to go back to America with her and her husband. He would like it, too. They are enormously rich; they could make me an heiress. The husband, John Haveril, is as honest and kindly a man as you could wish to find. He is a man who has made his own way; he has not the manners of society; but he is not vulgar; he is well bred by instinct.

"This is, I confess, a great temptation. It is more than a temptation, it seems almost a duty. I have found this poor, fragile creature; I know why she suffers. I think I ought not to leave her.

"If I accept their offer, I shall become one of the rich heiresses of America. It will mean millions. But then I really do not want millions. I shall have to give up all my friends if I go away to America. This would be very hard. I should also lose the happiness of desiring things I cannot now obtain. I believe that longing after things unattainable is the chief happiness of the impecunious. Only think of forming a wish and having it instantly realized! How selfish, how thoughtless of other people, how fat and coarse and lazy, one would become! Dick has often spoken of the terrible effect produced upon the mind by the possession of wealth. Perhaps he has prejudiced me.

"The next temptation comes from a certain young man. He besieges me—he swears he cannot live without me. He wants me to be engaged secretly—he says that I have promised. But I have not. As for keeping any secrets from you, and especially a matter of this importance, it is ridiculous. The young man is, in fact, one of the cousins—Sir Humphrey."

At this point Hilarie started, laid down the letter, looked up; read the words again; went on, with a red spot in either cheek.

"I confess humbly that the position which he offers attracts me. That so humble a person as myself should be elevated without any warning, so to speak, to this position—his mother is a great leader in the philanthropic part of society—is a curious freak of fortune. It is like a story-book. As for the man—well, for my own feeling about him, it is certainly quite true that I could very well live without him. I certainly should not droop and languish if he were to go somewhere else; yet—you know him, Hilarie. He is clever in a way. He thinks he has ideas about Art—he paints smudges, puts together chords, and writes lines that rhyme. He also plays disjointed bits, and complains that they do not appeal to me. That is harmless, however. His manners are distinguished, I suppose. He is quite contemptuous of everybody who has work to do. If you talk to him about the world below, it is like running your head against a stone wall. He loves me, he says, for the opposites. And what that means, I don't know. I suppose that, as a gentleman, he could be trusted to behave with decency and kindness to his wife. At the same time, I have found him, more than once, of a surprising ill temper, moody, jealous, violent, and I think that he is selfish in the cultivated manner—that is to say, selfish with refinement.

"I cannot and will not be guilty of a secret engagement; while a secret marriage, which he also vehemently urges, unknown to his mother or my friends, and to be kept in retirement, concealed from everybody, is a degradation to which I would never submit. I cannot understand what my lover means by such a proposal, nor why he cannot see that the thing is an insult and an impossibility.

"However, I have refused concealment. Meantime a most romantic and wonderful discovery is going to be disclosed. I must not set it down on paper, even for your eyes, Hilarie. It is a discovery of which Humphrey knows nothing as yet. He will learn it, I believe, in a few days. When he does learn it, it will necessitate a complete change in all his views of life; it will open the world for him; it will take him out of his narrow grooves; it will try him and prove him. Now, dear Hilarie, am I right to wait—without his knowing why? If he receives this discovery as he ought—if it brings out in him what is really noble in his character, I can trust myself to him. At the same time, it will deprive him of what first attracted me in him; but I must not tell you more.

"Lastly, my dear old Dick has been making love to me, just as he did when I was fifteen and he was seventeen, going about with my father, practising and playing. Such a Conservative—so full of prejudices is Dick. I confess to you, dear Hilarie, I would rather marry Dick than anything else. We should never have any money—Dick gives away all he gets. He will not put by. 'If I am ill,' he says, 'take me to the hospital.' 'If I die,' he says, 'bury me in the hedge, like the gipsy folk.' He never wants money, and I

The Changeling

should sometimes go on tramp with him, and we should sit in the woods, and march along the roads, and hear the skylark sing, and yearn for the unattainable, and go on crying for we know not what, like the little children. Oh, delightful! And Dick is always sweet and always good—except, perhaps, when he speaks of Humphrey, who has angered him by cold and superior airs. Dick is a philosopher, except on that one side. When I think of marrying Dick, dear Hilarie, my heart stands still. For then I get a most lovely dream. I close my eyes to see it better. It is a most charming vision. There is a long road with a broad strip of turf on either side, and a high hedge for shade and flowers, goodly trees at intervals; a road which runs over the hills and down the valleys and along brooks; crosses bridges, and has short cuts through fields and meadows; overhead the lark sings; from the trees the yellow-hammer cries, 'A little bit of bread and no cheese;' clouds fly across the sky; all kinds of queer people pass along—vagrants, beggars, gipsies, soldiers,—just the common sort. On the springy turf at the side I myself walk, carrying the fiddle—in the middle of the road Dick tramps, going large and free; over his shoulders hangs the bag which contains all we want; now and then he bursts out singing as he goes. In the coppice we sit down on the trunk of a tree and take lunch out of a paper bag. Sometimes, when we are quite alone in a coppice, far away from the world, Dick takes his fiddle out of the case and plays to me, all alone, music that lifts me out of myself and carries me away, I know not whither. Who would not marry a great magician? And in my dream about Dick I am never tired. I never regret my lot—I never want money. Dick is never savage, like Humphrey—he despises no one; he is loved by everybody. Oh, Hilarie, I would ask for nothing—nothing better than to give myself to Dick, and to follow him and be his slave—his grateful slave! Is this love, Hilarie? Write to me, dear Hilarie, and tell me what I ought to do."

Hilarie laid down the letter with a sigh. "Strange," she said. "Molly sees her own path of happiness quite plainly; yet she cannot follow it. What she does not know is that she has shattered my own dream."

She opened another letter in her hand. "I should have known," she said. "He is base metal, through and through. I should have known.

The Changeling

Yet what a son—of what a mother! Who would suspect?" She read the letter again.

"It has been my dream ever since the fortunate day when I met you in the churchyard, to unite our branches of the house. You have thought me cold about your very beautiful projects and illusions. I am, perhaps, harder than yourself, because I know the world better, and because I have always found people extremely amiable while you are giving them things—and exactly the reverse when you call upon them to give to others. However, you will never find me opposing the plans suggested by your nobility of character. I have spoken to my mother upon this subject——" She stopped short—she tore the letter in halves, then, with another thought, put back the torn sheet into its envelope. "Wretch!" she cried, "I will keep your letter!"

She sat there, alone, looking out upon the porch. The sun went down and the twilight descended, and she sat among the graves, thinking.

Presently she got up, feeling cold and numbed. "It was a foolish dream," she said. "I ought to have known—I ought to have known."

She walked slowly homeward. As she came out of the coppice into her own park, she saw the old house lit up already, and through the windows she saw figures flitting about. They were her students, and they were gathering for afternoon tea.

"Why," she said, "I want to be their leader, and I dream an idle dream about a worthless man!"

With firmer step and head erect she entered the porch of her house, and found herself in the midst of the girls. Her dream was shattered—she let it go: there are other things to think about besides a worthless man.

One knows not what were the actual intentions of this young man. Fate would not, as you will presently discover, permit him to carry them out. We may, however, allow that he was really in love with one of the two girls—the one who attracted all mankind, not so much by her beauty as by her manner, which was caressing; and by her conversation, which was sprightly. He was in love with her after the manner of his father, who felt the necessity for an occasional change in the object of his affections. To desert one woman for another was

The Changeling

part of his inheritance—had Hilarie known it. One should find excuses for hereditary tendencies; those who knew the truth would recognize in this treatment of women the mark of the changeling.

As for Hilarie, she wrote a brief note to Molly. "Let us talk over these things," she said. "Meantime, I implore you not to enter into any engagement, open or secret, with a man who could venture to propose the latter." She folded the note. She rose; she sighed.

"An idle dream," she said, "about a worthless man!"

CHAPTER XVII.

THE SECOND BLOW.

Three days after this conversation, the amateur detective on his first job arrived in London with the midday train from Birmingham. He was in a state of happiness and triumph almost superhuman. For he brought with him, as he believed, the conclusion of the matter. Alone, single-handed, he had discovered the plot; the proofs were in his hands. He was on his way to compel the guilty to submission, to subdue the proud, to send the rich empty away. Poetical justice would be done; his half-brother would be restored to his fraternal arms; and Molly would be free.

I say there was no happier man than this poor credulous Richard to be found anywhere than in that third-class carriage. He wanted no paper to read; he sat in a kind of cloud of glorious congratulations. Everything was proved; there was but one step possible—that of surrender absolute.

Two letters preceded his arrival.

One was for Molly. "Expect me to-morrow evening," he said. "I bring great news; but do not say anything to Alice. The news should be still greater than what I have to tell you."

The other was for Lady Woodroffe.

"MADAM" (he wrote)

"I have to inform you that I have made a discovery closely connected with you. The discovery is (1) that the only son of the late Sir Humphrey Woodroffe, the first baronet, died at Birmingham, on February 5th, 1874, and is buried there; and (2) that he died at the Great Midland Hotel, where your name is entered as being on that day accompanied by an Indian ayah and a child. There is a note to the effect that the child died the same night. The child is entered in the register as born on December the 2nd, 1872. I observe in the Peerage that the present baronet was born on that day.

"I propose to call upon you to-morrow afternoon at about three o'clock, in the hope of obtaining an interview with you on this subject.

"I remain, madam, your obedient servant,

"RICHARD WOODROFFE."

Now you understand why Richard Woodroffe came to town in so buoyant and jubilant a mood. He saw himself received with shame and confusion by a fallen enemy. He saw himself playing, for the first time in his life, a part requiring great dignity—that of the conqueror. He would be chivalrous towards this sinner; he would utter no reproach: to lay his proofs before her, to receive her surrender, would be enough. Richard was not a revengeful person; wrongs he forgot; injuries he forgave. At the same time, he would have been more than human if he had not contemplated, with some kind of satisfaction, the reduction of the second baronet to his true level, which would leave him with no more pride and no more superiority.

Alas! He was not prepared for what awaited him. Had he asked himself what kind of woman he should meet, he would have imagined a person broken down by the discovery of her guilt; throwing herself at his feet, ready to confess everything—a woman with whom he would be the conqueror. That the tables would be turned upon him, he never even thought possible. Who would? He had discovered that the real heir to the name and title of Sir Humphrey Woodroffe had actually died at Birmingham twenty-four years ago. Who, then, was the present so-called Sir Humphrey?

"Thou art the woman!" "Alas! alas! I am the woman."

This was the pretty dialogue of conquest and confession which he fondly imagined.

What happened?

At the hour of three he called and sent in his card.

He was taken upstairs to the drawing-room, where a lady of august presence and severe aspect, who struck an unexpected terror into him at the outset, was sitting at a table with a secretary. This severe person put up her glasses curiously, and icily motioned him to wait, while

The Changeling

she went on dictating to the secretary. When she had finished — which took several minutes — she dismissed her assistant and turned to her visitor, who was still standing, hat in hand, already disconcerted by this contemptuous treatment, and expectant of unpleasantness.

She pushed back her chair and took a paper from the table.

"You sent me a letter yesterday, Mr. Woodroffe."

"I did," he said huskily. Then, with a feeling of being cross-examined, he cleared his throat and tried to assume an attitude of dignity.

"This is the letter, I believe. Read it, to make sure."

"That is the letter."

"Oh! And you are come, I suppose, to talk over the matter, to see what you can make out of it. Well, sir, I have taken advice upon this letter. I was advised to have the door shut in your face; I was advised to send you to my lawyers; but I am not afraid, even of the black-mailer. I resolved to see you. Now, sir, you may sit down, if you like." Richard sank into a chair, his cheeks flaming. "Go on, then," she added impatiently. "Don't waste my time. Explain this letter, sir, instantly."

She rapped the table sharply with a paper-knife. The triumphant detective jumped.

"I can—I can explain it." The poor young man felt all his confidence slipping away from him. For it looked as if she was actually going to brazen it out—a contingency that had not occurred to him.

"One moment, Mr. Woodroffe. I am the more inclined to give you an opportunity to explain personally, because I hear that my son has already met you. I can hardly say, made your acquaintance—met you—and that you are, or pretend to be—it matters nothing—a distant cousin of his. And now, sir, having said so much, I am prepared to listen."

"I can give you the whole story, Lady Woodroffe."

"*The* whole story? *A* whole story, you mean. Call things by their right names. But go on. Do not occupy my time needlessly, and do not be tedious."

153

The Changeling

"I will do neither, I assure you." He plucked up some courage, thinking of his proofs, but not much. "I even think I shall interest you. First of all, then: my father, who was a comedian playing under the name of Anthony, which was his Christian name, married, as his first wife, a London girl. My father was not a man of principle, I am sorry to say. After a time, he deserted his wife, and left her alone with her child in the streets of Birmingham—Birmingham," he repeated.

Lady Woodroffe winced. It might have been his fancy, but she certainly seemed to wince at the mention of that great city. She sat upright, with hands crossed; her face was pale, her eyes were hard, though she still smiled.

"Go on, sir," she said; "left his wife in Birmingham. I dare say I shall understand presently what this means."

"This was twenty-four or twenty-five years ago. The deserted wife could not believe that she had lost his affection; but she knew that the child's presence annoyed him. That fact, perhaps, influenced her. There was also the certainty of the workhouse before her for the child; she was therefore easily persuaded to consent to an arrangement, by means of some doctor of the place, to give her child into the charge of a lady who had lost her own, and was willing to adopt another. She did this in ignorance of the lady's name."

"Did she never learn the lady's name?" The question was a mistake. Lady Woodroffe perceived her mistake, and set her lips tighter.

"Never. She had no means of finding out. She went after her husband, and followed him from place to place, till she finally caught him in some town of a Western State. Here, as soon as she appeared on the scene, he divorced her for alleged incompatibility of temper. Afterwards he married again. I am the son of the second marriage."

"Yes. This is, no doubt, an interesting story. But I am not, really, interested in your—your pedigree," she sighed. "Oh, do go on, man! Why do you come here with it?"

"It is the beginning of the story which ends with that letter of mine."

"You promised, Mr. Woodroffe"—she smiled icily, and her eyes remained hard—"that you would neither bore me nor waste my time. Are you sure that you are keeping your word?"

The Changeling

"Quite sure. I go back to the story. I concluded from the story as it was told me, that the lady's child had died in Birmingham—in some hotel, probably——"

"One moment. May I guess that your object is, apparently, to find this person who bought or took charge of the child?"

"It is on behalf of the mother, who is now in England. Above all things, she desires to find her child. That is natural, is it not?"

"Perfectly natural. Let us hope that she may succeed. Now go on, Mr. Woodroffe. Of course, a woman who would sell her child does not deserve to get it back again."

Perhaps the last remark was also a mistake. At least it showed temper.

"Perhaps not. This woman, Mrs. Haveril, however, who is married to an extremely wealthy American——"

"Haveril! Can it be the millionaire person whom my son met—with you—at Sir Robert Steele's house?"

"That is the lady."

"Indeed! I always tell my son that he should be more careful of his company. Well, go on."

Richard smiled. The insolence of the observation did not hurt him in the least. It lessened the power of the presence, and gave him confidence.

"This lady," he continued, "fancies or discerns an extraordinary resemblance to her husband, my father—and to myself—in your son, Lady Woodroffe. The resemblance is very striking. He has most undoubtedly my father's face, the same colour of his hair—his figure even more strongly, it is said, than myself. Yet I am considered like him."

"And because there is this resemblance, she imagined——"

"Hardly imagined. She dreamed——"

"Dreamed! What have I to do with her dreams? Well, she has only to ascertain the real parentage of Sir Humphrey—my son. Oh, I have your letter in my mind! Sir Humphrey, you said, the second baronet. We shall come to your letter presently."

The Changeling

"One would think——"

"Has she any other reason to go upon besides the resemblance?"

By this time it was evident that she understood exactly what was meant.

"She had, until yesterday, no other reason. Yet, from one or two simple facts that I have discovered—they are in my letter—I am certain that she is right."

"Indeed! Do you understand, Mr. Woodroffe, the exact meaning of those words, 'that she is right.' Then what is my son?"

"He would be no longer your son. He would be her son."

"Then what am I?"

"That, Lady Woodroffe, is not for me to say."

"I promised to give you an audience. Therefore go on."

"Since there was no kind of proof of this imagining—or this dream—I thought that I would go down to Birmingham to search the registers."

"You are a detective, or a private and secret inquirer?"

"No; I am acting only for this lady."

"She is a millionairess. I hope she pays you well. But the facts—the facts. And you found——"

"A great deal more than I hoped. The facts which I set forth in my letter."

"An entry in the register, purporting to record the death of my son, and an entry in a hotel-book, giving my name,—that is all!"

"Is it not enough? The child was about the same age as the one adopted. There are not many children of that age who die every week—even in Birmingham. Again, if the child died in Birmingham at all, it must have been at a hotel. There are not many children of the same age likely to die in the same week in a Birmingham hotel. I had the register of deaths searched, and found—what I told you. Copies have been taken. I went to the hotel nearest the station, and had the visitors' book searched. I found—what I told you. Copies have been taken."

The Changeling

"Very good. What next?"

"I sent you that letter, and I came to hear what you say about it."

"What should I say about it?"

"Who is this young man who calls himself the second baronet?"

"He is my son."

"Then who is the child that died?"

"How am I to tell? You must ask some one else."

"And who was the Lady Woodroffe who came to the hotel?"

"How do I know? You must ask some one else."

"Oh!"

He might have considered this attitude as possible at least. But he had not. His face expressed bewilderment and surprise.

"You actually suggest to me—to *me*, of all people in the world!—that I, actually I myself, a woman of my position, bought a child in place of a dead child! That is your meaning, is it not, sir?"

"Certainly it is," he answered with creditable valour. "I know you did it! There's no way out of it but to confess!"

"Why, you miserable little counter-jumper!"

Dick stepped back in some alarm, because it looked as if she were going to box his ears. She was quite capable of it, indeed, and but for the guilty conscience that held her back, she would have done it. As it was, her wrath was not feigned. It maddened her to think that this man should so easily discover a whole half of the thing she thought concealed for ever.

"You wretched little counter-jumper!" she repeated, with reginal gesture, tall and commanding—taller than poor Richard, and, dear me! how much more commanding! "And you pretend a trumpery resemblance! Why, my son is half a foot taller than you! My son's father was a gentleman, and his face and manners show it. Yours—— But your face and manners show what he was. Leave the house, sir!" Dick dropped his hat in his surprise. "If you think to black-mail me, you are mistaken. Leave the house! If you dare to speak of this again, it shall be to my lawyers."

Richard picked up his hat. The action is a trifle, but it completed his discomfiture.

"No; stay a moment. Understand quite clearly, that you can make any use of these entries that you please. But you may as well understand that I have never been in Birmingham in my life; that persons in my position act and move among a surrounding troop of servants, to speak nothing of friends and relations. That the heirs of persons like Sir Humphrey do not die and get buried unknown to their friends—perhaps you have not thought of all this."

He heard this statement with open mouth. He was struck dumb.

"Understand at once, make your principal—who is she? the rich person—understand that I have never been in Birmingham in my life; and that every hour of my life can be accounted for."

"Who was that child, then?"

"Find out, if you can. It has nothing to do with me. If, twenty years ago, some woman chose, for purposes of her own, to personate the wife of Sir Humphrey—who was then in Scotland—while Sir Humphrey was on his way home from India, do you think I am going to inquire or trouble my head about her impudence?"

Richard murmured something indistinct. He did not know what to say. How could this majestic woman have done such a thing? Yet who else could have done it?

Lady Woodroffe sat down again. "I have been wrong," she said, "in getting angry over this matter. Perhaps you are not, after all, a blackmailer."

"Indeed, I am not."

"I have heard my son," she said, in a softer voice, "speak of you, Mr. Woodroffe. But I must warn you that any attempt to bring this charge will be met by my solicitors. One word more. Miss Hilarie Woodroffe has also, I believe, taken some interest in you. I would suggest, Mr. Woodroffe, that it would be foolish to throw away the only respectable connections you possess in a wild-goose chase, which can

The Changeling

lead to nothing except ignoble pay from a woman who, by your own confession, threw away her own child or sold it to a stranger. Now you can go, sir." She did not ring the bell for the servant. She pointed, and turned back to her desk. "Have the goodness to shut the door behind you."

It was with greatly lowered spirits that Richard walked down those stairs and out of the door.

CHAPTER XVIII.

A GRACIOUS LADY.

Once removed from the presence of the great lady and the overwhelming authority of her manner, her voice, and her face, Richard began to consider the situation over again. The lady denied any knowledge of the fact. He might have expected it. Why, how could such a woman, in such a position, face the world, and confess to having committed so great a crime? He ought to have known that it was impossible. So he cursed himself for an ass; steadied his nerves with the reflection that she *had* done the thing, whatever she might say; considered that people can always be found to believe great and solid and shameless liars; and remarked with humiliation that on the very first occasion in his life, when he wanted dignity to meet dignity, and authority to meet authority, he had come to grief.

"Serious comedy, however"—by way of consolation—"is not my line."

In the evening, after dinner, he repaired to the hotel, but not with the triumphal step which he had promised himself.

Molly was reading a letter aloud to Alice. "Dick," she cried, "perhaps you can explain what this means. It has just arrived."

"Dear Madam,

> "I have had an interview with a certain Mr. Richard Woodroffe, who calls himself a distant cousin of my son. He brought me a strange story of a strange delusion, which he seemed to consider supported by a certain discovery of an entry in a register of births and deaths. I cannot believe his allegation without further evidence, because it is so extremely improbable—on the face of it, one would say impossible—and I cannot understand it, even if it rests on the strongest evidence. I have, however, forwarded the case to my solicitors, who will probably communicate with Mr. Woodroffe. With him personally I do not desire any further speech. The circumstances of the case, as first placed before me, naturally awaken a woman's sympathies. A mother bereaved of her son is, at all times, an object of pity, even when her

The Changeling

bereavement is not due to the common cause, but to her own conduct; and that conduct not such as can be readily excused.

"The story which this person brought me is to the effect that you have seen my son at a theatre; that you afterwards met him at the house of Sir Robert Steele; that you observed or imagined certain points of resemblance with your own first husband; and certain others with the man Richard Woodroffe. It certainly did not occur to me, when he called, that he could claim the honour of the most distant resemblance to my son. However, I learned from him that you have jumped to the wonderful conclusion that he is actually none other than your son, whom you lost, not by death, but by sale—that you sold your child, in fact, for what he would fetch—as a farmer body sells a pig. I do not venture to pronounce any judgment upon you for this act; the temptation was doubtless great, and your subsequent distress was perhaps greater than if you had lost the child by act of God. I write to you only concerning the strange delusion.

"Apart from the imaginary resemblance on which this delusion is founded, your adviser, this Mr. Richard Woodroffe, has discovered, he tells me, this entry, to which I have already referred, in the register of deaths at Birmingham. It states, he says, that on a certain day there died in that place one Humphrey, son of Sir Humphrey Woodroffe. On that day, as I find by reference to my diary, and to certain letters which have been preserved, I was staying with my father, Lord Dunedin, at his country seat in Scotland. My child, then an infant, who was born at Poonah, in India, was with me. A few days later I travelled south, to London, in order to meet Sir Humphrey, who was returning from India. And, of course, the boy came with me.

"It is not my business to inquire, or to explain, why this entry was made in the register, or why it was thought by any one desirable that a dead child should be entered under a false name. That the child could have been Sir Humphrey's was unlikely, first because he had been in India for ten years before his return, and next, because he was a man of perfectly blameless life.

"Observe, if you please, that these facts can all be proved. My father still lives; the dates can be easily established. Even as

161

regards resemblance, it can be shown that the child was, and is, strikingly like his father—of the same height, the same hair, the same eyes.

"When a delusion of this kind seizes the brain, it is likely to remain there, and to become stronger and deeper, and more difficult to remove, as the years go on. I have therefore thought it best to invite you to meet me. We can then talk over the matter quietly, and I shall perhaps be able to make you understand the baseless nature of this belief. I need hardly say that I should feel it necessary, in case of your persisting in this claim—that is, if you propose advancing such a claim seriously—to defend my honour with the utmost vigour, and in every court of law that exists. You cannot, of course, be ignorant of the fact that more than the loss of my child is concerned; there is the loss of my good name, because you would have the world to believe that a woman, born of most honourable and God-fearing parents; married to a man of the highest reputation, herself of good reputation, should stoop so low—one can hardly write it—as to buy a baby of a woman she had never seen, of a poor woman, of a woman of whom she knew nothing except that she was the deserted wife of a strolling actor; and to pass this child off upon her husband and the world as her own.

"I say no more by letter. Perhaps I have spoken uselessly; in that case, words must give place to acts. However, I will confer with you, if you wish, personally. Come here to-morrow afternoon about five; we will try to discuss the subject calmly, and without the prejudice of foregone conclusions. In offering you this opportunity I consider your own happiness only. For my own part, it matters very little what any one chooses to believe as to my son. There is always within my reach the law, if injurious charges or statements are made against my character. Or there is the law for your use, if you wish to recover what you think is your own.

"I remain, dear madam, very faithfully yours,

"LILIAS WOODROFFE."

The Changeling

"What *is* the meaning of this letter, Dick?" Molly repeated. "What is this entry that she talks about?"

"Molly, I thought I was coming home with a discovery that was a clincher. And I believe I've gone and muddled the thing."

"Well, but tell us."

He told them.

"But what more do we want?" asked Molly. "The child that died was hers."

"So I believe—I am sure. I remember how she took it—and her lies, and her pretences, and her rage. It wasn't the wrath of an innocent woman, Molly; it was the wrath of a woman found out and driven to bay. I am sure of it."

"Then what does she mean by this letter?"

"It's her reply. It means defiance."

"Ought we to go, then?"

"I don't know. I think that I was wrong to go. But that may make it right for Alice to go."

Alice did go. She took Molly with her because she wanted support. She went filled with doubt. The woman's letter was confident and braggart; but there was the discovery of the child's death, and there was the resemblance. She came away, as you shall see, in certainty, yet more in doubt than before.

They found themselves in a room in which not only the refinement which may be purchased of an artistic decorator is visible, but the refinement which can only be acquired by many generations of wealth and position and good breeding. Books, pictures, curtains, carpets, furniture,—all bore witness to the fact that the tenant was a gentlewoman. The Anglo-American, born and brought up in the poverty of London clerkery; accustomed to the bare surroundings of poverty in the Western States; able to command, after many years, and to enjoy, the flaunting luxury of a modern hotel; felt with a sense of sinking, that her son—if this was her son—must have been brought up with social advantages which she could never have given him. On

The Changeling

the table lay a small bundle tied up with a towel; curiously out of place this simple bundle looked among the things beautiful and precious of this drawing-room. You know how a little matter will sometimes revive an old recollection. What had this parcel wrapped in a towel to do with that time, twenty-four years ago, when the mother, broken-hearted, laid her child in the arms of the doctor who carried it into the railway station? Yet she was reminded of that moment—that special moment—in the history of her bereavement. To be sure, the mind of the woman was easily turned to this subject. It possessed her; she could think of nothing else, except when Molly came to talk and sing to her.

The door was opened and a lady came in. She was not dressed in nearly so costly a manner as her visitor, but her appearance impressed. She was a great lady in manner and in appearance. She was also gracious. Though a speaker on platforms, an advocate of many causes, she was still feminine and dignified.

She produced the effect which she desired without apparent effort. She carried in her hand a bundle of letters and papers. She bowed to her visitors.

"It is very good of you," she said, "to come. If you will excuse me one minute——" She sat down and touched a hand-bell. It was answered by a young lady. "These are the letters," said Lady Woodroffe. "I have indicated the replies. You can let me have them at six." Then she turned to Alice again. "You will forgive a busy woman, I am sure," she said. "I am for the moment greatly occupied with rescue work of all kinds. It is a beautiful thing to snatch even one poor woman from a life of crime."

One may observe that she received Alice as she had received Richard—with a great show of important philanthropic work. The effect produced was not quite the same, because Alice was thinking of something else, and to Molly it was only good play-acting. She was not in the least impressed by the presence or the authority. She only considered that the business was well done.

Lady Woodroffe finished. "Now," she said, smiling sweetly, "we will begin to talk."

The Changeling

"I have brought my cousin, Miss Pennefather," said Alice. "She knows why I am here."

"Oh yes!" Lady Woodroffe recognized Molly's presence with the inclination which asserts a higher place. "Shall we take some tea first?"

She was disappointed in the appearance of the woman who claimed her son. One expects of a woman who would sell her baby a face of brass and eyes of bronze; one expects vulgarity in a highly pronounced form—perhaps with ostrich feathers. She came in expectant of a battle with a red-faced, over-dressed female. She found a woman dressed quietly, yet in costly stuffs, a pale face, delicate features; no sign of the commoner forms of vulgarity; a woman of apparent refinement. Of course, we all know that a person may be refined yet not a gentlewoman. Many there are who take comfort in that reflection.

She rang the bell for tea and began to talk. "It is very good of you to come," she began. "Tell me, have you been long in the old country? Do you find it altered since you left it—so long ago? I believe you are not an American by birth. Have you any children? Do you soon return to the States?"

She went on without paying much attention to Mrs. Haveril's replies.

"I hear that your husband is a millionaire. We shall soon begin to think that all Americans are millionaires. It must be strange to have unlimited command of money. I am sure you will do a great deal of good with it. The sense of responsibility when there is so much waiting to be done must be overwhelming. Here in this country we are all so poor—so very poor. We have our country houses, you know, which are very fine houses—some of them, and our parks and gardens. But then, you see, the houses and gardens cost so much to keep up, and our farms remain unlet. However ... here is the tea."

Then she plunged into the subject. "My dear lady," she began. "I do assure you that I feel for you. It is the most extraordinary case that I have ever heard of. I believe, if I remember right, there is an account of a woman in Béranger's Autobiography, who had made her baby a foundling, and spent the rest of her life in looking for him, and became mad in consequence. Do let me implore you not to begin looking for your boy; the case is hopeless—you will never succeed—you will only

The Changeling

make the rest of your life miserable. It is quite impossible that you should ever find him, and if you did find him, it is utterly impossible that you should be able to prove that he is your child. You will, I assure you, heap disappointments and miseries upon your head."

Alice said nothing. Lady Woodroffe glanced at Molly. She was looking straight before her, apparently quite unmoved.

"Now let us argue the point calmly and quietly. You see a resemblance—you jump to a conclusion. Now, first, as regards the resemblance. There is a very remarkable family resemblance among many of the Woodroffes. Three cousins, at least—Miss Hilarie Woodroffe, whom you know, perhaps; my son; and this Mr. Richard Woodroffe, who appears to be a play actor of some kind—claim kinship after five hundred years—five hundred years. They met by accident in the old church of the family—they made acquaintance—both young men curiously resemble the young lady——"

"It isn't only the face," said Alice; "it's the voice, and the eyes, and the manner. My husband had most beautiful manners when he chose."

"On the stage, I believe, they learn to assume some kind of manners, supposed to be those of society, when they choose. My son, however, always chooses to have beautiful manners. But we must, I am sure you will admit, take into account differences as well as resemblances. For instance, I gather from the whole history that your husband was, in some respects, especially those which most touch a wife's sense of wrong—a—what we call a wretch—a disgraceful person."

"He was. He deserted me. He divorced me. He married an American actress. He deserted her. Richard Woodroffe is his second son."

"My son is quite the reverse. He is a young man of the highest principle and of perfectly blameless character."

Molly smiled, looking straight before her.

"Again, your husband, I believe, was a low comedian—a singer, a dancer, a buffoon—anything."

"He was a general utility actor. Sometimes he had a variety entertainment."

The Changeling

"Humphrey, my son, has no talent for acting at all; like his father, he would conceive it beneath the dignity of a gentleman to make merriment for his friends."

Alice sighed. Molly sat looking straight before her, either unmoved or unconcerned.

"Another point. Was your husband a bookish man?"

"No; he was not. He never opened a book."

"My son is essentially studious, especially in the history of Art."

Molly smiled again, but said nothing. To call Humphrey studious was, perhaps, stretching the truth; but there certainly were the rows of French novels.

"Now, my dear madam, I will ask you to set these points down side by side. That is to say, on one side resemblance in face, real or imaginary; on the other side dignity, good breeding—hereditary breeding, a constitutional gravity of carriage, studious habits, ambition, a total absence of the acting faculty. I ask you which of these qualities he could inherit from your husband? As we are here alone, I would ask you which of these qualities he could inherit from you?"

She paused for a reply. There was none. Alice looked at Molly and sighed. Molly smiled and looked straight before her.

"I do not say these things offensively," Lady Woodroffe continued, in soft and persuasive accents. "My sole desire is to send you away convinced that my son cannot possibly—cannot under any possibility—under any imaginable possibility—be your son. To return to the points of difference. I will ask you one more question. Was your husband a man of unselfish habits and even temper?"

"He was not."

Lady Woodroffe smiled. "I am sorry to hear it, for your sake. My son, on the other hand, is absolutely unselfish, and always sweet-tempered."

She looked sharply at the girl. Why did she smile? What did she mean? What did she know about Humphrey? However, Lady Woodroffe went on, still bland and gracious—

The Changeling

"Do not delude yourself any longer, madam. For the sake of your own peace and quiet, put it away from you. Oh, this dreadful delusion will possess you more and more! You will yearn more and more for the possession of the son you have lost. Your mind will become so filled with this delusion that you will be able to think about nothing else. It will drive you to some desperate act; it will poison your daily life; it will turn your wealth into a heavy burden. I implore you, for the sake of those you love, to abandon this baseless belief."

"Oh! If you only knew! If you only knew!"

The tears rose to the eyes of the woman who sought her son.

"After all these years, I thought I had found him again. I recognized him at the theatre and at the doctor's dinner."

"My poor dear lady"—again Lady Woodroffe took her hands and soothed her—"it was indeed strange that you should find such a resemblance. As I told you, see how impossible it is to find anything out. Nevertheless, if I can be of any help to you, I will willingly do all I can. Only, my advice is that you let bygones sleep, and remain contented with the wonderful gifts that Heaven has poured into your lap. To desire more is surely a sin."

"I would give them all to the first beggar in the street, if I could only get back the boy."

"We will suppose"—Lady Woodroffe got up and stood before the fireplace, looking down upon her visitor, who was now trembling and tearful—"we will suppose, I say, that you take some steps. I hardly know what steps you can take. Would you go to a lawyer? Perhaps. Would you go to my son? Perhaps. In either case the evidence will be examined. On your side a fancied resemblance. Why"—she pointed to a portrait on the wall—"that is my husband at the age of thirty. Whose eyes, whose face, whose hair, do you see in that portrait? Is it, or is it not, like my son?" There really was a strong resemblance. Lady Woodroffe, however, did not explain that she had copied it herself from an early portrait, perhaps with additions and slight alterations. "This portrait alone will meet the case. Besides—a chance resemblance—again—what is it?"

Alice shook her head sadly. She was shaken in her faith.

The Changeling

"Next, you find an entry in a register. Who made that entry? You do not know. Why? You cannot tell."

"Yet Mr. Woodroffe says——"

"Never mind Mr. Woodroffe. Listen to what I say. You then come forward yourself, and you tell the very disgraceful story of how you sold your own child—your own boy. Oh, a terrible—a shameful story!"

"Who was the child that died?" Molly put a word for the first time.

"Who was that child? I cannot tell you. Some one, for purposes unknown, chose to represent a dead child as my husband's child. I say that I do not choose to offer any explanation of this personation. I will tell you, however, how Mr. Woodroffe explains it, which you know already."

She waited for a reply. There was none.

"He supposes that the child was my child; and he supposes, next, that the person who bought your child was myself. That is what he calls certainty."

"Who was the child, then?" Molly repeated.

"Even supposing that my own child died at Birmingham, which is absolutely false—how will you connect the dead child's mother with the transaction which followed?"

"I don't know." Alice looked to Molly for support, and found none. Molly sat with cold, impassive face.

"When you have made it quite clear that you sold your child, you have then to fix your crime upon me as well. How will you do it? For I have letters showing where I was. The dates prove that I could not be in Birmingham at the time; they prove also that I was at my father's house in Scotland with my boy. Now, what have you got to say?"

"I want my son."

"Find your son," she replied, with a touch of temper. "He will be proud indeed of his mother when you do find him!"

Alice shuddered.

The Changeling

"I can do nothing to get that delusion out of your mind, then?"

"I want my son."

The woman's face was obstinate. She had left off crying and shaking; her eyes were fierce, her pale face was set; she meant fighting. The interview had been a failure.

"Who was the child that died?" Molly's question made all clear and plain again.

In moments of great and serious importance we think of little things. Lady Woodroffe saw, in this set and serious face, in the lines of her mouth, in the determination of the eyes, something that reminded her of Humphrey. She should have asked the woman what other qualities, apart from those she had enumerated, he might have inherited from her.

She was now certain that the interview was a failure. No persuasion, no soft words, could prevail against the certainty in this woman's mind.

"I want my son," she repeated.

Lady Woodroffe turned to Molly. "You have heard everything," she said. "What is your opinion, Miss— —? I did not catch your name."

"We must find out who that child was—the dead child," Molly replied, with tenacity.

"Then we will talk no more." She smiled again, but showed her teeth. She then did the boldest thing in her power, a thing which deliberately confessed the truth and bade them defiance. Like every bold stroke, it was a stroke of genius. Yet, like every stroke of genius, perhaps it was a mistake. For she had brought down the very clothes in which the child had come to her. And now she showed them to the mother, and claimed them for her own. "I am only going to delay you one minute, Mrs. Haveril. It is a foolish thing, perhaps; but it is an appeal to sentiment. I suppose that there is nothing a woman treasures more than her son's baby-clothes. I am going to show you a bundle of things that I made with my own hands, for my baby—mine—woman—do you hear?"—with the real ring of temper—"mine!

The Changeling

"These things"—she untied the towel slowly—"are my son's clothes when he was about twelve months of age. They are made of quite common materials, after the old Scotch fashion. The very things I made myself—with my own hands—for the child." She laid back the corners of the towel. She took up the things one by one. "His frock— he had gone into short frocks—his flannel, his shirt, his socks, his shoes, his cap." She held them up, and she looked at her visitor with mockery in her eyes and defiance in her words. "My things—that I made. You would like to have the baby-clothes of your own son— whom you sold—would you not?"

Alice started and sprang to her feet, gazing upon the baby-clothes.

"You see," Lady Woodroffe went on coldly and calmly, as if every word was not a lie, "the work is not very fine. There is his name in marking-ink. I did this embroidery. I made everything except his socks and his shoes. There is his rattle." It was a cheap common thing. "Here is his little cap. You have made such things, Mrs. Haveril, I dare say, for your child—the child you sold. I thought I would show them to you, to prove better than any words of mine, that my child is my own."

"Oh!" It was the scream of a tigress. "Oh, mine—mine—mine!" Mrs. Haveril threw herself literally over the clothes. She clutched and dragged them, and with quick fingers huddled them into the towel again and tied the corners. "Mine!" she repeated, standing up again, her hand on the bundle. "Mine!" Her voice was like a roar of rage, sunk down deep and low and rough—not like her customary voice, which was gentle and sweet. "Mine!" She held the bundle to her heart.

Molly rose at this point and laid her hand on her cousin's shoulder.

"Keep quiet, dear—keep quiet! Let us leave this house." She turned to Lady Woodroffe. "It is a house of lies."

Lady Woodroffe looked at her as if she were not present, and had not spoken.

"The delusion is stronger than I thought," she said, affecting surprise and wonder.

Alice recovered and stood up, still holding the things to her heart.

171

The Changeling

"Oh," she cried, panting and gasping, "you are a bad woman! a false woman!"

"For Heaven's sake," said Molly, "keep quiet! You have said enough. Think of yourself."

"I had better ring the bell, I think." Lady Woodroffe laid her finger on the knob, but refrained to press it.

"Oh! What can I say?"

"Say nothing, dear," said Molly.

"Will you give me back those things?" Lady Woodroffe moved as if she would take them. "No? Then keep them. After all I have—my son—mine—my son. That is the main thing."

"I made these things—every one—I made them. See, Molly—here is the very paper I wrote. I pinned it to his little frock." She kissed the frock. "'His name is Humphrey.' I wrote it. His father said there was always a Humphrey in the family. I wrote that paper—now!"

Lady Woodroffe smiled sadly. "Poor creature! But perhaps you had better go at once."

"Where is my son?"

"I have done my best to relieve you of a most remarkable delusion. You reward me by robbing me of my child's things. I cannot fight you for them, and I do not like to make my servants take them by force. Keep them."

She rang the bell.

"They are my things."

Lady Woodroffe continued to follow her movements with eyes of compassion.

"It is indeed wonderful!" she murmured. "All this great fortune! And this most miserable delusion to spoil it!"

Alice moved towards the door. She was trembling. She leaned upon Molly. She clung to the bundle. She turned.

"You have given my son back to me. I want no further proof."

The Changeling

Molly bore her down the stairs, as she retired, with some loss of dignity, her face tearful, her cheek flushed, but clutching the bundle.

"Now she knows the whole," said Lady Woodroffe. "And I defy her to move a step. She may look at the boy from afar off." She rang her handbell, and called her secretary, and resumed her struggle against sin.

CHAPTER XIX.

A CABINET COUNCIL.

"I don't like it," said Richard. "The thing is proved down to the ground. But I don't like it."

On the table lay the bundle of baby-clothes recovered by the true mother. It was untied. The little flannels, the little frock, the little woollen socks, the little cap—a touching little bundle to one who had memories of the things. And near the table, as if guarding the spoil she had carried off, Alice lay upon the sofa, slowly recovering from the excitement of the afternoon.

"Not like it, Dick?" Molly asked. "Why?"

Alice laid her hand upon the things. "I want no other proof," she said. "I made these things; I made them all. What more would you have?"

"What more can we desire?" asked Molly.

"I say that I don't like it." Dick rubbed his chin. "I don't like it at all. It means defiance. I was in hopes that she would climb down when she saw the copy of the entry. But she didn't. I understand now. She can't afford to climb down; so she must defy us. She will fight, if we make her. She sends for the mother of the child. She actually gives her another weapon, and she says, 'Do your worst. I defy you!'"

"What do you mean by not being able to climb down, Dick?"

"Why, she's not only a great lady, rich and well born, and in society. She is also a leader in all kinds of religious and philanthropic movements. A certain religious paper, for instance, called her, the other day, the Queen of the White Lilies. Exposure would be a terrible thing for her. But if she can make it look, as she will try, like an attempt on my part to get money out of Alice or herself, the thing might do her no harm. However, there's the register. They can't say I forged that entry."

"Well, but, Dick, what do you mean? You prove that her son is dead, and that he was buried under his own name without any concealment, just before the adoption; and we've got the baby-clothes, and we

The Changeling

recognize them. What more *can* you want? She must climb down, as you call it."

"We have got lots more, if you come to that. We have got the man who found the child. I wonder how Sir Robert would like going into court and deposing that he bought a baby for adoption by an unknown person. We have also got the mother of the adopted child. Unfortunately, there is nothing at all to connect Lady Woodroffe with the adoption. Without that connection the case breaks down. There's the point."

"Does Humphrey know anything about it?"

"I believe not. Lady Woodroffe is not likely to tell him."

"You must not set my son against me," said the mother.

"Not if we can help it. But about the value of this evidence. Now, Molly, please go into the witness-box." She stood up behind a chair, placing her hands on the back. "I am counsel. The jury are sitting over there; the judge is on your right. Keep your eyes on counsel. Now, you are Alice first—Alice Haveril. You swear, madam, that you know these clothes. How do you know them? Because you made them with your own hands. Are they made of rare or uncommon materials? Are they not made of stuff commonly used for the garments of infants? Is there anything distinctive in the materials used? They are also made in the fashion commonly used for children, are they not? Nothing distinctive, then, in the fashion? So that, for materials or for shape, there is nothing to make them different from any other baby-clothes? Nothing. Then, madam, how do you know that they were made by your own work?"

"Because I know," said Molly.

"Because you know. But how do you know?"

"Because I remember."

"But you cannot tell me how you remember them—by what mark?" He took up the frock. "Here is a crest in red silk. Did you work that? No. Yet it is on the frock."

"Well, Dick," said Molly, "you needn't take so much pleasure in knocking the case to pieces."

The Changeling

"I am only showing you what it amounts to. Now, get into the box again. You are Mr. Richard Woodroffe, the expert in sagacity. What have you got? A certified copy of an entry in the register of births and deaths. You place, I believe, great reliance on that entry? It records the death of the child of Sir Humphrey Woodroffe. Your theory is that the child who died was immediately replaced by the child who was adopted. Very well. But if there was no concealment of the death, how could there be substitution?"

"There's an answer to that," Molly replied quickly. "The woman never thought of hiding her name until after the child was dead and buried—until she thought of the substitution."

"That is your theory. When you come to proof—how do you know that the child whose death is recorded was really the son of Sir Humphrey? Was the death announced in the papers? They have been searched, but there is no mention of the event. Yet, when a man of such great importance as Sir Humphrey Woodroffe loses his only son, the announcement of the event would be made in all the papers, both here and in India. How do you explain that omission? It is not for us—I'm on the other side, Molly—to find out the reason of this lying entry; it is sufficient for us to prove the continuous existence of the child from his birth to the present day. Who made that declaration? We do not know; we do not care. It is sufficient for our purposes to prove that Lady Woodroffe at the time was with her father in Scotland."

"Oh, Dick, this is too horrible!"

"When such a child dies, everybody knows. Did her ladyship's family hear of it? It appears not. Evidence will be brought to show that she set out for London with her boy, that she wrote on arrival, and that she wrote immediately afterwards announcing the return of her husband. When such a child dies, the servants all know. Evidence will be given to show that none of the servants knew, or heard about, the loss of the heir—the only child. We are to prove that so terrible an event was not even announced in the servants' hall. But you shall hear Lady Woodroffe's own statement. Molly, you are now Lady Woodroffe, but I am speaking for you. 'In the autumn of 1873 I was staying at the country seat of my father, Lord Dunedin, in Scotland. I had just returned from India, and was waiting for the arrival of my husband, who was retiring from Indian service. Early in the month of

The Changeling

February I received a telegram from Brindisi, to the effect that my husband had arrived there, and was coming home as fast as he could travel. I was to meet him at the house I had taken in London. I therefore left my father's, went on to Edinburgh, stayed the night there, and came on next morning to London, bringing with me the child and my ayah. The next day, or the day after, my husband arrived. I have never been in Birmingham in my life. My child, as an infant, never had any serious illness. As to the entry in the register, I heard of it for the first time from Mr. Richard Woodroffe, calling himself a distant cousin, a vocalist, who seems to have conceived and invented some kind of conspiracy for duping Mrs. Haveril, who is wealthy, and getting money for himself out of her!'"

"Oh, Dick," said Molly, "you haven't!"

"'You ask me'—you are still Lady Woodroffe—'what proofs I have of these assertions. I have the clearest proofs possible—the letter of my husband, telling me when he would arrive, the evidence of my father that I left Dunedin Castle in time to arrive in London a day or two before my husband—not more.' The evidence of an aged, white-haired, venerable peer will be conclusive, Molly. 'I have old servants who can prove that they have known the child from day to day, and must have discovered the fact immediately had there been any change.' Do you hear, Molly? An aged father, aged servants, a lady with a commanding and queenly presence, a brow of brass, and a voice steady and limpid as that of Truth herself. Poor Truth! she may get down into her well again."

"Well; but about the hotel and the register?"

"Let us ask Lady Woodroffe. She says, 'I know nothing about either. I cannot understand or explain who the woman was that personated me, and said her child was the son of Sir Humphrey. It has been suggested that she may have been the mistress of my husband. I cannot for a moment allow that my husband, the most blameless of men, whose life was passed with open windows, could have carried on an illicit connection. It is impossible and absurd. I have no theory to offer about the personation. I cannot understand it.' That is all."

"She is the most shameless, most abominable, creature alive!" said Molly.

The Changeling

"She has her reputation to maintain. Well, what have we got on our side? The entry; the fact of the adoption; and the resemblance. Put Sir Humphrey, the second baronet, in the box. You are now that worthy, Molly. Look at him, gentlemen of the jury. Look at him well. Turn him round slowly like a hairdresser's waxen effigy. Observe the fall of his hair and its colour; the colour of his eyes; the shape of his head. Here is a portrait of Anthony Woodroffe, who, we maintain, was his father: could there be a more striking resemblance? Here is the respectable Richard Woodroffe, also a son—an unworthy son—of Anthony, and who, we maintain, is the half-brother of the baronet. You observe again a startling resemblance? Then up jumps the other side, with the portrait of Sir Humphrey. Same hair—same eyes. Where is your other resemblance then? Which of the two is his father? He is curiously like them both. See?

"'Resemblance,' the learned counsel continued, 'is not enough. Let us hear the evidence of Sir Robert Steele, M.D., F.R.S., Ex-President of the College of Physicians, author of the Lord knows how many treatises. Take the book, Sir Robert.' We know what he will say about the child and the adoption. Now, listen. He goes on, 'The business over, I thought no more of the matter. Nor did I know the name of the lady, nor did I inquire. It was for me a matter of business partly, because I charged a fee, and of charity partly, because the child would otherwise have gone into the workhouse. I should not like to identify the lady after all these years, when she must have changed greatly; she wore a thick veil while we talked, and I remember only a pale face and regular features.' Or stuff like that," Dick explained. "'Yes, I am now acquainted with Lady Woodroffe, and I know her son. I cannot explain his resemblance to Mr. Richard Woodroffe. The two young men are said to be distant cousins. I never knew Mr. Anthony Woodroffe. I know nothing more about the case; I express no opinion upon the claim. The lady, in adopting the child, did not express her intention of substituting it.' That is the evidence of the medical man, if he would acknowledge that he remembered anything whatever about the transfer!"

"Dick," said Molly, "Humphrey must not know anything until—unless—the case is complete. Don't make him your enemy."

The Changeling

"My dear child, in the event of either success or failure, my half-brother will most certainly regard me with a fraternal feeling, compared with which Cain was loving and Richard the Third was loyal."

Molly looked at Alice doubtfully. She lay back in silence, her eyes shut, paying very little attention to what was said. What, Molly thought, would be Humphrey's attitude towards his new mother, when the truth was disclosed to him? With the mother would come the relations. Molly remembered how her own father, the disinherited, used to laugh over his own cousins; over the family pride; how one was parish clerk of St. Botolph's; how one had a select Academy at Homerton; and one had a shop in Mare Street; and one was pew-opener; and one was a Baptist Minister in some unknown but privileged corner of the earth. And it occurred to her, for the first time, that the introduction of Humphrey to his new relations would be a matter of some difficulty and delicacy.

"I don't want any proof," said Alice. "I recognized my child when first I saw him. His father was in every feature and every look. And these are my things—mine: I made them." She laid her hand again on the bundle which brought her so much certainty after so much doubt.

"But it won't do. It isn't enough. We want proof that will convince a judge and a jury."

"If you haven't got it," she said, "I don't mind in the least. I shall send for my son and tell him all. He may stay where he is, if he likes. But I shall tell him all."

"I think," Dick continued, without heeding these words, "that we must continue to advertise."

"And then?"

"Then—I don't know. I should like to bring an action. I don't know what for. We didn't bargain for fraudulent substitution, but for open adoption. I should think there ought to be grounds for action. But, of course, I don't know. They certainly would not court publicity—at least, I should think not. Whether they lost the case or won, the evidence is so circumstantial that the world would certainly believe in the fraud. I cannot believe that even Lady Woodroffe would care to face the footlights."

"You talk as if you were at the same time perfectly certain, and also in great doubt."

"I am both. I am perfectly certain, not only from the evidence of the register and of these clothes, but from the lady's manner. How should we hear and receive such a thing on the stage, Molly? Consider. You are receiving the discovery of a thing you thought hidden away and buried for ever—a discovery which will blast your whole life."

Molly presented immediately a stage interpretation of the emotion thus rudely awakened. She started, threw up her left hand, pressed her heart with her right hand; she opened her lips and panted; her eyes dilated.

"That is very good. But Lady Woodroffe didn't do that at all. She was much more effective. Sit bolt upright in your chair; stiffen yourself; turn your eyes upon me quickly; at the mention of the dead child, let all the colour go out of your face; at the word 'substitution' let your head swim, clutch at the arms of your chair—so—recover in a moment. Look at me again with strangely troubled eyes—so—you remember you are going to fight; harden your face; set your lips firm; let your eyes be like flints for resolution—so. Molly, my dear, if you were to practise for a twelvemonth you couldn't do it half so well as Lady Woodroffe herself. As a study she was most valuable. If there had been any doubt before in my mind, there would be none now."

"How will Humphrey take it?"

"Are you concerned about him still, Molly?—after that midnight walk of ours?"

"Well, Dick, he has not had my answer yet. I must consider him a little. And he is your half-brother, remember."

"He will become, like his half-brother, an outsider—ha! an outsider, a cad, a bounder!" Dick snorted. Forgiveness and tenderness to the man who was trying to take his girl from him could not be expected.

Just then a telegram was brought in. It came from a certain firm of solicitors at Birmingham, and was addressed to Richard Woodroffe—

The Changeling

"Have found the medical man who attended the child. He has his notes, remembers the case, has identified lady from photograph; will swear to her!"

"Good Heavens!" Richard waved the telegram over his head. "We have got the next step. We can identify Lady Woodroffe with the woman whose child died."

He read the telegram.

"Is there anything more wanted, at all?"

"There is one thing wanted. It is the identification of the lady as the adopter of the child, and that lies in the hands of Sir Robert."

"Do you think he knows?"

"I am certain he knows. Why did he ask us all to dinner, if he does not know? I am pretty certain, too, that he won't let out, unless we make him."

"How can we make him, Dick, if he won't?"

"There is only one way, Molly. The case is strong, circumstantially — that if we make it public, the world will be forced to believe it, whatever the lady may say and swear. Nothing could be stronger."

"I want no proof," said Alice. "If you cannot bring my son to me, I shall go to him and tell him all."

"The one thing that will weigh with Sir Robert and the lady is the fear of publicity. I will make one more attempt, Molly. I will go to the lady first and to the doctor afterwards. If they remain obdurate, I will take advice as to the best way of obtaining publicity. And that will ruin the one and damage the other."

There was one other person present at this council. It was John Haveril. He said nothing, but he listened, with far-away eyes, like a gardener over a strawberry-bed. When Dick concluded, he took his hands out of his pockets and walked out of the room.

CHAPTER XX.

JOHN HAVERIL CLEARS UP THINGS.

John Haveril was a man of few words, and these came slowly; but of ready action. He followed the course of the inquiry, with doubt at first, but, as one point after another came to light, he began to be interested; when the child's clothes were brought home, he had no more doubt on this point: he became impatient. Why should there be any more hesitation? If the lady persisted in her denial, why not go straight to the young man and lead him to his mother? As for what might follow after that, if he thought about it at all, should be left to Providence. Therefore, bearing in mind the agitation and anxiety in which his wife was kept by these delays, he resolved upon independent action of his own. And that was the reason why he took his hands out of his pockets and left the room.

Humphrey Woodroffe sat in his study, getting through the hour before dinner with the help of a French novel. The field of human interest occupied by the kind of French novel which he and his friends chiefly studied, is so limited that one is surprised that its readers never seem to tire of it or to ask for more. The study—which was behind the dining-room—was furnished by himself, and was an excellent example of the day's taste. In the higher æsthetic circles, the members of which are very limited in number, the first and most important rule is that true Art, and with it, of course, the highest expression of Art, changes from year to year; what was last year the one and eternal treatment, is now Philistine and contemptible. His piano was littered with music—mostly in MSS.—his own; weird and wonderful daubs of colour hung upon the walls—they were the pictures of the New School—they called themselves the New School—the school of to-day, of whom he was one. His table was covered with books bound in dainty white and gold, or grey and gold: they were chiefly books of poets—old poets—forgotten poets, who sang of love; it has been reserved for our age to disinter them, and to go into raptures over their magnificent and fearless realism. Poetry, like painting, music, furniture, and wall-paper, changes its fashions for the young every year.

The Changeling

In a word, the study was a temple. For such a temple her worshippers must all be young—under seven and twenty. It is sad to think that they will one day become old—old—old—thirty years old, and that new poets will write, new musicians compose, new painters paint, for younger æsthetes. Sad to reflect that they will then be *passés*, their utterances Bohemian, their views contemptible, their standards ignoble.

John Haveril advanced into this shrine of the æsthetic muse with more of his later than of his earlier manner. The gardener was, perhaps, below the man of consideration.

"Mr. John Haveril?" Humphrey read the name from the card as if he had never heard it before, and received him with the studied chill which most effectually keeps off the outsider. "I met you, I believe, at Sir Robert Steele's?"

"Yes; I was there."

He looked about for a chair that would bear his weight. There was one which seemed equal to the task. He sat down without being invited. Humphrey remained standing, with his most repellent manner.

"I was there, young man; I was there," John Haveril repeated. "We had not much conversation; but I presume if you do meet a man once, and you have something to say to that man, you may call upon him."

"Surely. Though what Mr. Haveril, the man of millions—is it twenty millions?—and more?—I hope much more—can have to say to me, I cannot guess. Briefly, sir, I have no money; I never speculate; and I can take none of your shares."

John Haveril opened his mouth twice. Then he shook his head. "Best not to meet bad manners with worse," he replied, with dignity quite in his best manner. "I understand, young man, that you mean some kind of sneer which, let me tell you, sir, ill becomes your youth in the presence of my age."

Sir Humphrey leaned his elbow on the mantel-shelf, and adjusted his pince-nez with his unoccupied hand. This took time. In fact, he was thinking of a repartee. When the operation was finished, he turned to his visitor a face of deliberate insolence.

"You came to teach me something beside manners, I believe. Not, I am sure, that one could desire, even in manners, a more competent instructor."

"I did. Perhaps it may be worth your while to listen. Perhaps not. If it is, you may take your elbow off the shelf, and try not to look as if you were gazing at a chipmunk in a cage. Understand, sir that I will receive neither your pity nor your contempt. If you do not change your manner, I will show you, by a highly practical method, that you have made a mistake."

There was something in the man's eyes which compelled obedience. Besides, although he was forty years older than the other, there was a toughness about his build which might be formidable.

Humphrey instantly changed both his look and his attitude, and took a chair.

"You may go on," he said sulkily, "as soon as you please."

"When I heard about you, sir, in connection with the little transaction we know of, I began to inquire secretly whether we were wise to go on. 'If he turns out unworthy,' I said, 'we'd better stop where we are, and take no further steps in the matter.'"

"I shall probably understand as we go along," said Humphrey. "At present— —"

"You will understand, presently. I can't say, sir, that the character I have obtained of you is encouraging."

"Kind, however, of people to give one a character at all." He threw back his head into his hands, and stretched out his legs, and looked up into the ceiling.

"I don't understand," John Haveril replied, "the talk that says one thing and means another. I like plain and straightforward things. However, I hear of you that you gamble and drink, and that you run after dancing-girls; and that you believe, like many young Englishmen of fortune, that you belong to a separate caste, and not to the world, like common people."

"Unfortunately, Mr. Haveril, we have to belong to the world. I assure you that I would much rather not."

The Changeling

"You've got to. However, we did go on; I have not told the person chiefly interested all I'd heard about you, nor the half. We've now brought our business to an end. That is, we've proved up to the hilt what was at first only a suspicion."

"Again, I dare say I shall understand you presently."

"The question is, whether you know the secret. 'If,' I said, 'he does know the secret, and still carries on the pretence, the chap isn't worthy of our notice. Let's wipe our feet on him, and go on our way.'"

"Wipe—your—feet? You like plain and straightforward things, Mr. Haveril. Surely it is a poetical and an imaginative case—'wipe your feet'—upon—a—'chap.'"

"'If he carries on the pretence in ignorance,' I said, 'let us tell him, and see how he takes it. If he takes it worthily, we shall know what to think of him.'"

"To think of him?" murmured Humphrey.

"Yes. Well, the time has come for you to learn the truth, if you don't know the truth already."

Humphrey smiled. "I really cannot read that riddle. No; I do not know the truth. Whether I shall take it worthily, as you say, or whether I shall receive the wiping of muddy feet, I cannot foretell."

"You don't know? Well, I don't think it's my business to tell you. Very likely some one will tell you. Meantime, the person principally concerned does know it, and you will understand, when you do learn the truth, how much it has unsettled her. Also Dick knows it."

"Who is Dick? Fiddler Dick? Dick the Tramp? Dick who goes out in white-thread gloves, like a waiter?"

"And Molly knows it. And I know it. Very well. Now, I want you to remember very carefully what I say. If you don't understand these words now, you will later on. First of all, whatever happens, you are no relation of mine."

"Thank you! thank you!" Humphrey changed his position, sat up, and clasped his hands. "Thank you, *so* much! I began to fear, Mr. Haveril, that you must be a long-lost uncle."

The Changeling

"And no claim can be set up on me. You are not my son, but hers."

"That is at least true. I am hers. And I certainly am not yours. This grows exciting."

"Hers, I say, not mine."

Humphrey jumped in his chair. "How the devil, man, can I be your son? What drivel is this?"

John Haveril paid no attention to this question. He was putting his own case in his own words.

"And not being my son, there's no claim," he went on slowly. "But, young man, as the thing has to come out, you will have to behave according."

"'Behave according'? Come, Mr. Haveril, I have given you a patient hearing. Pray, what do you mean by 'behave according'? But please—please tell me what you mean, or go away." He spread his hands helplessly. "I wish some one would come," he murmured, "and carry off this person."

"When you learn the truth, remember what I say now. I don't like you, nor the looks of you, nor the language of you, nor the ways of you. But there you are, and I'm bound to do something for you. Now, sir, make your mother happy; do what she wants, make her love you. And, well, your sort, I take it, is always wanting money; you never make any, and you are always spending. Make her happy, and you shall have as much as any young man can want in reason or out of reason. I know your manner of life, sir, and it's an expensive manner of life. You are in debt again; Lady Woodroffe has already paid your debts once or twice; champagne and cards and painted Jezebels—you shall have them all—all; I don't care what you want, you shall have everything, if you only behave properly to your mother."

Humphrey heard these words with real and breathless astonishment. There had been, it is true, many expostulations from his mother about extravagance and scandals; but could she have complained to this rough, coarse creature?

"I cannot for the life of me understand what you mean."

"Remember what I say, then."

The Changeling

"Mr. Haveril"—for once the young man spoke quite plainly and unaffectedly—"I assure you, although you assume that I know what you mean—I do not in the least. Can you explain why you take such an interest in my relations with my mother, not to speak of my personal character?"

"No, sir. You will understand, very well, in a day or two. Let me conclude, sir. I intended to explain that I married late in life."

"Oh!" Humphrey groaned. "It is like a bad dream. What does it matter to me whether you married late in life or early? Man alive! Will you take a drink—two drinks—to go? There's whisky in the cabinet."

"I say," John Haveril repeated slowly, "that I married late in life. Over forty I was; therefore I've had but small experience of women. But of your mother I must say she's the very best woman that lives—the very best."

Humphrey gasped. "Good Lord!" he cried.

"The best and the tenderest and the most pious."

"Oh! The most pious!"

"And the most beautiful. Pity that she keeps fretting about you."

"Well, it is a pity. Do you mean to say that she sent you—you—you—to tell *me*—*me*—*me* that?"

"Otherwise, naturally a happy nature, full of sunshine, and well-mannered."

Humphrey laughed aloud. "Well, she is well-mannered. That's a good shot."

"And speaks like a lady."

"Yes, yes; she certainly does."

"Well, then"—John Haveril rose—"I believe I've said all I came to say."

"I'm glad of that. Perhaps you'd like to say it all over again. You have told me my character; you have assured me that I am not your son; you have offered me millions if I behave properly; and you have been so good as to praise my mother warmly."

The Changeling

"I've said, I think, all I came to say," he repeated, in his slow manner. "Don't tell your mother—when you know the truth—what I said, nor why I came here. Best for her to believe that you behave, as you are going to behave, out of your own good heart—you can pretend a bit, I suppose, without any thought of the dollars. And when you get those dollars, you can say to yourself, young man, that you wouldn't have had them if it hadn't been for your mother."

With these words John Haveril offered his hand. Humphrey looked straight through him, taking no notice of the proffered salute.

"I was once in the service of an English gentleman," he said—"in his garden. But for that I should believe that the English aristocracy was more unmannerly than any New Mexican cowboy. Sir, to use what I understand is your favourite expression where manners are concerned, you are yourself nothing better than a cad and an outsider. But do not tell your mother, when you know the truth, that I said so. Let it be a secret between ourselves that I have found you to be a cad—an unmannerly cad."

He then departed with dignity.

Humphrey looked after him with surprise rather than anger. To be called an outsider by a beast of a self-made Dives who had formerly been a gardener! It was astonishing; it was a new experience; it was ludicrous.

He ran upstairs to the drawing-room, where his mother was alone, writing.

"If I may interrupt," he said. "Thank you. One moment. Mother, I've had a most remarkable visit."

"Who is your visitor?"

"I wonder why they ever invented America," he said. "I wonder why we tolerate Americans—rich Americans—who have been English mechanics. Why do we admit them into our houses?"

"It is a mistake. But it is useless to protest. Why do you ask?"

"My visitor was a man who came last from America, where he has made a great fortune—robbed the people by the thousand, I suppose—a man named Haveril."

The Changeling

"Haveril!"

"I met the man the other night at Sir Robert Steele's."

"Vulgar, of course."

"Not so vulgar as ignorant—say, common. He told me he was a gardener's boy originally. Seemed to think it was a meritorious thing."

"It is the mock-humility of the purse-proud. But what did he want with you?"

"He is mighty mysterious about some secret which is going to be sprung upon me. It is now, he said, completely discovered."

"'Completely discovered,' you said, my son?"

"And I am to be told in a day or two. After which, everything depends upon my behaviour."

"Oh! Of what nature is the wonderful secret?"

"I don't know. Then he went on with a rigmarole about my being no relation of his—as if such a thing were possible! And he promises a mountain of dollars if I obey the wishes of my mother. Have you any special wishes, mother?"

"None—except those which you already know, and do not respect."

"I live as other men in my position are expected to live."

"Go on about your mysterious visitor."

"He began to talk about you, mother. Spoke of your good manners. I ought to have knocked him down for his impudence."

"Did he reveal his secret?"

"No. He gave me a warning—as I told you—and he went away."

Lady Woodroffe looked up, with a perfectly calm face.

"I believe I could tell you something about his secret." Truth was stamped plainly on that marble brow, with all the other virtues which belong to the *grande dame de par le monde*. "The woman Haveril is, I believe, crazed. The man is a fool, except in making money, where he is, I dare say, a knave. They are aided and abetted by a man of your name, a Richard Woodroffe, who is clearly making money by the conspiracy—and a girl they call Molly Something."

"What? Is Molly in it?"

"Pray, are you concerned with that person as well as— —?"

"She is a *protégée* of Hilarie. It was there I met her. As for the fellow, Richard Woodroffe, he is just a horrid little cad."

"Well. That will do. You need not worry yourself about it, Humphrey. I am busy now." She turned to her work, having been interrupted in an essay on the treatment of hardened sinners, considered in connection, I believe, with the case of Jane Cakebread.

CHAPTER XXI.

"TO BE OFF WITH THE OLD LOVE."

Once more, guest night at the college. A good many guest nights had passed since the first. The thoughtful and the curious no longer came; they were not missed by Hilarie and her friends at the place about which there had been at first so much discussion and derision. A college which taught nothing, and was only a place of culture, and consolation, and rest, and good breeding—a mere establishment for reminding women perpetually of their very highest functions and duties—was sure to excite derision. Meanwhile, it went on doing its own work, and nobody derided any longer. This is the way of the world, and it is like one of the three—nay, four, things which the Proverbial philosopher found too wonderful for him—things which he knew not. A man proposes to found, or establish, or create, something new—something which will, perhaps, cause changes small or great in the current order and the current talk. It is immediately fastened upon and he is held up to derision. Nothing is so truly ridiculous as a thing which is new; besides, it makes admirable "copy." If the man kicks out in return, he is jumped upon again. The world is then called upon to observe how completely the creature is squelched, how he lies flat and lifeless on the arid sand. Presently the world observes that the man, so far from being flat and lifeless, is going on just as if there had been no jumping at all; he bears no apparent mark of bruises, no bones are broken, there are no patches of diachylum on his head; he just proceeds quietly with his plan. Then comes another but a fainter sound of derision, because, when people do get hold of a good thing to worry, they like to keep at it. But the dead man, twice killed, goes on, without paying any attention. Then silence falls. It is unwise to let the world understand that the man you have just killed is going about alive and quite unhurt, and that the theory you have covered with contempt is flourishing like a vigorous vine, already bearing blossoms and rich with promise of purple clusters.

"Yes," said Hilarie, "my simple college is going on; we are quite full. We teach nothing except the true functions of woman, and her place in the human comedy. We admit all those who have to work. Here

The Changeling

they learn that work for money and a livelihood is a kind of accident for woman. For man it is necessary; his nature makes him crave for activity. For woman it is an accident, which belongs to our imperfect social system. She ought not to work for pay. And in the case of many women, perhaps most, it degrades and lowers them, because it turns them from what should be the main object of their lives. In this place we warn, and here we daily strive to hold before them the necessity of keeping before themselves a standard. They must never lose sight of the fact that woman is the priestess of civilization. We do our best to prevent our girls from being degraded by the unhappy accident of having to work for wages. All women's work should be work for love."

"But it is said that you pauperize them by taking them in for nothing."

Hilarie laughed. "If the gift is a gift of love, repaid by love, what harm? But there is a rule about payment, and nobody knows except myself who pays and who does not. They come when they like; they go when they like. It is a college in the old sense of the word, not the new—a place of residence."

She left her guests and spoke to Molly. "I have asked my cousin Humphrey to come," she said. "Will you give him an answer to-night?"

"I thought I would wait to see how he would receive— —"

"Yes; you told me. It is a most wonderful story, Molly. But I do not believe that it will be allowed to go beyond those who know it at present. I do not believe that he will ever be told this story at all. If he were, I know very well how he would behave. There is another reason, Molly dear; you will understand presently, when I show you a letter. Take him into the library, when the people are going away. Do not answer him until I come to you. I promise you, Molly, that after I have shown you a certain paper, you will thank God that your doubts and your temptations were all removed."

"But if he were to go through this ordeal? It is a trial that would prove the noblest nature."

"It is. But there is another ordeal. Will you trust me?"

"Why, Hilarie! If I am to begin by distrusting you!"

The Changeling

Dick was present, and had brought his fiddle, on which he presently discoursed, to the joy of everybody except his distant cousin.

Later on Molly led Humphrey to "sit out" in the library, where two or three other couples were already occupied in the same selfish evasion of duty.

The young man was in a most ill temper—perhaps on account of Dick's presence—— He made no pretence at concealing this ill temper.

"I have every reason to complain," he said. "You avoid me; you will not answer my letters."

"I am waiting to give you your final answer."

"You gave that long ago."

"I did not. I have told you all along that I was not certain whether the thing would tend to your happiness or my own. Above all, I refused to have any concealments."

"This objection to concealment is a new thing. Before, you consented."

"No; I never did consent. I have always told you that I would not be hidden away, like a thing to be ashamed of."

"And I have always told you that my only reason was respect for my mother's prejudices."

"Let me have my own prejudices, too; and I mean to have them respected."

"You know that I love you, Molly."

"That is no reason why you should insult me. If I am ever married, it must be openly, and in the sight of the world. I think I should ask my relations to be present. You would like to meet the parish clerk, and the pew-opener, and the ragged bankrupt. Don't use bad language, Sir Humphrey. Poor and lowly they may be, but perhaps—I'm sure I don't know—they are virtuous as well."

"I don't mind what you say, Molly."

"Then there are the Haverils."

"The rich people! The man called upon me the other day, and talked conundrums. What have you got to do with them?"

193

The Changeling

"They are my cousins. I am a great deal with them just now."

"Oh! Is that what makes you so infernally independent?"

"Shall I become the heiress of millions, or shall I be hidden away in a box by a husband who is ashamed of his wife? I have this choice."

"Oh! Their heiress! If they will do that! But have you told them of your engagement?"

"I am not engaged."

"Don't be silly, Molly. How can you refuse what I offer you? Why did the man call on me, then?"

"Did he call? What did he tell you?"

"He talked about some tremendous secret—talked about my mother. I thought he meant you and the engagement. Then he told me—which was a most curious thing—that if I followed the wishes of my mother, I should have as much money as I want. Wishes of my mother! Why, if I told her that I was engaged to a lady named Pennefather, she would ask what your county was, and with whom you were connected, and where your people's property might lie. And if I said— you know—why, it would be a case of cutting me off with a shilling. Yet that respectable Dives went on talking about my mother's wishes."

"Perhaps you did not understand him. At all events, he could not mean my engagement, because I am not engaged. This is the tenth time that I have reminded you of that fact, Sir Humphrey."

"My mother would certainly like me to back out—I mean, not to go on."

"Pray do back out."

"I believe you want to take up with that detestable cad—the man you call Dick—loathsome worm!"

"You are doing your very best to be pleasant this evening, and to ingratiate yourself! All the world are cads, are they not? except a small class. But it is quite true. Dick wants me to marry him."

"You'd better, then, and go off on the tramp with him."

The Changeling

"Perhaps I shall. But now, Humphrey, just to come back to ourselves. You continually insult my people—the class to which I belong—whenever you open your lips to speak. You have nothing but contempt for the people who work for their living, to whom I belong, and the people outside your own little circle. What do you want to marry me for? To make me happy by having to listen to this continual flood of contempt?"

"Because, Molly"—the young man's artificial smile vanished and his pince-nez dropped—"because you are unlike everybody I know. None of the girls that I know are in the least like you. It pleases me to see you get indignant in defence of cads. It is like coming into a different atmosphere. I like to feel like coming down into another class. When we are married, I mean to go on living with my mother and her set, and to keep you apart—don't call it concealment—in some cottage away from the West End."

"And my own people?"

"Well, of course you won't have them to your house, I suppose. You can go and see some of them, if you like. You can't possibly want to see all——"

"And my old friend Dick?"

Humphrey turned red; he lost his repose; he flushed a vulgar red.

"You shall not associate with that abominable cad, Molly. I shall forbid it altogether. You must promise——"

"When I promise anything—perhaps——"

"Then you know, Molly, you are soothing to the nerves. After seeing a bad picture, or hearing a bad piece of music, or listening to the cheerfulness of that—that BEAST they call Dick, only to watch you consoles, and to talk with you restores."

"I am glad to have some qualities, in spite of my birth."

"You have risen above that misfortune, Molly. If you would only refuse to know these people——"

"Certainly not."

"Give me your promise, Molly."

The Changeling

She rose. "Well, at all events, I understand exactly what you mean. If you are so good as to marry me, I am to be hidden away; I am to serve as a soothing syrup for shattered nerves; I am to be an antidote to bad music; I am to be ashamed of my own people, and to give up my old friends. That is understood, is it not?"

"We exchange sacrifices—mine the sacrifice of marrying beneath me; yours, that of giving up an ignoble troop of relations."

To plain persons every word that this girl had spoken would have been a clear announcement of her decision. To this young man no such intention was conveyed. Still in the fulness of his self-conceit, the sacrifice he himself proposed in actually marrying a girl with such family connections seemed so enormous, while the prospect of becoming his wife seemed to him so dazzling, that he was totally unable to understand any hesitation. Molly was whimsical; she did not like to surrender her independence. He liked her the better for it. No meek submissive maiden, however lovely, would be able to command that sacrifice. And, besides, there was that strange magic about the girl's face and eyes and voice, that in her presence, as has been explained already, the young man's mind was full of yearnings after transports unspeakable—after the Flowery Way, where the dancers are, with the castanets and the champagne and raptures that even the newest Art cannot bestow.

"Humphrey," she said, "suppose that in a moment—all in a moment—the things you value most in the world should vanish?"

"My Art? My genius?"

"No; not such genius as you may possess. That is not what you value most. I mean your birth and rank and position in the world. Suppose that were to vanish suddenly away?"

"You talk nonsense."

"I say, suppose it were to vanish suddenly away—suppose you were to become—say—one of my cousins—born like them——"

"Molly, don't waste time in talking nonsense."

"Well, perhaps—— Oh, here is Hilarie."

The Changeling

The library was now deserted, save for these two, when Hilarie appeared at the door. Her face, always grave, was now stern. Humphrey saw the look on her face and coloured, conscience-stricken. With her came his other cousin, also looking grave.

"Molly dear," said Hilarie, "has Sir Humphrey been pressing you?"

The young man became confused and agitated. He understood.

"He has. He wants me to promise to go into hiding with a secret marriage. He is unable to understand that the sacrifice could not be compensated even by his society."

Hilarie turned to Sir Humphrey. "I asked you here to-night," she said, "in order to arrange this little scene. Molly, you can read this letter."

Molly read it, and looked up from the page into the shamefaced cheeks of Humphrey.

"I—I—I must go," said the double lover. "Good night, Molly."

"No, sir. Not before Molly has read the letter."

Richard moved a step towards the door.

Molly read it, and looked up amazed. She read it again, and her cheek flamed. And a third time. Then she returned the letter to Hilarie.

"Wretch!" she said.

Since Hilarie used the same word to express the same idea, there is no doubt that the dictionary ought to have a special line on this meaning of the word "wretch."

"Do you understand it, Molly?"

"There can be no doubt about it, Hilarie. Won't you make him go?"

Hilarie pointed to the door contemptuously, as one dismisses a messenger or a boy; not in the tragic vein at all, but by a little gesture of her forefinger. Dick threw the door open with a gesture of command.

Humphrey obeyed, with an effort at preserving some appearance of dignity. To be found out under such circumstances, to be exposed in such a manner, to be ordered off the premises so contemptuously, would make the proudest of men leave the room with the appearance of ignominy.

"Molly, my dear," said Hilarie, "when you think of the man and what he is, you will never regret him."

She laid her head upon Hilarie's shoulder with a deep, deep sigh.

"One doesn't like a man making love to somebody else at the same time. But I dare say I shall get over that. And then—oh, my dear Hilarie, it is such a relief! I cannot tell you what a relief. For, you know, sometimes I seem to think that I did consent."

"And as for my other cousin here?"

"Dick," said Molly, "the fiddle is very light to carry. I shan't feel the weight of it—not a bit. Are you satisfied, Dick?"

CHAPTER XXII.

THE CLAN AGAIN.

Once more the relations met together, this time by invitation. They would have preferred separate and individual treatment. Each one received a letter, inviting him or her to the hotel on the afternoon of such a day. Each came expectant, hopeful, confident; and their faces dropped when they found, each in turn, that all had been invited together. They mounted the stairs; they entered the room; they stood about or they sat down in silence. If they spoke, it was to remark in murmurs on the interesting motives of certain persons in connection with rich cousins. The broken one, shabbier than ever, sat hanging his head. "I wouldn't ha' come," he said aloud, "if I'd expected a crowd like this." But the draper of Mare Street, Hackney, stood erect, his hand thrust into his bosom, as one who is gently rocked and lulled upon his own motives, as upon the cradle of the deep.

Presently John Haveril came in, accompanied by Dick, who attended as a kind of private secretary, and took no part in the proceedings until the end.

John carried in his hand a bundle of papers. "Well," he said, "you're all come, I think—all come." He turned over the papers, and nodded to the writer of each letter in turn. "All come. I invited you all to come." He spoke gravely and with dignity—in his most dignified manner.

"First, sir"—the self-constituted spokesman offered his hand—"we trust that you continue in good health, in the midst of your truly colossal responsibilities."

"Yes, sir, yes—I continue pretty well." Again he looked round. "Perhaps you will all sit down."

"I, for one, should be ashamed to sit." The draper spoke with reproach in his voice, for the rest had taken chairs. "Ashamed, sir, while you are standing."

It was something like the old-fashioned reading of the will, but before the funeral instead of after. They sat expectant, hungrily expectant.

The Changeling

Out of so many millions, surely, surely something would come to every one! Would it take the form of hundreds?

"Alma," said the pew-opener, coming along in the omnibus, "he's got a good heart; you can see it in his deep blue eye. He's bound to give us what we ask—and Alice my own first cousin and all, and you but one removed."

"Perhaps Cousin Charles has been at him behind our backs."

It is disheartening to observe the readiness with which young ladies on a certain social level ascribe and suspect the baser springs of action.

"Trust him!" The lady of the pews should have learned more Christian charity. "But I hope he won't be able to poison Cousin John's mind against honest people. I call him 'Cousin-John-by-marriage,' not 'Mr. Haveril,' and I say he took us over with Alice when he married her. A man marries, my dear, into his wife's family. Alma!"

"What is it, mother?"

"They've got no children. Somebody must have it when they go. Why not you and me?"

"Why not, mother? We could make a good use of it."

"We could. Ah!" She closed her eyes for the space of a furlong.

"Mother, how much did you ask for?"

"A hundred and twenty pounds. I could do it for less, perhaps, because there's my own furniture. He must give it; he can't refuse—and me Alice's first cousin, and you but one removed. My dear, I've always longed to have a Margate lodging-house since I stood upon Margate jetty as a girl, and paid a Margate bill as a grown woman, before you were born."

"I've asked for seventy pounds. I believe I could start respectably for less; but seventy would be plenty. And oh! to sit behind your own counter, covered with dolls and fancy-work and pretty things, and have no work to do! Oh!" She clasped her hands in ecstasy.

"Yes, Alma; it's all very well if the people come in to buy your things. But what do you know about shops and what to charge?"

"Come to that, mother, what do you know about keeping lodgings?"

The Changeling

It was with speculations such as these, with castles in the air or in Spain, that the cousins beguiled their way towards the Hôtel Métropole. The fancy of the broken one dwelt upon the tobacco-shop. It seems that this kind of shop attracts many of the best and brightest. There is so little to do; the money drops in all day long; you can smoke your own tobacco morning, noon, and night, while the laughing hours dance along and strew the way with roses. The bankrupt looked, indeed, as if roses would be a change for him after his long staying among the flagons and the apples.

"I asked you, when you were here last"—John Haveril remained standing—"to send me letters if you wanted me to do anything. I wanted to know quite clearly what you wanted. You have done so. I find, as I expected, that you all want me to give you money."

"Excuse me, sir," said the spokesman, "we distinguish between begging and borrowing. To give—to bestow alms—upon unworthy persons"—he looked severely at the bankrupt, who paid no heed—"or upon persons who are best left in their own humble station in life"—he waved an insulting hand towards the pew-opener—"is one thing; to advance capital which will be regarded as a loan, to be repaid with interest, is quite another thing. To solicit alms, as has been done, I fear, by some in this room, is one thing; to offer an investment, on the solid security of a sterling and established place of business, is quite another thing."

"Very true," said John Haveril. "Very true."

"Where the security is a concern—a concern, sir, improving every day, with four and twenty young ladies as shop-assistants——"

"Fed on scrag of mutton and margarine!" observed the pew-opener, aloud.

"—in a promising suburb and in a crowded highway, with the electric light, a carriage often at the door, and the proprietor a churchwarden—a very different thing," he concluded, running down and forgetting the construction of his sentence.

The others said nothing; but the Board school teacher examined the pictures on the wall, and was absorbed for the moment in art criticism.

"You all want money," John Haveril repeated; "that is the reason why I invited you here to-day."

"Why shouldn't we?" asked the broken one. "You are the only one of the family who has got any money. As for this fellow"—he indicated the draper—"hollow, hollow! There's no stability in him, I know. Where I am there he ought to be—down among the dead men."

"Where a few pounds would be the making of us, and them not so much as missed," said the pew-opener, "why not?"

"I don't know," continued the capitalist, "that you've got any claim on me. You cut your cousin Alice off—out of the family—for her first marriage."

"What else," asked the spokesman, "could we do? She married an actor, sir—a common actor. No doubt she has long since repented her early choice. How different from her second venture—her second prize! Ah! a prize indeed."

"Some of us were not born then," said the Board school teacher. "I'd as soon marry an actor as a draper—sooner, too." She was a sharp-faced girl, quick and ready—perhaps too quick—with woman's most formidable weapon. "Actors don't sweat shop-girls."

"Alice tells me," John Haveril went on slowly, "that none of you ever made any kind of inquiry after her, or answered her letters—except one—Will—also an actor, who is now deceased."

"How could we, when some of us hadn't even got into the cradle?" asked the teacher.

"I didn't quarrel with Alice," said the bankrupt. "I never saw her nor heard of her. And I didn't quarrel with Cousin Will. Why," he added conclusively, "I borrowed money of him."

"If she had been in want," John Haveril added, "would you have helped her because she was your cousin?"

"Since I, for one, never heard that she was in want"—again the teacher—"how can I tell what I should have done? It's like this, Mr. Haveril—you must know it yourself. It isn't respectable to have cousins ragged and in want. If I could afford it, I would give them money to go away. Look at that Object"—she pointed to the bankrupt. "Object, I call him."

"Object yourself!" retorted the broken one.

"Is he a credit to the family? No; I've got no money to spare, or I'd pay him to go right away. Same with Cousin Alice. Don't talk to us about cousinly love. We like respectability."

"Very good," said John Haveril.

"Cousin Alice has brought you a lot of relations," Alma continued, emboldened. "Here we are, fawning, like Cousin Charles; begging, like Cousin Alfred; and telling you the truth, like me."

"One, sir, one at least"—this was, of course, the draper—"has ever been ready to acknowledge the tie of blood."

"I'm sure," said the pew-opener, "if Alice had come to my humble place, which she never did— —"

"Never," her daughter added.

"—there'd have been a cup of tea made in no time, and a chair by the fire."

"You have among you"—John Haveril pointed to the bankrupt—"a cousin who is poor and distressed. What have you done for him? Which of you has helped this unfortunate man?"

"Not one," the unfortunate replied for all; while Charles regarded his fallen relation vindictively. "Not one," the bankrupt continued. "And now your guilty hearts are exposed and your greedy natures brought to light. Grabbers and grubbers—every one. And this to me—to me—Mr. Haveril, the only gentleman of the lot! What do they care about gentlemen?"

"You ask me, all of you, to help you with gifts or loans of money. On what pretence? Because I am your cousin's husband— —"

"Cousin-John-by-marriage," said the pew-opener. "You took us over as your own when you married Alice. You married into the family. That you can't deny."

"If that is the reason why I am to help you, why don't you help this cousin?"

The Changeling

"Hear! hear!" from the cousin indicated.

"He is in the last stage of poverty and misery."

"Because it serves him right." The draper once more stepped forward, while the rest of the family murmured assent.

"Outside," said John, "it is raining, with a cold wind; he has no great-coat,—nothing but a thin jacket; the soles of his boots are parting — —"

"Help him? He's always been a disgrace to the family," said the pew-opener.

"You ask me, however, to help you, and you offer no reference as to character."

"Reference? What reference do you want?" asked the Board school teacher. "Haven't I got a responsible situation? Isn't mother in a responsible situation? Mr. Haveril, I wouldn't talk about this poor ragamuffin, if I were you. It's beneath you. Give him a great-coat yourself, and in ten minutes it will be five shillings, and in an hour it will be drunk. Help him? I wouldn't help Cousin Alfred if I had hundreds—nor Cousin Charles if I had millions."

"You wouldn't," said the bankrupt, "if it was an angel from heaven; you'd see him starve first."

"Some of us, my dear sir," the draper explained sadly, "have to draw the line at disgrace. Character, in business, goes a long way. Bankruptcy brings disgrace even upon those members of the family who are otherwise regarded with respect."

"You think it is a mistake to give money?"

Cousin Charles retracted. "We must distinguish between giving and advancing. I would recommend the advance—the advance only—of capital to those who can help themselves."

"My friend, if you can help yourself, you want no help."

"In a sense, most true; in fact, profoundly true," Cousin Charles replied. "I will make a note of those words. They shall become my motto: 'Those who can help themselves want no help.' So truly wise."

The Changeling

"And if so," John continued, "to help those who cannot help themselves is throwing money away."

"It is—it is." He pointed to the bankrupt. "Why help him? He cannot help himself. I have always felt that to help my cousin Alfred is a sin—if waste of money is sinful. He failed, sir; he became a bankrupt in Mare Street, only five doors from my place of business; with my surname over his door. I wonder I survived it."

"You'll survive your own failure next," said the bankrupt.

"Come back to your own case, mister. You agree that one should not help those who can help themselves. Let us lay hold on that. If you can help yourself, why do you want help? You've helped yourself, I understand, to a flourishing business. You are evidently, therefore, beyond the necessity of further help. You want me to advance you a large sum of money. Why? You have shown that you can help yourself. Very well; the best thing you can do is to go on helping yourself."

Cousin Charles changed colour. His face dropped, to use the familiar expression.

"Sweating four and twenty girls in black with white cuffs," murmured the teacher.

"This," John continued, slowly and with weight, "is my answer to your letter. Go on, as you have already begun, trusting to yourself alone. It is best for you. If you are on the downward grade, you would only be saved for a time. If you are going up, the advance you ask would not help you. That is my answer, mister, to your letter."

The draper grew very red in the face. "Then," he asked, "you—you—you refuse—you actually refuse this trifling assistance?"

"Actually."

"You hear, Charles," said the bankrupt.

"Am I in my senses?" He looked round him. "The husband of my cousin Alice, much loved—'sweet Alice, Ben Bolt'—a man of millions, refuses me an advance, upon undeniable security, of a simple thousand pounds. Why, the bank will do it for me with alacrity."

"Then go to the bank."

The poor man changed from red to white. His cheeks became flabby. His arms, which had been folded, dropped. He suddenly grew limp. It is rather terrible to see a confident, aggressive man become suddenly limp. Perhaps he had built confidently on this advance; perhaps he was not quite so substantial as he boasted and as he seemed; perhaps that great shop, with four and twenty girls in black with white cuffs, all in a row, was haunted by the spectre of which nobody talks, though it is seen daily by so many—the grisly, threatening, lean, gaunt, fierce-eyed ghost called Bankruptcy.

He clapped his hat on his head. He recovered a little. He tried to smile. He assumed some show of dignity. He even laughed. Then he replied, with genuine heartfelt emotion, "The Lord forgive you!" and walked out of the room.

John Haveril turned to the pew-opener. "Here is your letter," he said; "I return it to you. Why should I give you anything? You are fifty years of age, you say. You have a son in good employ. You have a daughter—this girl, I suppose—in the School Board service. You have a reasonably good situation."

The lady's face dropped and lengthened. "Oh!" she cried; "don't refuse! don't refuse! It's such a trifle to you; you would never miss it, and never feel it. And it would be the making of me—it would indeed."

John Haveril shook his head with the deliberation and the expression of a bear. His mind was made up. The woman went on, but feebly—

"You can't like to own—you so rich, and all—that you've got a cousin in such a humble place as mine."

"You might help her to be respectable," her daughter put in.

"You can be respectable in any situation. I am quite as proud of you in your present situation as if you were what you want to be—a lodging-house keeper at Margate." He turned to her daughter. "My dear," he said kindly, "you are a little fool."

"Why? Oh, why?"—and her heart sank.

The Changeling

"Because you want to give up the best work that a woman can do, where there's pay enough, and holidays, and respect——"

The girl shook her head. "You don't know," she moaned, "the work and the drudgery."

"And to change it for the worst work in the world. My dear, you should be proud of being what you are. If you were in the States, you would feel proud of your work. What? Give up that work for a miserable little shop, where you must cheat to make both ends meet? Don't be silly. Go back and thank God, my dear, that He has put you where you can do some good."

She sat down and pulled out her pocket-handkerchief. Her mother stood beside her, her lips moving, her cheek flaming.

"Shall I give you back your letter?" John Haveril asked.

She took it, tore it up, threw the fragments on the floor, seized her mother by the arm, and dragged her out; whether in repentance or in anger the bystanders could not know.

They were all gone now, except the bankrupt.

"You've got my letter, too," he said. "What are you going to do for me?"

"The kindest thing would be to drop you in the river. Alice has left it to me. Well, you are a hopeless creature. Whatever is done for you will be money thrown away. I did think of asking your cousin, the draper, to give you a place in his shop. You might sweep it out and water the floor, and carry out the parcels—or you might walk up and down outside in uniform, and a gold band to your cap."

"Mr. Haveril—sir—I am a gentleman. Don't insult a fallen gentleman, sir; I've employed my own shop-assistants."

"But I fear he would do nothing for you."

"I came here—one day three weeks ago—you were away—I knew that. I gave Alice some secret information just for her own ear, not the kind of thing she would tell you."

"Get on, man!"

"I told her — you don't know, of course; I told her you ought to know — you suppose he's dead."

"Man! man!" said John.

"Alice's first husband — Anthony Woodroffe. You think he's dead. I told her where he was."

"Where?" Dick sat up, suddenly. "Anthony Woodroffe?"

"Why should I ask whether he's dead or alive?"

"That's what Alice said. As for me, I told her I was astonished. 'Alice,' I said, 'I did think you were respectable.'"

"What does this man mean?" asked Dick. "Anthony Woodroffe?"

"Well, boy," said John, "this chap brought us the news where he was. We thought, on the whole, there was no need to tell you — so we didn't tell you. I've been to see him. He's pretty comfortable."

"He is pretty comfortable," said Anthony's late companion between the boards. "If Abraham's bosom is better than the cold kerb, and softer than the doss-house, he is quite comfortable — for he died this morning."

"Where did he die?" asked Dick.

"In the Marylebone Workhouse Infirmary." The man got up and shuffled away. As he went out of the room, he held out his hand, and there was the chink of coin.

"My father dead!"

"Ay, lad, he's dead. What better for you and everybody? I've seen him, on and off, most days. He was a hardened sinner, if ever there was one."

"Dead! I have been taught to regard him with a kind of loathing; but — we can only have one father. Dead! In a workhouse infirmary!"

"He has left two sons. You are not the only one."

"Two sons. Yes" — concerning his half-brother Dick could not choose but speak vindictively — "the other will hear to-morrow who his father was. He shall hear also that his father is dead. He and I will be the mourners at the pauper's funeral."

208

CHAPTER XXIII.

ONE MORE ATTEMPT.

"That man again!" Lady Woodroffe threw the card into the fire. "Tell him I will not see him. No. Let him come up."

It was Richard Woodroffe, proposing to make his last attempt. Before doing so, he had run down to Birmingham and seen the newly-found witness. He was a most trustworthy person; he picked out the photograph of Lady Woodroffe from a bundle of photographs; he remembered the case and the lady perfectly well. There was, therefore, no doubt possible that she had been in Birmingham at that time, and that she had lost her own son.

"Sir"—she sat up in her chair with angry eyes—"this is persecution! I have already given a patient hearing to your most impudent story."

"You have, Lady Woodroffe." Neither her angry looks nor her presence disconcerted him now. He was so perfectly certain of his cause, and of her shameless falsehood, that he stood before her at ease, and even with some appearance of dignity.

"I even took the trouble to invite your friend, the person for whom you profess to act, the woman with the delusion——"

"You did." He did not wait to be invited. He took a chair and sat down in it.

"In order to convince her of her absurdity."

"In which you failed. Because, after all your talk, there remained the solid fact—the death of Sir Humphrey's son."

"Sir Humphrey had one son only, who is still living. I was wrong in thinking that a plain statement of facts could move the poor mad woman. She brought with her a young person, who encouraged her to insult me. They even attempted to assault me, I believe. After the grossest abuse, they carried off a bundle of baby-linen, and things that I had treasured, for reasons which I fear you are incapable of understanding."

"No, Lady Woodroffe, on the contrary, I understand them very well. You brought them out on this occasion with the intention of showing this poor lady what I must venture to call your defiance."

"My defiance? Certainly; I accept the word. My defiance. You appear to be almost as polite as your friends, Mr. Woodroffe."

"You could not have chosen a more effective manner of announcing your intentions. 'There!' you said, 'these clothes which you made with your own fingers show that it is your boy; yet you shall not have him, and I defy you to prove that he is yours.'"

"You are correct on one point. I do defy you to prove that fact."

"Very well; I am here to-day to tell you that I have advanced one more step, and a very important step it is."

"Important or not, I defy you to prove the fact. This is not, however, exactly an acknowledgment. But I shall not argue with you; I believe I ought to hand you over at once to my lawyers, to be dealt with for conspiracy."

Richard Woodroffe smiled. "I wish you would," he said. "I should like nothing better than the publicity of an action."

"Oh," she groaned, "the pertinacity of the black-mailer!"

"I shall not be insulted, whatever you say. I am here to tell you that the proofs have now closed round you so completely, that there is not left, I verily believe, a single loophole of escape."

Lady Woodroffe rose with dignity. "You talk to me, sir—to *me*?—of escape and loophole. Go, sir—go to my solicitors."

"Certainly." Richard continued, however, to occupy his chair. "I will go to your solicitors whenever you please. I would rather go to them than come here. But for the sake of others, I would prefer that you should acknowledge the fact, and let the son go back to his mother. He is my own half-brother, but it is not fraternal affection that prompts me in this research, I assure you. If you refuse to hear me, I shall have to go to your solicitors through Mrs. Haveril's solicitors."

"Oh, go on, then!"

The Changeling

She sat down again, and crossed her hands in her lap, assuming something of the expression of a person bored to death by a very bad sermon.

"I have certain evidence in my hands, then"—he could not avoid a smile of satisfaction—"which connects you with the dead child—your child."

Lady Woodroffe caught her breath and started, as if in sudden pain.

"Go on, sir."

"I will tell you what it is. You arrived one evening at the Great Midland Hotel, Birmingham, with an Indian ayah and a child. You engaged three rooms—a sitting-room and two bedrooms; you explained that the child had been taken suddenly and alarmingly ill in the train; you sent out for a medical man; he came; he kept the maids running about with hot water, and the boys going out for remedies and prescriptions; he stayed with you all night, watching the case; in the morning your child was dead; three days afterwards you buried him. There is no monument over the child's grave, because you made an arrangement with the help of Dr. Robert Steele, and substituted another child for him, and you went away two or three days after the funeral, and disappeared. The rooms were taken in your name; the books of the hotel prove so much."

"Oh! This man is tedious—tedious—with his repetitions."

"I have been down to Birmingham again. I have now found an old waiter who remembers the circumstance perfectly well—Indian ayah and sick baby and funeral. He says he remembers you, but that I doubt. I have also found the medical man who was called in. He not only remembers the case, which he entered at the time in his note-book, but he also remembers you ——"

"After four and twenty years——!"

"—and picked you out of a bundle of photographs. I think you will admit that this is an important step?"

She made no reply. Her face was drawn and twisted with the pain of listening.

"What is wanted now," Richard added, "is the connection of yourself and the child. If we fail there— —"

"You will fail."

"We shall ask Sir Robert."

"You will fail."

"Then we shall give publicity to the case—I don't quite know how. All the world shall understand. You will have to explain— —"

"All the world? It is the High Court of Justice that you must address. I shall look to the judge to protect me. Remember it is in my power to prove that I was in Scotland at that very time."

"On that very day when the child died?"

"On that very day," she replied, firmly and without hesitation.

"Lady Woodroffe, I cannot believe what you say."

"You can prove what you like," she repeated, "but you cannot prove that I bought the child."

"To speak plainly, I don't believe one word about your proving an *alibi*, Lady Woodroffe, any more than I believe that remarkably bold falsehood about the child's clothes. We shall prove the death of the child beyond a doubt. You can then, if you please, find out something that will amuse the world about Humphrey. As for the publicity— —"

"Since you will only prove that a woman took my name, I care nothing. My reputation is not likely to be injured by such a story. Who will believe against my word—that I—Lady Woodroffe—a leader, sir, in a world of which you and your like know nothing—the world which advances humanity—the world of religion and of charity—the world which combats vice unceasingly—should condescend to a crime so ignoble and so purposeless?"

"I am not concerned with your credibilities, Lady Woodroffe. I learn that you made a large use of them with Mrs. Haveril, and only desisted when they proved a failure. Then you took to defiance."

"The publicity will fall upon the fashionable physician, the great man of science, the head of his profession, who will have to acknowledge

The Changeling

that he found a child and bought it for a certain unknown person—a noble way for a young physician to earn a fee! The publicity will also fall upon the now notorious lady who has got up in the world since she sold her only child for fifty pounds, to keep it and herself out of the workhouse. No injurious publicity will fall upon me, other than the discovery of some woman who once took my name."

"You are identified by your photograph. You forget that."

"Can I? After four and twenty years? Can any woman of my age—forty-nine—be identified, by a stranger, with another woman of twenty-five or thereabouts? Now, Mr. Richard Woodroffe, what else have you got to say?"

"I have only this to say. I came here to-day, Lady Woodroffe, in the hope that what I have told you would show you the danger of your position. For the sake of this lady, who is worn almost to death by the anxiety of her situation, I hoped that you would confess."

"Confess! I to confess! You speak as if I were a common criminal."

"No," said Richard, "not common by any means."

Lady Woodroffe left her chair and stepped over to the fireplace. She looked older, and the authority went out of her very strangely. She laid her hand on the shelf, as if for support, and she spoke slowly—with no show of anger—slowly, and with sadness.

"I think, sir, I do think, that if you could consider the meaning of this charge to a person in my position, the suffering you inflict upon me, the mischief you may do to me, and I know not how many more, by persisting in this charge, you would abandon it."

"I cannot; I am acting for another."

"You are playing a game to win. I don't accuse you of sordid motives. You want to win."

"Perhaps I do."

"Have you asked yourself the simple question, whether it is possible for me to commit such a crime, and then to confess?"

"I have to win this game, Lady Woodroffe. I think I have won it."

"It is not won yet. And believe me, sir, it will not be won unless I choose."

"We can place you in a very awkward position, anyhow."

"Mr. Richard Woodroffe, you came here to make a final appeal to me; it is my turn to make a final appeal to you. I am a woman, as perhaps you know, of very considerable importance in the world. Such a charge as you bring against me would not only crush me, if it were proved, but it would dislocate or ruin a great many associations and institutions of which I am the very soul. Thousands of orphans, working girls, Magdalens, and sinners, would lose their best friend. I am their best friend; my tongue and my pen keep up the stream which flows in to their relief. Is it not possible for that woman to think of these things? Or, there is the boy. He is partly, I suppose, what he is by education, partly by his nature; take away from him his position as a gentleman of rank and family, send him out disgraced to make his own way in the world, and he will sink like lead. You call him your half-brother. Well, Mr. Woodroffe, he is not a young man of many virtues; in fact, he has many vices."

"That I can well believe."

"If he has seven devils now, after this disclosure he will have seventy-seven devils."

"That also I can well believe. But, of course, I do not think about him."

"Then, Mr. Woodroffe, can you not persuade that poor woman to go home, to be content with what she has seen and you have proved?"

"No, I cannot."

"Can you not remind her that she sold the child on the condition that she would never trouble about him, or seek to know where he might be living?"

"No, I cannot. She has seen her son; she knows who he is; she wants your acknowledgment. Give her that, and, I don't know, in fact, what will happen afterwards."

Lady Woodroffe sat down and sighed heavily. "Be it so," she said. "You will go on; you will do your worst."

The Changeling

Richard Woodroffe regarded her with a sense of pity, and even of respect. The woman had supported her position by a succession of shameless lies; she was now virtually confessing to him that they were lies. But she had so much to lose—her great position among religious and charitable people, her reputation, the respect which her blameless life and her great abilities had won for her. All these things were threatened.

"Madam," he said, his face full of emotion, "if it were only your son to be thought of, I would retire. But there is this poor lady, who is only kept alive, I believe, by the hope and belief that her son will be restored to her. Believe me, if I may speak of pity for you——"

"Pity?" She sprang to her feet with fire and fury in her cheeks and eyes. It is, happily, the rarest thing in the world to see a woman—I mean a woman of culture—overmastered by passion. Yet it lies there; it is always possible. In the heart of the meekest maiden, the most self-governed and most highly bred woman, there lies hidden the tigress, the fish-wife, the scold, the shrew. Formerly, whenever women were gathered together, they quarrelled; whenever they quarrelled, they fought—sometimes with fists, cudgels, brooms, chairs, sometimes with tongues. Men were so horribly frightened by the scolding wife, that they ducked her, put her in a cage, carried her round in a cart. The little word "pity" was the last drop in the cup. Lady Woodroffe raged and stormed at the unfortunate Richard. For the time her mind was beyond control; afterwards, he remembered that such a fit of passion showed the tension of her mind. He made no reply. When her torrent of words and threats was exhausted, she threw herself into her chair, and buried her face in her hands.

Then Richard quietly withdrew.

CHAPTER XXIV.

A HORRID NIGHT.

Richard Woodroffe walked away with hanging head. A second time he had learned that his proofs might not be so convincing, after all. The defence set up by a woman of the highest social position, character, and personal influence, that she had never been in Birmingham in her life, that on the day of the alleged death of her child she was in Scotland, that she knew nothing of the person who was said to have assumed her name, could only be met by evidence concerning that person by an identification of that person with Lady Woodroffe by an old man, speaking of an event of four and twenty years ago, and by an alleged resemblance; as to the packet of clothes, that would certainly be no evidence at all. He himself was perfectly certain of the fact; there was no doubt left in his own mind. But would his proofs be accepted in a court of justice?

As he walked along with these heavy reflections, he was startled by a hand upon his shoulder—a thing which, in former times, caused the sufferer to swoon with terror, because it was the familiar greeting of the sheriff's officer, the man with a writ. That part of the officer's duty is now, however, gone. It was, in fact, the hand of Sir Robert Steele, who, his day's work finished, was taking the air.

"Dick," he cried, "I haven't seen you since—since—when?"

"Since the day when you made a study of heredity."

"Oh, you mean when you dined with me? Yes, Dick, my boy, I have heard things about you—the Strange Adventures of a Singer."

"Of course you have. Lady Woodroffe has told you."

"How you are fishing in troubled waters, and catching nothing. Yes, I have seen Mrs. Haveril—a most interesting woman; but she ought to go home and keep quiet. Keep her quiet, Dick. Put down your fishing-rod, and make that good lady sit down, and keep that good lady quiet."

The Changeling

"I will as soon as I have restored her son to her. We have found him, you know."

"You tell me so. You think it is Sir Humphrey Woodroffe, is it not?"

"We are perfectly certain it is. Lady Woodroffe has told you, I dare say, what we have done."

"Something—something. You are working, no doubt, in the interests of the second baronet?"

"Yes, oh yes." Dick grinned. "He is my half-brother, you know. I am anxious to restore him to his real rank, which is mine. He shall become what he is pleased to describe me—an outsider and a cad."

"Two Cains and no Abel. A slaughterous pair. Well, have you proved your case yet?"

"To our own satisfaction, perfectly. To the complete satisfaction of the world as soon as the story is told. For lawyers—well—there is one point lacking."

"That one point! That one point! Always that one point! It is like connecting your family with illustrious ancestry—always the one point wanting. I need not ask what that point is."

"No, because you are the person who can supply the link."

"Is that so?" asked the doctor, dryly. "Then, while you are waiting for that link, my dear Richard, I advise you to tie up your papers and go back to legitimate business." He stopped, because they were arrived at his own door. "Come in," he said. "Now then, my dear boy, sit down and let us have it out. First of all, however, understand that you cannot establish that link. You say that I am the only person who can supply it. Well, if that is so, remember that I shall not."

"You mean, will not."

"Just as you like. The distinction between *will* and *shall* is sometimes too subtle for the rules of syntax."

"But, my dear Sir Robert, just consider what a lot I can prove. Lady Woodroffe goes to a hotel in Birmingham. She drives in hurriedly; her child is ill. She sends for a medical man. She takes two bedrooms and a sitting-room. She has an ayah. The medical man stays with her the whole night. In the morning the child dies——"

"How do you know all these things?"

"By the note-book of the man who was called in, by the books of the hotel, by the evidence of the medical man himself, by the evidence of a waiter who remembers the case, by the register of deaths."

"All this looks strong, I admit."

"So that we can actually prove the death of Sir Humphrey's only son. And we can call upon Lady Woodroffe to inform us who is the man calling himself Sir Humphrey's only son."

"You prove that a woman calling herself Lady Woodroffe did all these things."

"And we can produce a witness who will swear to her identity."

"After all these years I doubt if you could—if that evidence would be received. I admit that you have a case. As it is, you could make a *cause célèbre*. You are able to make things horribly uncomfortable for Lady Woodroffe; and you are able to inspire the young man, her son, with a lively animosity against yourself."

"I don't mind that in the least. I shall go and see him. I shall say, 'You are my half-brother. You are first cousin to a collection of common folk, whose commonness will rejoice your heart. I will introduce you to them. You shall take tea with them—the tea of shrimps, periwinkles, and watercress, that you have yet to learn—and to love.' I shall exhaust myself in congratulations."

"With the domestic affections I never interfere. Here, however, is a difficulty. You say 'we' will do this and that. Who is 'we'? You yourself? Suppose you spring all this upon the world? And suppose nobody takes any notice?"

"I may advertise the whole history, and offer a reward for the discovery of the identification of the woman."

"But nobody can identify Lady Woodroffe."

"My old doctor——"

The Changeling

"Your old doctor would break down. Lady Woodroffe has only to deny absolutely that she is the woman. Counsel can always suggest—man in India—another woman—assumption of name—real wife with her father, Lord Dunedin—letters to prove it—old nobleman swears it. Venerable old nobleman—ever seen him?—rather like Abraham."

"Well, we shall find some way of forcing the history upon the public. And a certain event has just happened which may give me an opportunity."

"What is that?"

"My father is dead. He died yesterday. He was also Humphrey's father."

"Oh, I am sorry."

"No one need express any sorrow on that account. As he left my mother when I was a baby, I have never seen him. I did not know that he was in England. It appears that he has been a sandwich-man for some time. And he died in a pauper infirmary. As for myself, I feel neither shame nor grief; he was to me, as to you, a stranger. But perhaps I can use the event in order to give publicity to our story, if we must court publicity."

"Well, let us hope —— But go on."

"As for Lady Woodroffe, she has actually confessed the thing."

He then proceeded to tell the story of the child's clothes.

The doctor became thoughtful. The audacity of showing and claiming the clothes astonished him.

"It isn't evidence, Dick," he said.

"No; but it's complete proof to the true mother."

"Perhaps—to her."

Sir Robert, in fact, admitted everything. But at this stage a mere admission of the kind meant nothing.

"It was a strange thing to do," said the doctor. "There is the audacity of despair about it. She had quite forgotten the fact that the register of deaths contained the name of the boy. If it had been a common name,

The Changeling

it would have mattered little. She did not tell me that the child died in Birmingham. That doctor—what is his name? Ah! I don't know him. Does he know the meaning and bearing of his evidence?"

"I believe not. He will not talk, however. He has undertaken to preserve absolute silence until he is called upon to speak."

"Keep the power of disclosure in your own hands, Dick. Above all things, do that. Why did she produce the child's clothes? Woman's wit is hard to follow. 'My word against all the world,' she meant, I believe. As if she must be believed on her bare assertion, against all the facts that could be brought against her. It was her pride. Like all female leaders, she is incredibly proud. She means to stand up and deny. On the other hand, the situation is harassing; there are points in the case which make it almost impossible——"

"The goings-on of my ill-conditioned brother, I suppose?"

"Perhaps—perhaps. I wish she had told me when and how the child died."

They dined together. Over an excellent bottle of Chateau Mouton they exchanged further confidences.

"My dear Dick," said the doctor, "it's a serious situation. You propose to cover a woman of the highest reputation with infamy. She says, in effect, 'You are quite right. I am that infamous person. But prove it.' You want to restore to another most amiable and honourable woman her son, and he would break her heart in a year. You want me to identify the lady, and thereby to confess my share in a transaction which might be made to look like complicity in a fraud and a conspiracy. I told her at the time that it looked like substitution, though she called it adoption. Well, I can imitate the lady's frankness; that is to say, I do not in so many words confess the truth, but I show it; I allow you to conclude that the thing is true. And, like the lady, I defy you. You will find out nothing more. And if you were to put me in the box—if you were to make me tell the truth about that infernal babe—never, never would I confess to knowing the name of the lady. And without that evidence you can never prove your case."

The Changeling

As a rule, the doctor was the last man in the world either to dream or to trouble himself with dreams; nevertheless, there fell upon him an incubus of the night which was so persistent, that, though he waked a dozen times and shook off the thing, a dozen times it came again. And so vivid was it that he saw it still when he awoke in the morning, and heard it, and remembered it, and felt it.

For in this dream he saw himself giving evidence in a court of law as to his own share in the substitution of another child for the dead child.

And in the dream he saw himself losing reputation, character, practice, everything. As the evidence was reluctantly given, he saw the face of the judge growing more and more severe, the faces of the jury harder, the faces in the court more hostile. He read in all his own condemnation.

This is what he had to say.

> "In the years 1873-1876 I was carrying on a general practice in a quarter of Birmingham. I was, in fact, a sixpenny doctor, charging that sum for advice and medicine, and having a fairly good reputation among the poorer class of that quarter. On a certain afternoon in February, 1874"—here the witness referred to his books—"a lady entered the surgery. She was deeply veiled, and in much trouble. She told me that she wanted to adopt a child in the place of her own, whom she had just lost by death. She asked me, further, if I knew of any poor woman who would give up her child. It was to be about fifteen months old. She gave the date of her dead child's birth as December the 2nd, 1872. And it must have light hair and blue eyes.
>
> "Among my patients was a woman left penniless by her husband, who had deserted her. She wanted, above all things, money to go in search of him. As he was an actor in a small way, she thought it would be easy to find him if she had money to travel with. The woman was mad with grief. She was ready to give up the child in return for the money she wanted. At the time, she would have given up her own soul for the money. The child was somewhere about the required age—a month more or less mattered little; it had blue eyes and light hair. I made the arrangement with her. I took the child, also by arrangement, to the Great Western Railway

The Changeling

Station, and gave it to an Indian ayah, who carried it into a first-class carriage, where the lady sat. Then the train went off, and I saw nothing more of the lady or the child for twenty-four years.

"I did not know, nor did I ask, the lady's name or address; only on a half-torn envelope, in which she had placed the notes—ten five-pound notes—for the mother of the child, was the word, 'Lady W——,' as part of an address.

"I did not know, nor did I ask, the lady's intentions. She said she wanted to adopt a child. I arranged this for her. I took the mother the sum of fifty pounds, and I charged the lady a fee of three guineas. The only question we discussed was that of heredity, and especially the danger of the child inheriting criminal tendencies.

"Four and twenty years later I received a visit—being then a physician practising in London—from the mother of the child, who had remembered my name. She was anxious to learn, if possible, what had become of her son. She had become rich, and would willingly claim the child.

"Upon her departure I began to think over the case, which I had almost forgotten. I remembered, first, the half-torn envelope. And then, looking at my note-book, I remembered the date of the dead child's birth—December 2, 1872. I took down a Peerage, and looked through the pages. Presently I discovered what I wanted, under the name of Woodroffe. The present baronet, the second, is there described as born on December 2, 1872. Now, the son of the first baronet, the late Sir Humphrey Woodroffe, who died early in 1874, was born on that day. It was so extremely unlikely that two women enjoying the title of 'Lady W.' should have a son born on the same day, that I naturally concluded the second baronet and the adopted child were one and the same person. So convinced was I of this fact that I ventured to call upon Lady Woodroffe, and satisfied myself that it was so.

"As, however, I had ascertained the truth in this unexpected manner, I assured Lady Woodroffe that the secret should remain with me until she herself should give me permission to reveal it.

"Meantime, one of Mrs. Haveril's friends began to make inquiries into the case. He ascertained that the son of Sir Humphrey

Woodroffe died, a child of fifteen months old, at Birmingham, early in 1874. He further learned that the so-called son, in person, figure, and face, closely resembled the father of the adopted child; and he learned also that the medical man who attended the dead child knew its name, and could absolutely identify the mother as the present Lady Woodroffe. In fact, the case was so far capable of proof that no reasonable person could entertain the slightest doubt on the subject.

"It was certainly open to Lady Woodroffe to perjure herself by denying that she had ever been in Birmingham. This she was going to do. I took no steps to dissuade her; nor did I take any steps to put an end to the fraudulent representation of this young man as Sir Humphrey's son; in fact, I became a party to the conspiracy."

He looked round the court in his dream, and read his own condemnation in all the faces.

When he awoke in the morning, the scene began all over again.

"Confound the baby!" he groaned. "Am I never to get to the end of it?"

He went down to breakfast, trying to shake off the feeling of disquiet that possessed him.

Just as he sat down, Richard Woodroffe called. "I am sorry to disturb you," he said, "but I have just been called to the Hôtel Métropole. Mrs. Haveril has had a miserable night. Molly sat up with her. She was weeping and crying all the night. This morning she is a wreck. There is, perhaps, no time to be lost— —"

"I knew something was going to happen."

"If she is to get her son back, it must be soon, or that dream of hers will not come true."

"Sit down, Dick. I've had a horrid night too. We will consider directly what is best to be done."

While he spoke there came a letter—"By hand. Sir Robert Steele. Bearer waits."

"Dear Sir Robert,

"Come to see me as soon as you can. I have had the most terrible night.

"Yours,

"L. W."

"Again! Three terrible nights for the three principal conspirators. The devil is in the business, I believe. Now, Dick, I have to call on Lady Woodroffe. Before I go to see this lady — —"

"I sincerely hope she will treat you as she did me. The manners of the aristocracy never showed to such advantage in my experience."

"Before I go to see this lady — —" Sir Robert repeated.

Again Richard interrupted him. "We cannot afford to wait any longer. Mrs. Haveril's condition forbids it. I have determined to write to Humphrey. I shall begin by informing him of his father's death. I shall invite him to join me in paying his father's debts. I shall then advertise the death of Anthony Woodroffe in the Marylebone Infirmary as the father of Sir Humphrey Woodroffe. That will make him do something. If he likes to go to law, we will meet him; if he wishes to see me, I will tell him everything."

"Why not go to him at once without any letter?"

"Because he will thus learn, in the most dramatic way possible, the name and the social position of his real father."

"Dick, you make this a personal matter."

"Yes, I do." He became suddenly vindictive. "The scoundrel wanted Molly to marry him secretly, and live secretly with him — you understand that — while he was making love to Hilarie Woodroffe."

"It is steep, certainly steep. But perhaps he did not mean — —"

"Doctor, you know the kind of men they are — this Johnnie and his friends. They have no honour, as they have no heart; they are rotten through and through — rotten and corrupt."

"Dick, there are others to be considered."

"I will make the whole story public — I will write a play on it."

"Is this revenge or justice, Dick?"

The Changeling

"I don't care which. Revenge is wild justice."

"When are these letters to be written?"

"To-day—this morning."

"Dick"—the doctor laid a persuasive hand upon his arm—"you don't understand what it is you are doing. Wait till this evening. Give me, say, eight—ten hours. Let me beg you to wait till this evening. If I can effect nothing in twelve hours—with the principals—the two—the three principals concerned—you shall then do as you please."

"Well, if I must—— If you really think—— Well, I will wait; but I will have no compromise. I could forgive him anything—his insolence and his contempt, but not——"

"Love has many shapes, my Richard. He may become a soldier—but a hangman, an executioner, he who brandishes the cat-o'-nine-tails—no, Dick, no—that *rôle* does not suit Love. Stay thy hand——"

Dick turned away. "Take your twelve hours."

"I am going, then, at once—to Lady Woodroffe."

CHAPTER XXV.

THE FIRST MOTHER.

There were once two women who claimed the same child. The case was referred to the king, who in that country was also lord chief justice.

"It is clear to me," said the king, after hearing the evidence on both sides, "that the case cannot be decided one way or the other; therefore bring me the child." So they laid the child before him. He called his executioner. "Take thy sword," he said, "and cut the child into two equal portions." The executioner drew his sword. Then said the king, "Give one half to each of the two women; they can then go away content." And the woman who was not the mother of the child said, "Great is the wisdom of the king. O king, live for ever!" But the other woman, with tears and sobs, threw herself over the child, saying that she could not endure that the child should be killed, and she would give it up to save its life.

Parables, like fables, belong to all time. This parable applies to the conclusion of the story.

Sir Robert found the lady in a condition closely resembling hysteria. She had sent away her secretaries; her letters lay piled on the table. She herself paced the room in an agony.

"I cannot bear it," she cried; "I cannot bear it any longer. They persecute me. Help me to kill myself."

"I shall help you to live, rather."

"I have resolved what to do. I will struggle no longer."

"Above all, do not struggle."

"You have deceived me. You told me that without your evidence they can prove nothing."

"That is quite true. Without my evidence they can prove nothing."

"They have found proof that I was in Birmingham at the time."

The Changeling

"Yes, yes; I know what they have found. They have found enough to establish a suspicion—a strong suspicion, difficult to dissipate—which would cling to us all."

"Cling? Cling? What would that mean—to me?"

"We must, therefore, avoid publicity, if we can. We are threatened with public exposure. That, if possible, I say, must be avoided. Are you listening? If there is still time, we must prevent scandal."

"I can no longer bear it, I say." She pressed her hand to her forehead. "It drives me mad! I thought, last night, I was mad." She threw herself on a sofa, and buried her head in her hands. "Doctor"—she started up again—"that man has been here again. He has found some one—I don't know—I forget—some one who remembers me—who recognizes me."

"So I believe—and then?"

"Day and night the thought is always with me. How can I bear the disclosure? The papers will ring with it."

"I hope there will be no disclosure. Believe me, Lady Woodroffe, no one can be more anxious than myself to avoid disclosures and scandals."

Lady Woodroffe, this calm, cold, austere person, whose spoken words moved the conscience of her audience, if not their hearts, whose printed papers carried conviction, if not enthusiasm, gave way altogether, and sobbed and cried like a young girl.

"It is all lost!" she moaned. "All that I have worked for—my position in the world, my leadership, my career—everything is lost. I shall have shame and disgrace, instead of honour and respect. Oh, I am punished—I am punished! No woman has ever been more punished."

"Perhaps," said the physician, "your punishment is finished. Four and twenty years is a long time."

"I have written out a confession of the whole business," she said wearily: "I had to. I got up in the middle of the night. My husband stood beside me. Oh, I saw him and I heard him. 'Lilias,' he said, 'what you did was in pity and in tenderness to me. I forgive you. All shall be forgiven you if you will confess.' So I sat down and wrote; and here

The Changeling

it is." She gave him a paper, which he placed in his inner pocket. "You know what I had to say, doctor. I was young, and I was in agony: my child was dead—oh, my child was dead! No one knows—no man can tell—what it is to lose your only child. All the time I wrote, my husband stood over me, his noble face stern and serious as when he was lieutenant-governor. When I finished, he laid his hand upon my head—I felt it, doctor, I tell you I felt it—and he said, 'Lilias, it is forgiven.' And so he vanished. And now you have got my confession."

"Yes, I have it. Give me—I ask your leave—permission to speak."

"Oh, speak! Cry aloud! Go to the house-top, and call it out! Sing it in the streets! I shall become a byword and a mockery!" She walked about, twisting a handkerchief in her hands. "My friends will have no more to do with me. I have brought shame on my own people!" She panted and gasped; her words came in jerks. "Doctor, I am resolved. I will turn Roman Catholic, and enter a convent. It is for such women as myself that they make convents. There I shall live out the rest of my life, hearing nothing and knowing nothing. And none of the scorn and shame that they will heap upon my name will reach the walls of my retreat."

"You must not think only of yourself, my dear madam. What about Humphrey?"

"He must do what he pleases—what he can. What does it matter what he does? Sir Robert, I assure you that he is a selfish wretch, the most hardened, the most heartless; he thinks about nothing but his own pleasure; under the guise of following Art, he is a cold sensualist. I have never detected in him one single generous thought or word; I have never known him do one single unselfish action. I have never cared for him—now, I declare that it costs me not one single pang to think that he will lose everything. Let the wretch who has made me suffer so much go back to the gutter—his native slime!"

"Stop! stop! my dear madam. Remember, in adopting the boy, you undertook to look after him. Every year that you have had him has increased your responsibilities. You owe it to him that since he was brought up as Sir Humphrey's son, you must make him Sir Humphrey's heir. In other words, whatever happens, you must not let him suffer in fortune."

The Changeling

Lady Woodroffe was silent.

"Do you understand what I mean? You adopted him. He is yours. It is not his fault that he is yours. He may be robbed of his father by this discovery; he cannot be robbed of his education and of the ideas which belong to your position; he may have to recognize for his father a most unworthy, shameful man instead of a most honourable man. Selfish—callous—as he may be, that will surely be misery enough. He must not, at the same time, be deserted by the woman who adopted him."

"I don't care, I tell you, what becomes of him," she replied sullenly.

"Then, madam, I retire." He rose as if about to carry the threat into execution. "Here is your confession." He threw it on the table. "Use it as you please. I am free to speak as I please. And things must take their own course." He moved towards the door.

"Oh!"—she flung out her arms—"do what you please—say what you please."

"The one thing that remains is to soften the blow, if that is possible. Do you wish me to attempt that task?"

"Soft or hard, I care nothing. Only, for Heaven's sake, take away that wretched boy—that living fraud—that impostor——"

"Who made him an impostor? It is not Humphrey that is a living fraud. It is yourself—yourself, Lady Woodroffe," he repeated sternly. "And I am your accomplice."

"Well, take him out of my sight. His footstep is like a knife in my side. I could shriek even to hear his voice. Oh, doctor! doctor!"—her own voice sank to a moan—"if I could tell you—oh, if I could only tell you!—how I have always hated the boy. Take him back—the gutter brat—take him back to that creature, his mother. He is worthy of her."

Sir Robert sat down again and took her hand in his. "Dear lady"—his voice was soft and soothing, and yet commanding; his hand was large and comforting, yet strong; his eyes were kindly, yet masterful—"your position is very trying. You want rest. In an hour or two, I hope, we shall settle this business. Then you will be easy in your mind again. Come. I shall send you news that will be worth the whole pharmacopœia, if I know the heart of woman."

The Changeling

She burst again into sobs and tears. "Oh, if you knew—if you knew!"

"Yes, I know. Now I am going. You will be better when I am gone. Once there were two mothers," he murmured, "in the parable." He looked down upon her bowed head. "One thought of herself—the other—— I go to see the other."

On the stairs he met Humphrey.

"Sir Robert? Been to see my mother? She's not ill, I hope?"

"Best not go to her just now. She is a little troubled about herself."

"Nothing serious, I hope?" He spoke with the cold show of interest in which one might speak of a servant.

"Anything may become serious; but we will hope that in this case——"

"Come into my room for a moment, if you can spare the time." He led the way to his study. "I want to ask you about a man I met at your house—that fellow with the money, who says he was a gardener once, and looks it still."

"What about him?"

"He's been here. He called here the other day. Sat half an hour—said he wasn't used to my kind of conversation."

"Well, he isn't—is he?"

"I dare say not. But as we don't regulate our discourse by the acquirements of gardeners, it doesn't matter. However, I asked him what he came for, and hinted that I wasn't going to take any shares, if that was what he wanted. Then he began to talk conundrums."

"What did he tell you?"

"Told me nothing. Hinted that there was a lot that I ought to know."

"He didn't give you any hint of what that was?"

"No. Why? I thought that you, who know everything, might know what he meant."

"My young friend, I learn a good deal about the private affairs of many people. They remain private affairs."

The Changeling

"Very good. This fellow seemed mad. He informed me, among other things, that he was no relation of mine."

"Unnecessary."

"Quite so. Then he began to speak in high terms of my mother, for which I ought to have kicked him."

"Of your mother?"

"Then he said that if I followed the wishes of my mother, there would be any amount of money for me. That was to come after I learned the truth. What is the truth?"

"How am I to know what he meant? Perhaps he called on the wrong Woodroffe. There's another man of your name, you know—Richard Woodroffe."

"I know. Little cad! Perhaps that may explain the whole thing. It never does to treat those outsiders as if they were gentlemen born, does it? Once in the gutter, always in the gutter, eh?"

"I don't know."

"Look here, Sir Robert, you come here a good deal. My mother says she knew you years ago——"

"Very slightly."

"Well, there's something going on. She's miserable. I had hints from Molly—from a girl—as well as this gardener fellow—that there's something going on. Is it a smash? Has my mother chucked her fortune? The girl said something about losing everything. I can't get my mother to attend to business, and I must have some money soon. You're a man of the world, Sir Robert. There's a row on, you know."

"Another? Why, man, I hear you were engaged to Miss Woodroffe and to Miss Pennefather at the same time. There are the materials for a pretty row. Is there another?"

"Well, if my mother has got into a mess, I was thinking that it might be as well to make it up with Molly, and stand in with the gardener, and get as much as I can out of him."

"Perhaps—perhaps." He considered a little. "Look here, Sir Humphrey, I am on my way to see Mrs. Haveril. Be here—don't go away—I shall come back in an hour or two, with something to tell you."

CHAPTER XXVI.

THE SECOND MOTHER.

When we are waiting for the call to do something—to say something—of cardinal importance; something that will affect the whole of our life, all that remains of it: when we are uncertain what will happen after or before we have said or done that something; then the very air round us is charged with the uncertainty of the time. Even the hall and the staircase of the Hôtel Métropole, when Molly entered that humble guest-house, seemed trembling with anxiety. Her cousin's rooms were laden with anxiety as with electricity.

"Come in, Molly," said Alice. "No, I am not any better; I try to rest, but I cannot. I keep saying to myself, 'I shall get my son back; I shall get my son back.' How long shall I have to wait?"

"I hope—to-morrow. Dick has prepared a way to tell him."

"Will he be ready to go away with his own mother, to America, do you think, Molly dear?"

"Perhaps. But you must remember. He has his own friends and his own occupations. And we don't know yet——"

"He will be glad—oh, how glad!—to get his true mother back. He's a handsome boy, isn't he, Molly? As tall as his father—Dick isn't nearly so tall—and stout and strong, like my family. He's like Cousin Charles."

"Don't tell him so, Alice."

"Why not? His face is his father's—and his voice. Oh, Molly! will he come to-morrow?"

"Dick was going to send his letter to-morrow." Her heart sank as she thought of the contents of that letter, which would reach its destination, not as a peace-offering or a message of love at all. The poor mother! Would her son fly to her arms on the wings of affection?

Their discourse was interrupted or diverted—there was but one topic possible that day—by the arrival of Sir Robert Steele.

The Changeling

As a skilful diplomatist, he began with the second of the two mothers where the first ended. That is to say, he sat down beside her, took her hand in his, and held it, talking in a soft, persuasive voice.

"We are such old—old friends, dear lady," he began—"friends of four and twenty years—that I have taken a great liberty. That is—I am sure you will forgive me—I have consented to act as ambassador on a delicate mission."

"He comes from Lady Woodroffe," thought Molly, "or perhaps from Humphrey."

"Yes," the doctor went on, his voice being like the melodious cooing of the stock-dove—"yes. As a friend of the past, I thought you would forgive this interference. Things have changed, with both of us, since that time, have they not? I was then at the bottom of the profession—I am now at the top. I was then a sixpenny doctor—fill your own bottle with physic, you know; with a red lamp, and a dispensary open from six to ten every evening. Now I am what you know. You are a great lady—rich—a leader. I am sure you sometimes think that 'not more than others we deserve'——"

"I do, doctor, constantly. But the loss of my boy has poisoned everything. Yet now, I hope——"

"Now, I promise and assure you. This day—this evening——"

She fell back on her pillow.

"I will not let you see him," he said, "unless you keep calm. Don't agitate yourself. Shall I go on? Will you keep as quiet as possible? Now, I've got a great deal to say. Lie down—so. We must remember our present position, and what we owe to ourselves. Think of that. There are three of us concerned."

"Oh!" cried Molly. "Then you own it at last!"

"First, there is Lady Woodroffe. Exposure of this business will ruin that lady."

"She deserves to be ruined," said Molly.

"Because she has taken a poor child and brought it up in luxury? Let us not inflame the situation by hard words."

The Changeling

"I don't wish to be hard on her," said Alice. "But she said my baby-clothes were hers."

"Forgive her, Mrs. Haveril. We must all forgive. Before I leave you to-day I must take your forgiveness with me."

"Oh, Sir Robert!" said Molly. "She will forgive you too, if you restore her son."

"As for myself, the second of the three. It will be a pleasing thing for the world to read, and for me to confess, that I was the person who found the child and arranged the bargain. And that afterwards, when I discovered that for 'adoption' I must read 'substitution,' I held my tongue until proofs had been discovered which rendered further silence impossible. I am an Ex-President of the College of Physicians; I am a Fellow of the Royal Society; I have written learned works on points of pathology; I am a leader in practice; I am a K.C.B. It will be a very delightful exposure for me, will it not?"

"Well," said Molly, "but you might have told us when you found it out."

"As for yourself, my dear madam, I believe that in the States they are curious about rich people."

"They just want to know even what you eat and drink."

"Then consider—you must—the effect upon your own reputation, which will be produced when you have to confess that you sold your child—sold: it is an ugly word, is it not?—sold your child for fifty pounds."

"Why should the story come to light at all?" asked Molly.

"There are secrets in most families. In my position I learn many. I certainly considered this as one of them. The only reason why this must come to light is that the young man must lay down his title. His name fortunately remains unchanged."

"Who cares for a title?" asked Molly.

"You would, young lady, if you had one. An hereditary title, however, cannot be laid down at will. It belongs to a man—to his father, to his eldest son. To lay it down would require explanation. And there is no

The Changeling

other explanation possible except one—that the man is not the son of his putative father."

"Doctor," said Alice, "I don't care what the world says. I shall not listen to what the world says. I want my boy."

"Very well. You shall have your boy, if you like. But we must have a little talk first about him—about your son."

"Ah! my son."

"Now, dear lady, I want all your sympathy." He pressed her hand again. "Your sympathy and your affection and your self-denial, even your self-effacement. I have to call upon all these estimable qualities. I have to ask of your most sacred affection—your maternal affection—a self-sacrifice of the highest, the most noble, the most generous kind."

He looked into his patient's eyes. As yet there was no mesmeric response. Alice was only wondering what all this talk meant. If there was any other expression in her eyes, it was the hungry look of a mother bereft of her children. The doctor let her hand drop.

"I shall succeed," he said. "Of that I have no doubt. But I fear my own power of presenting the case with the force which it demands."

He then, with as much emphasis as if he were on the stage, produced a manuscript from his pocket, and unfolded it with an eye to effect.

"I received this," he said, "half an hour ago. It is Lady Woodroffe's confession. It was written in the dead of night—last night. If the imagination of the writer can be trusted, it was written by order of her dead husband, who stood beside her while she wrote. The intensity of feeling with which it was written is proved by that belief."

"Ghosts!" said Molly, contemptuously. "Stuff with her ghosts!"

"My dear young lady"—the doctor felt that his ghostly machinery had failed—"will you kindly not interrupt? I am speaking with Mrs. Haveril on a subject which is more important to all concerned than you can understand. Pray do not interrupt."

But the impression which might have been produced by the vision of the dead husband was ruined by that interruption. If a ghost does not produce his impression at the outset, he never does.

The Changeling

Alice received the confession coldly. "Am I to read it," she asked.

She opened it and read it through. What it contained we know very well. It was written quite simply, stating the plain facts without comment. The concluding words were as follows:—

> "My husband never had the least suspicion. The boy's real nature, which is selfish and callous and heartless, did not reveal itself to him. To me it was, almost from the outset, painfully apparent. He is so entirely, in every respect, the opposite of his supposed father, that I have sometimes trembled lest a suspicion should arise. For my own part, I confess that I have never felt the least tenderness or affection for the boy. It has been a continual pain to me that I had to pretend any. So far as that is concerned, I shall be much relieved when I have to pretend no more. Whatever steps may be taken by his real mother, they will at least rid me of a continual and living reproach. I do not know how much affection and gratitude his real mother may expect from such a son in return for depriving him of his family and his position, and exchanging his cousins in the House of Lords for relations with the gutter. I wish her, however, joy and happiness from his love and gratitude."

"Molly dear," said Alice, "the woman confesses she took the child and passed it off upon the world for her own. What do you say now, doctor?"

"If necessary, I am ready to acknowledge publicly that Lady Woodroffe is the person who bought your child. However, when you came to me about it, I did not know that fact. I found it out afterwards by a remarkable chance. But she confesses, which is all that you desire."

"She confesses! Now—at last! Oh, Molly, I shall get back the boy! He will be my own son again—not that horrible woman's son any more! Oh, my own son! my own son!"

"The other mother," the doctor murmured. Molly heard him, but understood not what he meant. "Will you, dear madam, read the latter part of the document once more, that part of it beginning, 'My husband never had any suspicion.' Perhaps Miss Molly will read it aloud."

The Changeling

Molly did so. As she read it she understood the meaning of these words, "the other mother." She thought of Humphrey, with his cold disdainful eyes, his shrinking from display, his pride of birth, his contempt of the common herd, and of this warm motherly heart, natural and spontaneous, careless of form and reticence, which was waiting for him, and her heart sank for pity. The sham mother, glad at last to get rid of the pretence; her own lover Dick, eager to pull down the pretender, and full of revenge; the pretender himself maddened with rage and shame; and the poor mother longing in vain for one word of tenderness and kindness. Molly's heart sank low with pity. What tenderness, what kindness, would Humphrey have for the mother who had come to deprive him of everything that he valued?

"I have come here this afternoon," the doctor went on, "as a friend of both mothers. On the part of Lady Woodroffe, I have absolutely nothing to propose. She puts the case unreservedly in your hands. Whatever steps you take, she will accept. It remains, therefore, for you, madam, to do what you think best."

"I want my boy," she repeated doggedly. "So long as I get him, I don't care what happens."

"That is, of course, the one feeling which underlies everything. I will, if you like, see him in your name."

"Dick was going to write to him as the son of Anthony Woodroffe," said Molly.

"I know his proposals. We have to consider, however, the possible effect which the discovery of the truth will produce upon this unfortunate—most unfortunate—young man."

"Why is he unfortunate?" asked his mother jealously. "He will be restored to his own mother."

"I am going to tell you why. Meantime, you will agree with me that it is most important that the communication of the truth must not embitter this young man, at the outset, against his mother."

"No, no. He must not be set against me."

"Quite so. Dick proposes, I understand, to address a letter to him as the son of the late Mr. Anthony Woodroffe—better known as John

The Changeling

Anthony—and inviting him to pay certain liabilities. As to the wisdom of that step, I have no doubt. It can produce no other effect than to fill him with rage and bitterness against all concerned, all—every one—without exception."

He shook a warning finger at one after the other.

"But he must know," said Molly.

"Perhaps. In that case the subject must be approached with the greatest delicacy. Dick's method is to begin with a bludgeon."

"We must think of his mother first," said Molly. "We have been working all along for his mother."

"My dear young lady, you do not understand the situation. Because we must think first of his mother, and for no other reason, we must advance with caution. Had we not to consider the mother, there would be no reason for delicacy at all. And now, if you will not interrupt, I will go on."

The warning was now necessary, because the time had arrived for the final appeal. If that failed, anything might happen.

"We must consider, dear madam, the character, in the first place, of your son, and in the next place, the conditions of his education and position. As regards his character, he has inherited the artistic nature of his father, to begin with. That is shown in everything he does in his music and musical composition."

"I have heard him sing a song of his own composition," said Molly. "It had neither meaning nor melody; he said that it only appealed to the higher culture."

"Once more"—but he spoke in vain—"I say, then, that he has inherited his father's artistic nature. He sings and plays; he paints——"

"Landscapes of impossible colour," said Molly.

"And writes verses. He has a fine taste in the newer arts, such as decoration, bookbinding, furniture——"

"And champagne."

"All these qualities he inherits from his father, with, I imagine, a certain impatience which, when opinions differ, also, I expect,

The Changeling

distinguished his father. From his mother he seems to inherit, if I may say so in her presence, tenacity, which may become obstinacy, and strong convictions or feelings, which may possibly degenerate into prejudice. His mother's softer qualities—her depth of affection, her warm sympathies—will doubtless come to the front when his nature, still partly undeveloped, receives its final moulding under the hands of love."

All this was very prettily put, and presented the subject in an engaging light. Molly, however, shook her head, incredulous, as one who ought to know, if any one could know, what had been the outcome of that final moulding under the hands of love.

"This is his character," the doctor went on blandly. "This is the present character as it has been developed from the raw material which we handed over to Lady Woodroffe four and twenty years ago. Next, consider his education."

"Why?" asked his mother. "Hasn't he had his schooling?"

"More schooling than you think. He has been taught that his father was a most distinguished Indian officer, in whom his son could take the greatest pride; that his mother belonged to an ancient Scotch family, his grandfather being the thirteenth baron, and his uncle the fourteenth; he was taught that there is no inheritance so valuable as that of ancient family; as a child he imbibed a pride of birth which is almost a religion; indeed, I doubt if he has any other. His school education and his associates helped him to consider himself as belonging to a superior caste, and the rest of the world as outsiders. This prejudice is now rooted in him. If he had to abandon this belief——"

"But he must abandon it," said Molly. "To-morrow he becomes an outsider."

"When you parted with your boy, you gave him, without knowing what you were doing, statesmen and captains, great lords and barons that belong to history, even kings and queens, for ancestors. Now, without warning—how could one warn a young man of such a thing?—you suddenly rob him of all these possessions. You give him for a father, a worthless scoundrel, to use plain language—a man whose record is horrible and shameful, a deceiver and deserter of

The Changeling

women, a low-class buffoon, a fellow who met with the end which he deserved in a workhouse, after a final exhibition of himself as a sandwich-man at one and twopence a day. The mere thought of such a father is enough to reduce this unfortunate young man to madness. And for other relations, I repeat, you offer him, in place of his present cousins, who are gentlefolk of ancient birth, with all that belongs to that possession, such humble—perhaps such unworthy—people as Dick sums up under such titles as 'the pew-opener,' 'the small draper,' and 'the mendicant bankrupt.' Can you imagine Humphrey, with his pride of birth, calling upon the Hackney draper, and taking tea with the pew-opener?"

"They are my cousins, too, Sir Robert," said Molly. "And I get along without much trouble about them."

"Yours? Very likely. Why not?" he replied impatiently. "You are used to them. You were born to them. Sir Humphrey was not." He turned again to Alice. "Have you considered these things? You must consider them—in pity to your son—in pity to yourself."

Alice made no reply.

"Your son will be crushed, beaten down, humiliated to the lowest, by this revelation. Ask yourself how he will reward the people who have caused the discovery. Will he reward the hand which inflicts this lifelong shame—it can be nothing less to him—with affection and gratitude—or——? Finish the question for yourself."

Alice clasped her hands. Then she rose and bowed her head. "Lord, have mercy upon me, miserable sinner!" she murmured.

Molly laid her arm round her waist.

"Take me to my room," she murmured.

Her room opened out of the sitting-room. Through the open door Sir Robert saw her lying rather than kneeling at the bedside, her arms thrown upon the counterpane. Molly stood over her, the tears streaming down her cheeks.

The doctor beckoned the girl to leave her. "My dear"—his own eyes were dim with an unaccustomed blurr; he could walk without emotion through a hundred wards filled with suffering bodies, but he

The Changeling

had never walked the ward of suffering souls—"my dear, leave her for a while. We are all miserable sinners, you and Dick, with your revengeful thoughts, and I, and everybody. And the greatest sinner is the young man himself."

"I did not think," Molly sobbed. "I only thought—we only wanted to prove the case."

"It is the old, old parable. The false mother thinks only of herself; the true mother thinks of her son. Solomon, I thank thee!"

The true mother came back. "Doctor, do what you will—what you can—I will spare him. Let things remain exactly as they are."

He made no answer. He gazed upon her with troubled eyes.

"Tell me, doctor," she said, "what I must do."

"Will you do, then, what I advise?"

"If you will only save my son from his mother. It's a dreadful thing to say. Doctor, I would rather lose the boy altogether than think that he hates and despises his mother."

"When you put the child into my hands, when you undertook to make no inquiry after him in the future—then you lost your child. I told you so two months ago, when this inquiry began. Nothing but mischief could come of it—mischief, and misery, and hatred, and shame, and disappointment. This you could not understand. Now you do."

She sighed. "Yes, I understand."

"Our duty is plain—to hold our tongues. Humphrey will remain where he is. It is a family secret, which will die with us."

"And is he—Dick's brother—to go on holding the place to which he has no right?" asked Molly.

"There will be no change. It is a family secret," he repeated. "A close family secret, never to be whispered even among yourselves."

"He must never know," said Alice. "Yet I must speak to him once; I must hold his hand in mine once."

"If you can trust yourself. If you can only keep calm. Then, I will bring him—this very afternoon. I will go to him. You shall tell him briefly

The Changeling

that he is like your son—that is all—your son which was lost, you know. And, remember, there will not be the least show of affection from him. Let Sir Humphrey—Sir Humphrey he must be—leave you as he came—a changeling—with no suspicion of the fact."

The Changeling

CHAPTER THE LAST.

FORGIVENESS.

Alice lay patiently. It was done, then. Her punishment was ended; she was to see her son for once—only for once.

"My dear," she said, "my dream will come true. I shall see my son—to call him my son—for once—only for once. And then? But there will be nothing left."

Dick came bursting in. "I've drawn up the case, and I've got the advertisements ready. If by this time to-morrow the doctor makes no sign, I shall act. Here's the case."

He drew out a document in foolscap, tied with red tape—a most imposing document. "And here are the letters—

"'SIR,—I beg to inform you that the funeral of your father, the late John Anthony Woodroffe, who died yesterday, Tuesday, October 15th, will take place from that institution at twelve o'clock on Friday. Your half-brother, Mr. Richard Woodroffe, has ordered me to convey to you this information.'

"I hope he'll like that," said Dick, rubbing his hands. "And here is the second letter—

"'SIR,—I am requested by Mr. Richard Woodroffe to inform you that your father, Mr. John Anthony Woodroffe, has died in debt to a certain Mrs. Welwood, widow of a grocer, of Lisson Grove. The amount is about £60. He wishes to know whether you are prepared to join him in paying off the liability. Your obedient servants.'

"I hope he will like that," said Dick. "And here is the advertisement—

"'Died. On Tuesday, the 13th, at the Marylebone Workhouse Infirmary, John Anthony Woodroffe, father of Sir Humphrey Woodroffe, baronet, aged 55.'

"I hope he will like that."

"There is something more for you," said Molly. "Lady Woodroffe confesses. There is the paper."

The Changeling

"Confesses?" Dick snatched the paper, and read it through with a hunter's sense of disappointment. "Well," he said, "I thought better of her. I thought she would die game. Never trust appearances. Well, this changes these matters. Instead of sending the letters and the advertisement, I shall now go myself with the case and the confession, and bring him to his——"

"No, Dick," said Molly. "There is to be no shame for him, and no humiliation."

"*What?*"

"No shame for him at all. He is to be left in ignorance unless he has guessed anything. We shall tell him nothing. All will go on as before."

"Oh, Molly! have we given in? With victory assured? Don't say that!"

"You don't understand, Dick. Everything is changed. It is now Lady Woodroffe who would spare him nothing. It is his mother who would save him from everything."

Dick looked at the pale woman lying on the sofa. Then he understood, and a tear stood in his eye. 'Twas a tender heart. He went over to the sofa and kissed her forehead.

"Forgive me," he said.

"Oh, Dick!" she murmured. "Would to God you were my son! As for him, he is what they have made him."

They had made him grumpy and obstinate. At that moment the doctor was urging upon him compliance with a simple thing.

"You want me to go to the rooms of the gardener man who insulted me? I am to listen to some rubbish about his wife. What do I care about his wife? I tell you, Sir Robert, this is trifling. I won't go, there; tell them so. I won't go."

"Then, Sir Humphrey, I tell you plainly, Ruin stares you in the face. Yes; the loss of everything in this world that you value—everything. You will lose all. I cannot explain what this means. But you will have letters to-morrow which will change your whole life—and all your thoughts. They mean, I say, the loss of everything that you value."

The Changeling

"I don't believe a word——"

"You wanted to know what Mr. Haveril meant, what your mother meant, what Miss Molly Pennefather meant. They meant Ruin—Ruin, and loss of everything, Sir Humphrey—that and nothing else."

"Tell me more. Tell me why."

"I shall tell you no more. I shall leave it to your—to Richard Woodroffe, whom you love so well. He will tell you."

The young man hesitated. "What do you want me to do?"

"You are to come with me to Mrs. Haveril's rooms; she will receive you; she will make a communication to you. Whatever she says you are to receive with courtesy—with courtesy, mind. That done, you may return, and everything will go on as usual. You can then forget what you heard. Are you ready? Very well."

"If that cad, the fiddler, is there——"

"Hark ye, Sir Humphrey, if you behave or speak like a cub and a cur, I throw you over. By the Lord! I will have no mercy upon you. I will tell you myself what it all means. Now!"

Molly waited, sitting beside Alice, who lay with closed eyes. Perhaps she slept. Presently John Haveril came home. Molly told him what had happened.

"Ay, ay," he said. "Let him come. Let Alice have her say. They've made a cur of him between them. Let him come."

He sat down beside his wife, and whispered words of consolation and of soothing. They would go home again—out of the atmosphere of deception. They would be happy once more in their own home on the Pacific slope.

"John," said Alice, "it was good of you to bring me over on the strength of a dream, and a promise of a dream—to give over all your work——"

"Nay, nay, lass. What is work compared with thee?"

The Changeling

"I shall see my son again. I have prayed for that. I did not pray, John—I could not—for his love—that was gone. Yet I hoped. Now I must be satisfied only to take his hands in mine."

"We will go home again—we will go home again."

"My dream said nothing about going home again." She was silent for a while. "John," she said, "what was it you were going to tell Molly and Dick?"

They were all three standing over her.

"Why," said John, "Alice had a fancy—because she loves you both—to see you join hands—so."

Alice laid her thin hands across their joined hands, and her lips moved.

"And I was to tell you both that I would not give you a single dollar out of all the pile. You are happier without, she says. And so do I," he added.

It was a strange betrothal, with tears in the eyes of both.

At that moment arrived the doctor, with Humphrey. The young man looked dark and lowering; his cheek was flushed. He glanced round the room, bowed low to Alice, recognized Molly by a cold inclination, Mr. Haveril by a nod, and Dick by a blank stare, which did not recognize even his existence—the frequent employment of this mode of salutation had made him greatly beloved by all outsiders.

"Ah," thought Dick, "if you knew what I've got in my pocket, you'd change that look."

"Mrs. Haveril," said Sir Robert, "I have brought you Sir Humphrey Woodroffe, at your request. I believe you have something to say to him."

"Molly dear, give Sir Humphrey a chair near me—so. I want to tell you, Sir Humphrey, of a very strange dream, if I may call it—a hallucination."

"You may, madam," said the doctor, for the young man sat down in silence.

The Changeling

"Which has, I fear, given your mother a great deal of annoyance. I am, unfortunately, too weak at present to call upon her, or to explain to her. Therefore I have ventured to ask you to be so very kind as to come here, so that I may send a message to Lady Woodroffe."

"I am here," said Sir Humphrey, ungraciously.

"I will not take up much of your time. I had an illness in America which touched my brain, I believe. I imagined that a child which I lost twenty-four years ago was still living. He was the son of my first husband, whose name was Woodroffe. He was also the father of Richard Woodroffe here. More than that, I fancied that one person was that child. That person was yourself. I fancied that you were the child. I had not lost it by death. I surrendered it to a lady by adoption."

Humphrey started. He changed colour. He sat up in his chair. He listened eagerly. His lip trembled.

"He understands," Molly whispered.

"No; he begins to understand what was meant," Dick returned. "He cannot guess the whole."

Yes; he understood now that he was face to face with a great danger. Many things became plain to him—Molly's words, John Haveril's words, Sir Robert's words.

He understood the nature of the danger. He listened, while a horrible terror seized him at the mere prospect of that danger. He heard the rest with a sense of relief, equalled only by his sense of the danger.

Alice went on. "I first saw you at the theatre one night. You were so much like my husband that I concluded that you must be my son. I met you at Sir Robert's. I became certain that you were my son. We made inquiries. Please tell him, Sir Robert."

"These inquiries," said the doctor, "proved certain things which were curious and interesting. I may confess that they seemed to point in your direction. This lady became too hastily convinced that they did so. She is now as firmly convinced that they did not."

Humphrey sighed deeply.

The Changeling

"It was an awkward case," Sir Robert went on—"one that required tact."

"I gave a great deal of trouble"—Alice took up the wondrous tale again.

"But it is all over now," the doctor added. "Do not talk too much."

"Yes, all over. My bodily frame is weak, but my mind is clear again. Now, Sir Humphrey, I wish you, if you will be so kind, to go to Lady Woodroffe, and tell her from me that the hallucination has passed away, and give her my regrets that I disturbed her. Sir Robert will perhaps go with you, to make the explanation clearer, because he knows all the details."

"I will certainly call upon Lady Woodroffe this evening," said the doctor. "Indeed, Sir Humphrey is ignorant of certain facts connected with the case which will probably incline Lady Woodroffe to forgive and excuse the more readily."

"Will you do this, Sir Humphrey?" asked Mrs. Haveril.

"Yes, if that's all," he replied hoarsely. "Is that all? Was it, as you say, hallucination? Are you quite certain?"

The doctor felt his patient's pulse. "All hallucination," he replied. "Now, please finish this interview as soon as you can."

"I want Sir Humphrey to give me his own forgiveness."

"If there were anything to forgive."

"Since there is nothing," said the doctor, sternly, "you can even more readily go through the form."

"Well, if you wish it."

Humphrey held out his hand.

"Tell her, man," said the doctor, impatiently—"tell her what she wants."

"Since you desire it"—Humphrey obeyed, coldly and reluctantly—"I forgive you. Will that do?"

Alice raised her head; she pushed back her hair with her left hand. Molly held her up. She gazed upon her son's face; it was cold and hard

249

The Changeling

and pitiless. She stooped over her son's hand; it was cold and hard, and seemed as pitiless as his face—there was no warmth nor impression in the hand. She bent her head and kissed it. Her tears fell upon it—her silent tears. Humphrey withdrew his hand. He looked round, as if asking what next.

Dick went to the door, and pointed to the stairs, holding the door open.

Alice lay back on the pillow. The doctor took her wrist again.

"Doctor," she whispered, "I have never wholly lost my boy till now."

Her eyes closed. Her cheek grew white.

The doctor laid down her hand. "Never," he said, "till now."

THE END.

PRINTED BY WILLIAM CLOWES AND SONS, LIMITED,
LONDON AND BECCLES.

Copyright © 2023 Esprios Digital Publishing. All Rights Reserved.